T0357760

DEATH
in the
CARDS

ALSO BY MIA P. MANANSALA

TITA ROSIE'S KITCHEN MYSTERY SERIES

ARSENIC AND ADOBO
HOMICIDE AND HALO-HALO
BLACKMAIL AND BIBINGKA
MURDER AND MAMON
GUILT AND GINATAAN

DEATH
in the
CARDS

MIA P. MANANSALA

DELACORTE PRESS

Delacorte Press
An imprint of Random House Children's Books
A division of Penguin Random House LLC
1745 Broadway, New York, NY 10019
penguinrandomhouse.com
GetUnderlined.com

Text copyright © 2025 by Mia P. Manansala
Jacket art copyright © 2025 by Alex Cabal
Drawn tarot card by scarlet_health/stock.adobe.com, white paper texture by
srckomkrit/stock.adobe.com, and tarot card page design used under license from
Shutterstock.com

Penguin Random House values and supports copyright. Copyright fuels creativity,
encourages diverse voices, promotes free speech, and creates a vibrant culture.
Thank you for buying an authorized edition of this book and for complying with
copyright laws by not reproducing, scanning, or distributing any part of it in
any form without permission. You are supporting writers and allowing Penguin
Random House to continue to publish books for every reader. Please note that
no part of this book may be used or reproduced in any manner for the purpose of
training artificial intelligence technologies or systems.

Delacorte Press is a registered trademark and the colophon is a trademark of
Penguin Random House LLC.

Editor: Bria Ragin
Cover Designers: Ray Shappell and Liz Dresner
Interior Designer: Megan Shortt
Production Editor: Colleen Fellingham
Managing Editor: Tamar Schwartz
Production Manager: Liz Sutton

Library of Congress Cataloging-in-Publication Data
Names: Manansala, Mia P., author.
Title: Death in the cards / Mia P. Manansala.
Description: First edition. | New York : Delacorte Press, 2025. | Audience term:
Teenagers | Audience: Ages 12 and up. | Summary: "When a high school tarot
reader's latest client goes missing after a troubling reading, she must apply
everything she has learned from her private investigator mother to solve a case of
her own"—Provided by publisher.
Identifiers: LCCN 2024059995 (print) | LCCN 2024059996 (ebook) |
ISBN 978-0-593-89792-8 (trade) | ISBN 978-0-593-89793-5 (trade pbk.) |
ISBN 978-0-593-89794-2 (lib. bdg.) | ISBN 978-0-593-89795-9 (ebook)
Subjects: CYAC: Fortune telling—Fiction. | Missing persons—Fiction. |
High schools—Fiction. | Schools—Fiction. | Mystery and detective stories. |
LCGFT: Detective and mystery fiction. | Novels.
Classification: LCC PZ7.1.M3614 De 2025 (print) | LCC PZ7.1.M3614 (ebook) |
DDC [Fic]—dc23

The text of this book is set in 11.5-point Adobe Garamond Pro.

Manufactured in the United States of America
10 9 8 7 6 5 4 3 2 1

The authorized representative in the EU for product safety and compliance is
Penguin Random House Ireland, Morrison Chambers, 32 Nassau Street,
Dublin D02 YH68, Ireland, https://eu-contact.penguin.ie.

Random House Children's Books supports the First Amendment and celebrates the
right to read.

To young Mia, who maybe would've figured certain things out a lot sooner if she'd had a book like this.

And to anyone else struggling to figure out who you are or who feels like you're not enough—I see you.

THIS JOURNAL BELONGS TO:

DANIKA DIZON

THE 7 B'S OF
PRIVATE INVESTIGATING

1. Be observant and document everything.
2. Be prepared for any scenario.
3. Be logical, but don't be afraid to trust your gut.
4. Be a safe space for your clients but keep professional boundaries.
5. Be friendly and communicative—building relationships is the foundation of any good agency.
6. Be able to adapt, adapt, adapt.
7. Be sure your evidence is concrete!

WORDS OF WISDOM

"Trust your clients,
but don't always believe them."
—Angelica Dizon, aka my mom

HOW TO CONVINCE MY MOM TO LET ME BECOME A PRIVATE INVESTIGATOR

1. Fix up Veronica—reliable transportation = reliable detective.
2. Use my Kali skills to show I can defend myself in the field.
3. Develop my tarot knowledge to show I can attract clients, know how to be discreet with sensitive information, and am good at reading people and situations.

4. Practice my interview and research skills by helping Daddy with his mystery stories—even fictional cases require real research and problem-solving.
5. Find my USP (unique selling point, according to my business teacher)—what do I have to offer as a detective???

CHAPTER ONE

THERE ARE FEW THINGS I LOVE MORE THAN GIVING people advice and being 1,000 percent right about it. Even better? Giving people advice, them NOT following it, then having them come crying to me, asking why they didn't just listen to me from the start.

LOVE. IT.

Some people might find this behavior annoying, but for me, it means repeat customers. I promised myself this was the year I stopped relying on the CTA and got myself a working set of wheels. Don't get me wrong, the Chicago public transit system is fine and all (well, mostly), but I'm trying to level up to more dependable transportation. Thanks to my eccentric grandparents, I'm the proud owner of Veronica, a broken-down black 1994 Chrysler LeBaron convertible. I love it to death, but that old beater isn't gonna repair itself, which is why those advice-seeking repeat customers are so crucial.

Why do people pay me, a random seventeen-year-old high school student with zero social life, for guidance? Because I believe in the heart of the cards.

Tarot cards, that is. Danika Dizon, Lane Tech's resident

tarot reader and number one advice giver, at your service. For twenty bucks a pop, I'll counsel you on your love life, tell you how to handle that messy fight with your bestie, help you decide which university to go to (or whether college is even right for you), or simply talk about anything that's on your mind. I'm discreet, I mind my business, and I'm very, *very* good at what I do. Because of that, I've managed to build up a solid clientele and a reputation for being the go-to person when someone needs direction. Even though I'm the person who knows everybody's secrets, it's never caused any real drama.

Until today.

I'm doing a love reading for one of my regulars, a senior girl with the worst taste in guys, about her latest mistake/boyfriend when someone interrupts us.

"You're the reason my sister is missing."

In my line of work, I get blamed for stuff all the time—usually having to do with exposing lying-ass boyfriends and the subsequent breakups. But this is a first.

I look up from the tarot cards spread out in front of me to see who so rudely interrupted my reading with wild accusations and meet a pair of dark brown eyes surrounded by the longest lashes I've ever seen. I normally wouldn't care about a detail like that, but those mascara-ad lashes draw my attention to the girl's bloodshot eyes.

Oh great. Another crier. I'm used to my clients sobbing. Sometimes I wonder if I should become a therapist after I graduate since I'll make way more money and people love to tell me their problems anyway. But I still haven't figured out a good way to deal with the crying.

Stay respectfully silent? Talk about something off topic till they calm down? Give an awkward "there, there" shoulder pat? None of these options seem to go over well, but my clients keep coming back, so I must be doing something right.

I gesture to my client to wait a moment while I deal with this. "Sorry, who's your sister?"

Crying Girl ain't having it.

"This is a private conversation," she says to my client. "You'll have to come back later."

"I was here first! Wait your—"

Crying Girl glances at the cards. "He's cheating on you. There, now you can go."

My client flinches, and I feel oddly protective of her, considering I was about to tell her the same thing. "Do not talk to her like that, and do not pretend like you know what the cards say."

"I don't have to know what the cards say. This girl and her boyfriend are in my trig class. I see him all over other girls every day."

"He's just a big flirt! That doesn't mean he's doing anything with them."

Crying Girl and I exchange a look, and I decide to cut them both some slack. "You know what? The vibes are off right now. How about we do a new reading some other time? You don't have to pay for this one."

After my client agrees and clears out, I turn to Crying Girl. "You cost me a reading, so this had better be good."

"I told you that my sister is missing. Did you not catch that?"

"No, I heard you. I don't know what that has to do with me, though."

Crying Girl pulls out her phone and shows me a picture. "Eli. Mary Elizabeth Delgado. She's a senior here. I know she talked to you before she disappeared."

I glance at the picture on her screen, and she's right. I remember that girl.

Last week, she busted in during a session I was doing with another client by slapping down fifty bucks and demanding a reading. Crashing my consultations must be a Delgado sister thing. Anyway, usually I'd turn someone like that away because I'm not interested in people who don't respect me or my time, but who am I to say no to that much money?

My mom doesn't actually pay me for the work I do at our family's detective agency. The lack of funds wasn't a huge problem before since I never go anywhere or do anything. But now that I'm at the end of my junior year, I'm hoping my mom will give me some real work to do over the summer—work that'll require me to fix up Veronica because I'll need her to investigate all around Chicago. There's no way to convince my mom I can handle fieldwork without reliable transportation—apparently a Ventra card isn't good enough. Like, what, I can't be an environmentally conscious private detective? Who says I can't tail someone on public transit? So what started as a fun way to tell people what to do and keep my tarot reading skills sharp became a fast, simple way to earn money.

But this girl, Eli . . . she was anything but simple. I could tell her life was complicated with a capital *C*. I have no idea why she came to me. Typically, my clients ask their questions out loud to help me hone my readings. But she refused, and I didn't want to push too hard. Again, fifty dollars for what's usually a twenty-dollar reading—I wasn't gonna fight her. It's my policy not to dig too deep during my readings anyway. Everyone has a secret or two they want to keep, and it's better to keep a professional distance.

Besides, I have enough going on—helping my family out and maintaining my GPA—without caring about people who love my advice but don't actually give a damn about me. I'm barely keeping my head above water pretending I care about my AP classes, and it's not like I can afford a tutor. In my family, no scholarship means no college. Which I would be fine with, but the last time I suggested skipping college to work for my mom, she took off her house slipper and threw it at me. At least I don't need to worry about my mom's safety when she's in the field, considering how deadly she is with her tsinelas.

And let's be real. High school kid problems are boring AF. Nothing like the cool cases my mom takes on. She's a private investigator who specializes in family issues, and let me tell you, everyone likes to talk about teens and how dramatic we are, but what we do doesn't hold a candle to what the effed-up adults in Chicago are up to.

But this girl's sister was different. A high school senior like Eli would normally be hoping for a love reading or some tips about university. And even though she refused to ask her question out loud, I know she didn't come to me for anything so mundane. Call me melodramatic, but when you have a mom who's a private detective and a dad who's a mystery author, you learn to read people and piece together their stories.

Eli was scared.

I could see it in her eyes, the dark circles peeking through layers of hastily applied concealer. Her arms hugged close to her body, long sleeves pulled down past her wrists, which drew my eyes to her hands. Manicured nails that had been bitten down past the quick, a Band-Aid wrapped around one where she'd likely chewed too far and drew blood. An odd contrast to the cute and clearly expensive rose gold flower ring she wore on her right ring finger.

The three cards I dealt her are clear in my mind: the Ten of Swords, symbolizing loss, betrayal, and painful endings. The Tower, the herald of chaos and destruction and lightning bolt revelations. And, finally, Death.

I remember the expression on her face as she listened to my interpretations, her eyes lingering on Death, the card of change. I remember piecing together signs from her appearance and wondering if she sought me out over an abusive boyfriend, if this was a cry for help. And I remember praying that my reading would be the push she needed to get away.

Maybe it was.

Maybe that's why she decided to run.

CHAPTER TWO

"HOW LONG HAS YOUR SISTER BEEN MISSING?"

"Since Friday night. And before you ask, she left a note. That's how I know she ran away and wasn't, like, kidnapped or anything."

My eyebrows shoot up. "And she mentioned me in her note?"

The girl shakes her head. "No. But when I talked to her best friend to see if she knew where my sister went, she mentioned that Eli had been acting weird lately. And she brought you up. I figure you must be connected somehow."

I pull out my notebook and flip back to see if I recorded Eli's reading. I typically don't, partly for client confidentiality and partly because the readings aren't interesting enough for me to note. But I write down the ones that stick out to me, the ones that are harder than usual, so I can reflect on what I learned and improve my craft. I also journal my morning pulls and personal readings to see if I notice any patterns, a habit I picked up from my dad. My mom may be the detective, but my dad is the one who passed on his love of puzzles to me, the one who takes the time to help me hone my observation and analysis skills, the one who takes me and my training seriously.

Sure enough, I find an entry with the name "Eli Delgado" scribbled at the top. My clients don't give me their names unless they want to, and that girl hadn't. But the sheer terror in her eyes had made me curious, so I'd asked around about her and edited her file later. Ever since, I've wondered if my interest in her was because I sensed a case in the making.

I peer up from my notes to see the girl studying me. "What's your name?"

"Gaby."

"Okay, Gaby, why are you so sure I had anything to do with your sister?"

"What did she talk to you about?" she counters.

"Sorry, client confidentiality."

Her eyes flick down to the graffiti-scrawled student desk that I use as my tarot table, then flick back up as if to say, *Girl, are you serious?*

I shift the scarf that I use as my tarot cloth to cover up a surprisingly well-done drawing of a giant monster scrotum.

"I'm a professional."

Gaby rolls her eyes. "Yeah, whatever. Again, my sister is missing. And you don't even care?"

I shrug. "Sounds like you should go to the police. I don't have anything to do with it."

Her eyes shift. "No cops. My parents don't want them involved."

I lean forward, suddenly a million times more intrigued. "Why?"

"They don't want to risk this getting in the news."

"Wouldn't that be a good thing? Expand the search to make it easier to find her?"

She throws out her arms, nearly knocking over my reusable water bottle. "That's what I said! But they don't want people finding out. My parents are already upset that Eli's best friend knows they were looking for her, even though she doesn't know why."

"So how do they hope to find her?"

She tilts her head down and glares at me like I'm a fool. "Why do you think I'm talking to you?"

Sensing a business opportunity (no, I absolutely did *not* feel responsible for her sister going missing, why do you ask), I pack up my cards, wrap them in their scarf, and stuff them and my notebook into my backpack. "I can't help you, but I know someone who can." I pull a business card from my pen case and hand it to her. "Call your parents and tell them to meet you here."

GABY DRIVES US TO MY FAMILY'S DETECTIVE AGENCY, which is only twenty minutes from our school, but the Delgados still get there before us. Technically, it's my mom's agency since she's our only detective, but my dad and I are her only employees, making it a family affair. Sure enough, my dad is at the front desk while my little brother, Daniel, lounges on the floor next to him playing some card game I don't understand on my dad's phone.

"Oh, good timing, Danika. I'm on deadline, so Tita Baby

is picking you up for your Kali lesson. Can you get Daniel dressed—"

"Sorry, Daddy, but my classmate's parents are here, and I promised I'd go talk to Mommy with her," I interrupt, gesturing toward Gaby.

We don't have any classes together, but I know we're both juniors, so it isn't really a lie. Neither is the second part. In her car, she promised to let me be in the room while she and her parents talk to my mom. In exchange, I have to tell her about her sister's reading. As long as my mom gets a new case out of this, I consider it a fair trade. My aunt and our martial arts lesson can wait.

I knock on my mom's office door and wait for her to open it. For privacy (and to discourage my eavesdropping), my mom's office is pretty much soundproof and always locked. The door opens up a crack, and a white woman eyes me suspiciously.

"Yes?"

Gaby leans around me. "Mom, this is the classmate I told you about. Let us in."

The woman backs away from the door, and Gaby pushes past me into my mom's office. I follow more slowly, examining the Delgado parents to see if I can figure out their story. If they don't want to go to the police, it means they don't trust the cops or are hiding something. Or both.

Gaby's mom, a strikingly tall redhead, moves to stand next to a middle-aged Latine man of average height with dark brown skin and a great head of wavy black hair. Suddenly Gaby's sun-kissed skin, freckles, and auburn curls make sense, as well as the fact that she's even taller than me, though I'm pretty much a giant as a five-foot-eight Filipina.

My mom stands up and walks around her desk, a hefty Goodwill monstrosity that my dad refurbished for her, to shake Gaby's hand. "I'm Angelica Dizon. I'm so sorry to hear about your sister, but I'll do everything I can to help you find her."

Gaby's whole demeanor relaxes, and I can tell my mom's magic is working on her. Everything about my mom, from her calm smile and firm handshake to her perfectly fitted blazer and polished oxford pumps, gives off an aura of warmth and competence. You see her and think, *Now this is someone I can trust. This is a woman who gets shit done and looks amazing while doing it.*

At least, that's how I feel when I look at her.

"Your parents were telling me a little bit about Eli, but I was hoping you could fill in some blanks. You're less than a year apart, yes? You must have a lot of the same friends," my mother says.

Gaby glances at her parents. "Not really. I mean, we used to. But she got busy with some school club and preparing for college, so we're not really part of the same crowd."

"She's such a good girl. So smart. You know she skipped a grade?" her father says, raising his head, a proud smile spreading across his face. "Her advisor told her she should add more extracurricular activities to her resume for college, so Eli joined a club that focuses on volunteer work. She does so much good for the community."

His gaze turns toward Gaby, and his smile fades. "You should follow your sister's example. A scholarship—"

"We talked to the teacher in charge of the club," Mrs.

Delgado interrupts. "He said the last time he saw her was at a club meeting last Thursday."

"Did you talk to any of her friends while you were there?" My mom has her tablet open and is taking notes.

"No, we didn't want to ask too many questions and arouse any suspicions." Mrs. Delgado hitches her Goyard bag higher. "You know how people talk. Anyway, when do you think you'll find her? It's already the end of the school year. What will people say if she misses graduation? And senior prom! She can't miss prom."

My eyes meet my mom's, and I can tell we're both thinking the same thing: Mrs. Delgado is one of *those* parents. The ones who only care about how their family is perceived. We get a lot of those. That's the point of hiring a *private* investigator, after all.

My mom knows exactly how to handle those types because she's had lifelong experience. My rich, bougie grandfather wanted my mom to marry his business partner's gross son, but she eloped with my dad instead. My Lolo Ben was so ashamed of the gossip that spread throughout the suburban Chicago Filipino community (yeah, I know how ridiculous that sounds) that he disowned her, leaving her with nothing. So she and my dad moved into the city to start over and built the Dizon Detective Agency from scratch.

I glance over at Gaby, who's busy glaring at her mother, and suddenly I understand why she was so intense when asking me about her sister's reading. If Daniel went missing and my mom was too worried about what the neighbors thought to do anything, I'd be kicking down doors and doing whatever it took to find him myself.

I'm not saying Mrs. Delgado doesn't care about her daughter or that she'd go the lengths my grandfather did to save the family's reputation. But she doesn't care *enough*. That combined with the expression on Gaby's face lets me know that I want in. I've been trying to get my mom to involve me in her cases for a while now anyway.

I mean, I'm glad she trusts me to handle the phones, email, and paperwork. Whenever I complain about how boring it all is, my dad gives me some pep talk about how the work I do is what keeps the lights on, blah blah blah, I'm an indispensable member of the team, yadda yadda. That's easy for him to say when he spends most of his day working on his next novel, lost in the worlds that he creates, rather than covering front desk duty. I'm the one picking up the slack when he's on deadline.

But I want to be so much more than an administrative assistant. If they're going to make it so that I have no social life thanks to taking care of my brother and the agency, the least they can do is let me help for real and, I don't know, maybe pay me? It's not like I haven't proven myself before.

More than once, I've helped my mom comb social media for leads, and I even helped solve an infidelity case when I pieced together clues our client gave us and found the social media account for the cheating husband's sidepiece—complete with some VERY damning photos. I was maybe twelve when I cracked that case, and I've been chasing that high ever since. If there's a better feeling than having that last puzzle piece perfectly slot into place—and having your emotionally withholding mother tell you that she's proud of you—I sure as heck don't know about it.

After the Delgados answer a few more questions and make a follow-up appointment, they leave, and I mention that point. I have prepared three separate arguments to persuade my mom that I'll be an asset to this case, anticipating her potential problems and preparing rebuttals for them (the debate team captain keeps begging me to join after hearing me convince the security guards to let me use that stairwell as my tarot office).

So it's simultaneously thrilling and disappointing when my mom agrees to my assistance immediately after I suggest it, no convincing necessary.

"That's a good idea. It's not like I can roam the halls of your high school without raising eyebrows. The daughter definitely knows something. Did you see how she reacted when her mom claimed Eli left no note? And all the restrictions she put on who I can and can't talk to? Her mother is hiding too many details from us. She's entitled to her privacy, but I can't do my job properly without more information."

"And that's where I come in? Oh, and Eli did leave a note. Gaby told me earlier."

She smiles at me. "See? Helping already. It'd be smart for you to make friends with the sister and see what else you can find out. And check out the club Eli is supposedly involved in. But you can only handle the school connection, okay? I don't want you going around spying on their neighbors or anything like that."

My mom walks back to her desk and roots around in one of the fifty million drawers, finally pulling out her old tablet and attached stylus. "You can use this to take notes. It has special encryptions, so only certain people can use it. I expect you to keep me updated and to conduct yourself with the utmost professionalism. This is not a game." She holds the tech out but doesn't place it in my hand. "Do you understand me?"

She levels a look at me, a sweeping, discerning look, as if she's questioning whether I'm truly ready for this. I straighten my posture and nod as I reach out to accept the tablet. "Of course, Mommy. I won't let you down."

"You better not." Her expression lingers a moment longer before her eyes soften, and she gives me her usual smile. "Welcome to your first case, Danika. I hope you're up to the challenge."

Bestie Group Chat

> **Danika:** I GOT THE BEST NEWS

> When can we talk???

Junior: Read
Nicole: Read

I wait two minutes.

> **Danika:** YOU ALL DID NOT JUST LEAVE ME ON READ!!!!

CHAPTER THREE

MY PLANS TO IMMEDIATELY START WORK ON THE case are thwarted by my dad, who won't let me cancel my Kali lesson.

"Your Tita Baby is already here, and you know how much it means to Daniel. Besides, you've got your very first case. Don't you think it's even more important to keep up with your training now? You're going to be in the field. Not that you'll need it, hopefully, but it's always good to know how to defend yourself."

I glare at my dad. How dare he make such excellent points? I don't even get to respond before Tita Baby whacks me on the head with a Kali stick.

"Surprise attack!"

I quickly disarm her, and my favorite aunt rewards me with a big hug. My mom's family may have shut her—and, by extension, the rest of us—out, but my dad's family more than makes up for it. Tita Baby is a professional martial artist and the youngest sibling, as denoted by her nickname (I honestly have no idea what her real first name is). Then there's my dad, who writes mystery novels while also helping out at the detective agency and working odd jobs between deadlines. He's doing fine, but he's not exactly making bank. He describes himself as a "midlist" author, which basically means he makes more than zero dollars but less than Stephen King. Finally, we have Tita Myrna (an accountant) and Tita Linda (a nurse), their older twin sisters. We often joke that, as the older sisters, they were stuck choosing practical careers while their younger siblings got to be dreamers, but it wasn't really like that. My grandparents are both successful artists who travel the world, and they want their children to choose their own paths. Some people like stability, I guess.

Daniel has his own Kali sticks out and is wriggling with excitement. I started training at four years old, but my brother only recently began his lessons. He's got a bunch of health issues that prevented it when he was younger, but now that he's got his asthma under control, he's making up for lost time. "Let's go, Ate. Let's go!"

I grab my gear and head out with my aunt and brother while my dad and mom hold down the agency. I'm not a particularly skilled martial artist, and the few tournaments I participated in did not go well, but like Tita Baby says, that's not the point of my training. She's not expecting some dude on the street to follow exhibition rules when he's attacking me. I train so that the movements become second nature to me. So that muscle memory kicks in, allowing me to defend myself until I can run away or help arrives.

Based on how long it takes the cops to show up after a call in Hermosa—I find the name of my neighborhood ironic considering I live across the street from an abandoned factory and next to some run-down train tracks—I figure I'll have to work hard to get good enough to handle everything myself. I know better than to trust the police.

Luckily, I've never had to test my skills in a real fight, though I found out muscle memory is absolutely a thing after my best friend Junior jumped out of an alley and grabbed me as a prank in middle school. He learned real quick not to play like that, and my aunt got another student when Junior's parents signed him up for lessons, hoping he'd learn discipline and focus (he did not). We've been friends since kindergarten and were practically inseparable, but high school changed things. My parents said kindergarten through eighth grade was more than enough Catholic schooling, and it was up to me if I wanted to continue my religious studies (I did not). Junior didn't get that choice.

With him and our other best friend Nicole at DePaul College Prep and me at Lane Tech, these lessons are the only times we really get to hang out. You'd think since our schools are basically down the street from each other, there wouldn't be much of a difference. And for a good part of freshman year, that was true. But as the agency got more work and Daniel needed more care, I started to have less and less time for my friends. A point that's driven home when I get to Tita Baby's martial arts studio and unexpectedly see Nicole suited up next to Junior.

"What're you doing here? Is this why you two left me on read?"

"Wow, nice to see you too," Nicole says, taking a swipe at me. "I figured since you kept flaking on us, I'd have to get creative if I wanted us all to hang out. Especially since you got big news to share."

"I've never flaked on you! I just turn down all your invitations," I say.

Nicole rolls her eyes, but one of Tita Baby's assistants calls for the room's attention before she can respond. The assistant guides us through some warm-ups before the class separates according to skill level.

"No running off after class, okay? We seriously need to catch up," Nicole says before heading to the beginner section with Daniel.

Nicole hates sweating, and any and all forms of physical activity outside of dancing. I wouldn't put it past her to do this to impress a new crush, though I expect it to go as well as her basketball phase—poorly. But seeing as she's here for me, I must be an even worse friend than I thought.

Junior heads to the intermediate section, and I go to spar with Tita Baby and the two other advanced students, my twin cousins. Being her sons and all, they're the only other adults in this particular class besides Tita Baby's assistants. They've been studying Kali and other martial arts almost as long as they've been alive, as part of the after-school program Tita Baby runs for disadvantaged youth in our neighborhood. She knows how easy it is to get into trouble around here, so she teaches Kali and kickboxing classes for free every day after school for the kids in the neighborhood. She also has private and weekend classes for adult students, but that's only 'cause the adults are the ones who pay the fees that keep her studio open.

Andrew, Joemar, and I are perfect sparring partners since we balance each other's weaknesses. Andrew's the strongest, I'm the fastest, and Joemar has the best technique. You'd think a couple dudes in their early twenties would hesitate to fight a seventeen-year-old girl, but since we're family, we have no problems beating the crap out of each other. Besides, we know our limits and how to push each other past them. Tita Baby also likes to point out that it's not likely I'll get into a fair fight, and it's good to get used to fighting multiple attackers at the same time.

I can't get my dad's voice reminding me that I'm going to be in the field out of my head, so I keep at Andrew and Joemar until they're both begging for a break.

"What's with you? Usually we're the ones knocking you on your ass," Joemar says as Andrew pulls him up off the ground.

I grin as I wipe my face with the towel that Tita Baby tossed me. "I got my first case."

Andrew raises his eyebrows. "For real? Your mom's okay with you doing that kind of work?"

"Weren't you complaining last week that she was never going to take you seriously?" Joemar sips from the sixty-four-ounce water bottle he carries everywhere. "What made her change her mind?"

"The case involves someone from my school. Can't say too much, but I might need your help. Is that cool?"

Like I said before, my mom's side of the family sucks, but all the Dizons are super ride-or-die, my cousins included. My mom can't afford to hire them as full-time employees, but she often pulls them in for jobs that require a bit more . . . heavy lifting. They also work as her informants and can get into places where she'd stick out too much. On top of that, they take on the role of my honorary big brothers, which is why no dude in our neighborhood is brave enough to talk to me, let alone date me, once they find out who I'm related to.

"Since it's your very first case, we'll help you out for free. But once you become big-time, we gotta charge you the usual rate."

Considering these two are even more hard up for money than I am, that means a lot. "Thanks, Joemar."

"Anything for you, cuzzo. Now pick up them sticks. I can feel my mom glaring at us."

"SO WHAT'S GOING ON WITH YOU?"

Nicole helps herself to Vienna sausages and scrambled eggs before passing the platter over to the kid next to her. In addition to the free lessons, Tita Baby also provides meals for the kids who need them, as well as snacks to take home. Junior, Nicole, and I sit at the low table in the studio's back room as Tita Baby, Andrew, Joemar, and her assistants go back and forth refilling the platters and talking to the neighborhood kids. I usually help too, but Tita Baby let me be off duty for the night to hang out with my friends for once.

I'm only half listening to Nicole since I'm busy filling Daniel's plate with fried rice. "I want to see a clean plate, Daniel. Then you can go play your game."

He obediently starts spooning up the rice, and I glance over to see Junior and Nicole exchanging looks. "What?"

"Guess that answers my question," Nicole says. "This is what you've been up to. School. Kali. Work. Daniel. Rinse and repeat."

"You're such a mom," Junior adds, digging into his own

food. "These classes are the only fun thing you do, and that's still, like, tied into family time and work."

"I do fun things!" I say, racking my brain to remember the last fun thing I did. With how far back I'm going in my memory, they might be right, and I absolutely cannot let them know that. "I read tarot cards for people at school!"

"That's work," Nicole says. "You're charging people for it. And don't lie and say you read for friends. Andrew and Joemar already told me you don't have friends at school."

Another side effect of having such overprotective cousins who also work as informants on the side? Not only is my dating life affected but they also have people watching me at school to make sure I stay out of trouble. I need to have words with them because this is embarrassing.

I wave their remarks away. "I have people I eat lunch with every day, and I talk to my classmates all the time. They don't know what they're talking about."

Sure, those people aren't exactly friends the way Junior and Nicole are, but it's not like I'm some weird loner. I've got other stuff going on.

"Anyway, as I said in my text that you two so rudely ignored, I have big news. But you can't go spreading it around."

"You finally had sex?" Nicole asks.

Junior starts laughing so hard, he chokes, and Nicole has to slap him on the back a few times.

"I hate you both. And my news is way more important than that." I pause for dramatic effect before saying, "I've got my first case!"

Both of them pause midmotion, Nicole with her fork in the air, about to stab a sausage, and Junior with his water glass tilted, about to drink. He continues to move his glass even after he turns his head toward me and ends up spilling ice water all over himself.

"Gah! Look what you made me do."

I roll my eyes and grab a towel from the pile behind us so he can dry off. "Don't go blaming your cartoon clumsiness on me."

"I can't believe your mom is letting you have a case," Nicole says. "I thought she wanted you to stay away from the actual agency work so you could focus on college stuff."

That's the annoying thing. My mom has no issues using me as a free secretary and babysitter, but anytime I show an interest in the job she does, she brushes me off and tells me to hit the books. Hypocritical much?

"She thinks I should have the college experience and choose a 'real' job instead of being forced into an unconventional one like her. She's big on choice, supposedly. But when I tell her that I *want* to work at the agency, suddenly it's like my choices don't matter." I steal the last Vienna sausage off Junior's plate. "But since this new case involves a girl at my school, she wants me to help with, like, insider stuff."

"Oh cool. So this is your chance to prove yourself, huh?"

I already said as much to myself, but hearing someone else say it out loud makes it that much more real to me.

Junior knows better than to fight me over food and helps himself to more fried rice from the fresh platter that Tita Baby sets down.

My aunt must've overheard at least part of our conversation, because she sits down next to me. "Your dad told me about your new job. Asked me to make sure you could take care of yourself if things go sideways."

Contrary to what you see on TV and in movies, not all PIs carry a gun. My mom sure doesn't. She focuses on family issues because that's what she cares about. It's way less dangerous than handling criminal cases—she won't even tell me about the investigations she handled at her mentor's agency before striking out on her own—but that's not to say there isn't risk involved.

Lying spouses really don't like getting caught. And if someone has escalated to parental kidnapping, it's not like they're going to willingly hand over their child. My mom usually brings my cousins along if there's a chance of violence, but she's gotten into more than one fistfight, almost been stabbed a handful of times, and received countless death threats.

So yeah, I've been training in self-defense almost since birth. But does that mean I'm truly ready?

I'm about to answer with all the confidence that I definitely don't feel, but Tita Baby's not done yet. "You know your mom. She's not big on second chances."

I lift my chin. "I won't need one."

Tita Baby grins. "That's what I want to hear."

I finally have the opportunity I've been waiting for, and I'm not about to blow it.

I return her smile. "Don't worry about me, Tita. I got this."

THE CASE FILES OF DANIKA DIZON

CASE NO.: XX-135
DATE: April 8, 20XX
CASE TYPE: missing minor; presumed runaway
CLIENT NAME(S): Juan David and Caitlin Delgado
(parents)

CASE INFORMATION:

On the morning of Saturday, April 6, clients realized
their 17-year-old daughter, Eli, hadn't come home. A
search of her room led them to believe she had run away.
No sign of struggle, several bags and personal items
missing. Allegedly no note left behind (younger sister
claims otherwise).

REQUEST(S): Find Eli. Do not arouse the suspicions
of the school, friends, neighbors, relatives, or other
acquaintances. Avoid involving the police. May only
speak to approved people (Note: list with Angelica
Dizon).

CLIENT INFORMATION:

NAME: Mary Elizabeth "Eli" Delgado
DATE OF BIRTH: October 4, 20XX; 17 years old
STATUS: missing; presumed runaway
GENDER IDENTITY/PRONOUNS: female; she/her
HEIGHT: 5 ft. 5 in.

EYE COLOR: light brown

HAIR COLOR: dark brown with blond highlights

HAIR TYPE: medium length; naturally curly but often wears it straightened

SKIN COLOR: deep tan

BODY TYPE: curvy

ETHNIC/RACIAL BACKGROUND: biracial; Colombian and Irish American

OCCUPATION: student, senior in high school; no part-time job (according to parents)

KNOWN ASSOCIATES: Winston Chang (boyfriend); Eunice Kim (best friend)

KNOWN HANGOUTS: school volunteer club

[Recent high school photo attached]

CHAPTER FOUR

THE FIRST PLAN OF ACTION IS TO TALK TO ELI'S friends and see if they have any idea what happened to her. I told Gaby yesterday that I was perfectly fine taking the bus to school, but she insisted on picking me up the next morning to go over the details of my investigation.

"Something tells me that if I don't insert myself now, you're going to try and do everything on your own, and that's not why I came to you."

I wanted to argue with her—this is my investigation, and she has no idea what she's doing—but I remembered something my dad said when my mom was complaining about a difficult client not too long ago.

"I know it seems like your client doesn't trust you, but I don't think that's it. He may be nitpicking over every little thing you do, but I don't think he's trying to find fault with you. I think he's looking for something else."

My mom, knowing my dad gives great advice but only after a lot of buildup and talking around things, sighed and gestured at him to continue. *"And that is . . . ?"*

"A sense of control. If you can make him feel involved somehow,

if you can give him a task that'll keep him busy, that'll stop him from feeling so helpless. And I think you'll find he's actually quite an asset to your investigation." My dad paused, glancing over at me, and I quickly turned my attention back to Daniel's homework, pretending I hadn't been eavesdropping the whole time. *"I think you'll find that's true for a lot of your clients. Trust and a sense of control. That's all they really want."*

My dad knows his job isn't to fix things. If my mom wanted help, which she never does, she would ask for it. He's there for emotional support and to provide an ear while she brainstorms out loud and comes to her own conclusions. But once in a while, he steps outside his prescribed role and tells her what she needs to hear, whether she wants it or not. And she knows if he's offering advice, then it's worth listening to.

So far, he hasn't been wrong. Maybe his career as a writer gives him insight into people that the rest of us don't have. He spends months at a time getting into the heads of his characters, figuring out what makes them tick. Or maybe with three sisters, he's learned the power of being an active listener.

All that to say, maybe I shouldn't alienate Gaby right off the bat by trying to go total lone wolf. The whole point of my mom letting me in on the case is that I have access to people she doesn't. She even said Gaby knows more than she's letting on. So I might as well let Gaby think she has some control. I can steer her in the direction I want to go and let her think it was her idea.

It's actually a good thing that she picked me up this morning because (1) I was so busy searching Eli's social media for clues that I overslept, and (2) the Delgados came up with a cover story to excuse Eli's absence, and Gaby wanted to make sure I didn't accidentally blow her sister's cover.

As far as the school knows, Eli is out of town caring for a sickly aunt who lives in Michigan and requested Eli's company since she's near the end of her life and wants her favorite niece nearby. Gaby let me know in no uncertain terms what her parents would do if word got out that their precious, perfect angel ran away from home. That is, if word got out that Mrs. Delgado's parenting made her daughter run.

"They'd fire your ass. Then they'd leave a shitty review and spread the word that your family's agency isn't to be trusted."

"Because I accidentally let it slip that your sister ran away?"

"You saw what my mom is like. You ruin our family's image, and she has no problem ruining yours."

"Yeah, but it's not only our image she's trying to ruin. It's our livelihood."

Gaby pulls into a parking spot on Rockwell, near the McDonald's, and kills the engine before turning to me. "Then I guess you better not mess this up."

AFTER THAT CHEERFUL MORNING RIDE, I CAN'T WAIT to go to class so I can get away from Gaby. I spend first period formulating a list of questions to ask Eli's friends after school and think about what the most natural approach would be. If the Delgados don't want anyone to know what really happened to

Eli, drawing attention to her absence with a bunch of questions from some rando probably isn't the way to go.

I spend second period doing more of the same, but during homeroom, an announcement comes in saying that third period is canceled. Instead there's going to be a school-wide assembly memorial service for a senior who passed away recently. Everyone around me starts buzzing about the announcement, excited about the "free" period since they can chill or catch up on the homework they didn't do. The fact that the only reason we have this free period is because some kid died does nothing to dampen anyone's enthusiasm. I sure hope that nobody who knew the guy is in our homeroom because even I think that people are being insensitive as hell.

I often sit by myself at a desk in the corner because sometimes people in my homeroom want a tarot consultation, but the group of girls who often ask for readings is too busy gossiping about the guy who died.

"Did you hear? The memorial is for Marisa's ex."

"Marisa's ex? You mean Alberto?"

"Yup. I wonder how he died."

"Ohmigod, she must be so heartbroken. She was still super into him, wasn't she?"

"Yeah, from what I hear, he was a good guy but she never got to see him. He worked mad shifts at his job to help out his family and told her it'd only get worse after graduation. He broke up with her so she could find someone more available."

My ears prick up at this information. Alberto? For some reason, that name rings a bell, but I can't connect it to a face.

Then again, Alberto is a fairly common name. The chances that I know the guy are slim. There are over four thousand students in this school, and we weren't even in the same year.

I doodle in my notebook as I listen in and feel a pang in my chest for this boy's family. Bad enough to lose someone so young, but it seemed like his family depended on him. I feel a sad connection to this dead kid and start to question what happened to him when I overhear this next bit of gossip:

"Really? I heard she broke up with him because he was into some shady shit, and she didn't want to get involved. Maybe he was a drug dealer or something?"

"Wait, does anyone know how he died? If he was suspicious, maybe someone ki—"

"Excuse me, ladies, but it is in very poor taste to be gossiping about the deceased like that." Mr. Jones, our homeroom teacher, steps into the gossip circle that formed next to me. "I understand being curious about the loss of a fellow student, but take care not to spread rumors, especially when you don't know the whole story. It does a disservice to his memory, as well as to his friends and family."

The girls all flush and apologize to Mr. Jones, who gives them a kind smile. "I know you're processing the news. And if you need it, I believe grief counseling will be available. But do be careful about what you say, especially in public. Now get ready. Homeroom's almost over. You all have to head down to the auditorium."

I was so busy eavesdropping, I must've missed Gaby's first few texts. And now, she's blowing up my phone with single-word messages.

Gaby: WHY

AREN'T

YOU

RESPONDING

STOP

IGNORING

ME

I scroll up and see that she texted me right after the announcement, asking to meet up in front of the auditorium, so we can sit together during the memorial. With the whole school there, she thinks it might be a good time to wander around and talk to Eli's friends.

Danika: Don't we have to sit with our class?

Gaby: Its fine, just show up, get attendance, then come find me

Danika:

After I check in with my third-period teacher, I wait till her back is turned to slip away to meet up with Gaby. On the way, I hear speculation about the deceased similar to what the girls in my homeroom said. It runs the gamut from a simple car accident to a hit by the Chicago Mafia. One person says he was stabbed, another that he was shot. It's all so fantastical that I should ignore it and keep moving, but I feel myself slowing down to take in as much as I can.

The detective blood running through my veins longs to listen in on everyone's conversations, jotting down and sifting through the information until I figure out what really happened to this guy. But I'm here to solve a missing-girl case, not a death, one that probably isn't even suspicious to begin with, so I force myself to stop dragging my feet and head toward Gaby.

She's standing with a couple girls. I recognize a senior from my chemistry class, but I don't know her name.

The senior recognizes me too, because she says, "Hey, you're in Ms. Lewis's class with me, right? I'm Jana."

The other girl introduces herself as Eunice, and I realize she's Eunice Kim, Eli's best friend.

"Danika," I say.

Eunice says, "Gaby tells us you read tarot cards." When I nod, she continues. "What period do you have lunch? I'd love for you to read for me!"

"Fifth, but I usually don't—"

"Oh, perfect! I do too. So can you—"

"I didn't realize we had lunch the same period, Danika. We should sit together," Gaby interrupts. "Eunice, Danika charges for her services. She's not going to give anything away for free."

Eunice laughs. "I can pay. Now that I think about it, I've

heard of you. Wasn't Eli asking about some tarot reader here at school a couple weeks ago?"

Jana tilts her head. "Did she? She always made fun of me whenever I talked about horoscopes—Aquarius sun, Virgo rising—so I had no idea she was into tarot. But she's been acting weird lately, and maybe she needed to talk to someone who's not us."

My ears perk up at that tidbit. "Eli's been acting weird? How so?"

Jana gives me an odd look, probably wondering why I care, but explains. "Well, she broke up with Winston, for one. She says she's been too busy with work and doesn't have time to deal with him. *But* I'm pretty sure the real reason is she met a new guy at her job."

Eunice adds, "She's also always staring at her phone. More than once, I glanced over when she was texting, and she hid the screen. You only do that if you have a secret boyfriend, you know?"

Interesting. I didn't know Eli had a job. When my mom asked yesterday, Mrs. Delgado said her daughter was too busy with school to bother looking for work she didn't even need. Talking to Eli's friends is already paying off. I'll have to update her case file.

I glance over at Gaby, wondering if she knew this information, but her expression gives nothing away. "I see. Why would she keep that from you? You'd think she'd want to gush about a new boyfriend. Show him off or whatever."

I have no idea how to talk about romantic partners, since I've never dated anyone or been in love or anything like that, and my fictional crushes on Catra from *She-Ra* and half the cast of *Riverdale* don't count, according to my friends. But Nicole falls in love, like, every other week, and tells me and Junior everything about her new crushes. I mean EVERYTHING.

Jana and Eunice exchange glances and grin at each other. "Isn't it obvious? If Little Miss Goody Two-Shoes broke up with her perfect, boring boyfriend and is dating a new guy who she's keeping secret, someone she can't even tell *me* about . . ."

Jana finishes Eunice's sentence. "He's the type of guy she can't tell anyone about. Probably older, definitely a bad boy, someone her parents would loathe."

I flash back to Eli's reading, and the little signs that made me wonder if she had an abusive boyfriend. If her friends are right, then finding this new guy is our next step. After all, the partner is usually to blame in cases like this. Eli's ex-boyfriend is also a prime suspect, but there are now a bunch of question marks around Mystery Man . . .

"Have you noticed any other red flags?"

Eunice pauses. "I thought you were a tarot card reader, not a detective?"

Oof. "I'm a concerned citizen."

"Right. Well, she's been obsessing over her job. Taking on more shifts so we can never hang out, always spending time with the people at work. It's not like she needs the money, so something is going on."

That's the second time someone has mentioned Eli not needing to work for money. It's one thing for her mom to say that, but kind of weird for one of her friends to. The only time Junior,

Nicole, and I talk about money is to complain about not having it. Is Eli the type to flaunt her wealth? Maybe Eunice is like my mom and can clock who comes from money based on their clothes, speech, and mannerisms. I try to remember how Eli was dressed when I did her reading, but all I really remember is her expensive ring. Did her secret boyfriend give it to her? Or does she have a taste for luxury that led her to racking up debt, and that's why she ran?

"I think Eli was saving up so she could stay with our aunt. Our parents were against it, saying they're already helping our aunt with her medical bills and Eli needed to focus on school. Eli insisted she do more, with or without their money. She said senior year is a joke anyway since she took all the tests to get into college last year. And her attendance is good enough that she should be fine missing a few days." Gaby sighs. "I wanted to go too, but apparently junior year is more important to my parents than being there for our aunt."

I don't know Gaby well enough to know if lying comes naturally to her or if she practiced her story knowing people would have questions, but she delivers it with a smoothness that I can't help but admire. Most importantly, Jana and Eunice totally buy it. Partnering with her is definitely the right move.

After that, Jana changes the subject to ask me about my zodiac sign because she's super into astrology and figures it must be connected to tarot. Which it kind of is. Anyway, after she asserts, "Oh my God, you are SUCH a Libra," despite only knowing me for a few minutes, I promise to read their cards during lunch, and Jana and Eunice move to join their class. I wait until they're far enough away that I'm sure they won't overhear us to say, "Your mom told us that Eli didn't have a job. Was that a lie?"

Gaby sighs. "I suspected she was using her club as an excuse to go off and do other stuff, but I didn't actually know. Like I said before, we're not exactly close anymore."

Something about the way she says this makes me think of a million other questions, but the memorial is about to start, and I need to head back to my class before my teacher notices I'm gone. As I say goodbye to Gaby, I can't help rethinking my earlier assessment—partnering with Gaby IS a huge help . . . but only when I can tell if she's being honest. The way she handled the cover story her parents cooked up was so smooth, and now she's claiming she didn't know that Eli had a job . . . I'm not sure if I believe her.

Seems like deception is a common trait among the Delgados, and it's up to me to sift through the lies to figure out what really happened to Eli.

CHAPTER FIVE

I'M NOW BURSTING AT THE SEAMS TO FIND OUT IF Eli really does have a secret boyfriend and, if so, what his role is in her disappearance. But I still have to make it through the rest of the school day.

The memorial assembly finally starts, and after a few generic words from the principal about "our dear departed friend, Alberto Ruiz," the screen behind the principal changes from the image of our school to a yearbook photo of Alberto. With a start, I lean forward and study the picture.

I know him. Or, at least, I used to.

He wasn't from my neighborhood, but he lived close enough to stop by Tita Baby's Kali classes once in a while. He didn't attend regularly—I remember overhearing him and Tita Baby talking about his part-time job and how that would be taking up most of his free time, but he'd drop by anyway. We talked a couple times briefly after Kali class and would do the head-nod thing when we saw each other in the halls, but it's not like I knew him very well. He was a decent guy, though, and based on what those girls in my homeroom said, he was working hard to support his family. My aunt is going to be shook when I tell her about his death.

The principal steps aside, and Alberto's homeroom teacher comes to the podium to give a more personal remembrance, then informs us that grief counseling is available to students. The principal returns to the podium with an impassioned speech about how we're all in this together, and there's a moment of silence in honor of Alberto. "Take all the time you need. And remember: Counselors are available if you need anything."

BLESS MY THOUGHTFUL ENGLISH TEACHER, WHO let me leave class to process. Seeing Alberto's yearbook photo during the memorial gave me an idea. In the library now, I pull out the yearbooks from Eli's freshman, sophomore, and junior years, hoping to find a clue. Our school's pretty huge, with over four thousand students, but Eli's friends and parents mentioned Eli being a "good girl" and skipping a grade, which makes me think she's in the honor society on top of that volunteer club she allegedly attends. If I can figure out how Eli spent those last few days before her disappearance, I might get an idea of what led up to it. Or at least find people who know a different side of Eli, the side that has a secret boyfriend and no longer wanted, as her friends put it, a "perfect, boring" boyfriend. What's his name again? Winston?

Sure enough, she is in every National Honor Society pic, along with a Winston Chang. I check my case file and confirm that yes, Winston Chang is the guy her parents named as her boyfriend. There's no way for me to get my hands on his schedule, so I check to see if he's part of any other clubs.

He's on both the school newspaper and the golf team. I didn't even know we had a golf team. I also check to see which volunteer club Eli's part of. Who knew our school had so many different ones? Chi-Care, GIVE Student Group, Key Club . . . there are over a dozen clubs that mention volunteer work, and Eli isn't pictured in any of them. Maybe she joined after the club photos were taken.

Well, I have enough to go on for now. I can ask Gaby during lunch what else she knows about Eli's ex and extracurriculars. I don't need Gaby to talk to the volunteer club—unless she has no idea which one it is and we have to hit them up individually—but once I learn the meeting times for the school newspaper and golf team, we can go interrogate Winston together. I'm sure she'd love that.

"ABSOLUTELY NOT. YOU'RE WASTING YOUR TIME IF you think he has anything to do with this."

Gaby narrows her eyes at the limited selection on offer in the school cafeteria: burgers, chicken tenders, mushy green beans, and French fries. Salad, which is basically the lettuce, tomatoes, and onions they serve as toppings for the burgers. Their one vegetarian option today (other than salad, but salad doesn't count) is grilled cheese, which she plunks on her tray along with a basket of fries and a few slices of tomato. As she pays for her food, she mutters, "I can't believe you're making me eat here."

"You're the one who insisted I eat lunch with you! Sorry you're stuck with us poors," I shoot back defensively.

Most upperclassmen eat lunch off campus—the only students who *have* to eat in the cafeteria are freshmen and people like me, who can't afford to eat out. Yeah, the food here sucks, but you know what doesn't suck? Free lunch. The selection is the same every day, so sometimes I'll bring baon from the previous night's leftovers, or if Daniel's class is going on a field trip, my dad will pack lunch for both of us. But most of the time, I'm stuck with the school's greasy fare.

I hand over my student ID that has the "free lunch" designation on it and smile at the older Filipino woman at the register. I didn't think Dizon was that uncommon of a last name, but the first day she met me, she took one look at my ID and asked if I was related to her favorite author, Benigno Dizon, and ever since she chats with me about my dad's books and slips me something special. Today it's sapin-sapin, my favorite Filipino dessert.

My face lights up at the circle of sweet purple, yellow, and white sticky rice layers. "Thanks, Tita Jo!"

She smiles. "I know it's your favorite, but make sure to share with your family. Now go on, you're holding up the line."

"Salamat po," I say, thanking her politely in Tagalog before I follow Gaby to an empty table and place my tray down. "We're not sitting with your friends?"

Again, most upperclassmen avoid the cafeteria, but it's not like it's weird for us to be here. I eat lunch most days with a couple girls I'm cool with who are in my next period. When I told them I was meeting up with someone, they didn't question it.

She scrunches her nose. "How are we going to talk about my sister with other people around? And lower your voice."

"It's so loud in here, I doubt anyone will overhear us, but

you've got a point." I pick up my burger. "Where are Jana and Eunice? I thought they wanted a reading."

She tears a piece off her grilled cheese and pops it in her mouth before answering. "They'll come later. Gives us time to come up with more questions for them. You were a little obvious earlier."

I wince. I had a feeling I came on a bit strong. "It was my first time interviewing people, so I wasn't as smooth as I should be. It's different doing practice interrogations with my dad and doing it for real. It won't happen again, I promise."

"It's fine. You were able to get good info out of them. We just need to figure out if my sister really does have a new boyfriend, who knows about him, and if he's someone from work. Oh, and where she's been working."

"Why don't you want to talk to her ex?" I ask, bringing the conversation back to the original topic before I got distracted by Tita Jo's sapin-sapin.

She makes a face. "He creeps me out."

"Did he say or do anything weird to you?" I lean forward. "He never tried to . . . you know?"

Thankfully, she laughs and waves her hand. "No, he's never done anything I didn't want. He's just too perfect, you know what I mean?"

I do not.

"Like, nobody's really that nice. It felt like an act, you know? Even Eli complained that he was too much sometimes, and she, like, worships that guy. Or, at least, she did. I didn't even know they broke up. But whatever. I may not like him, but he's harmless. There's no way he did anything to my sister."

Which leads me to the question I've been wanting to ask but haven't had the chance to yet.

"You said you and Eli aren't close. How come?"

The fact that Gaby came to me about her sister's disappearance implies that they somewhat are, but I also know that sibling relationships can be complicated. Especially when close in age. Nicole has three sisters, and they're all two to three years apart. From what I've seen, she would die for her sisters, but she is also ready to throw hands with them at any given moment. That's love in the Castillo-Johnson household. I wonder if it's the same for the Delgado sisters.

"We used to be," Gaby finally says. "We had the same friend group when we were little, but once she got to high school, we started doing our own things. She became part of the super-high-achieving crowd while I went down the art route."

"You can be high achieving and do art," I say, thinking of Nicole and her fashion school ambitions. Like me, she's hustling to get good-enough grades for a scholarship, but at least she has a dream school she's aiming for.

"Yeah, I didn't mean it like that. I know plenty of people in the art program who are killing it at school. I'm just not one of them. I'm one of those 'doesn't live up to her full potential' types," she says with air quotes, "while Eli's out here building robots and doing whatever STEM kids do."

She says this as if it doesn't bother her, but it so obviously does.

"Did she ever try to get you to be more like her?"

The smile she gives me is as bitter as the ampalaya I pretend to like so my brother will eat it. "Nah, that's more my parents.

Eli would actually defend me. Told them to let me live my life, that I was smart enough to figure things out on my own. So even though we aren't close like we used to be, we always look out for each other. Which is why I came to you."

Now's not the time to properly interview her. It will look too weird if I break out my tablet and start recording our conversation in the middle of the cafeteria. But I'm starting to get an image of who Gaby is and, by extension, who Eli is. My mom and dad both say that the better you understand your subject, the more you can get in their head and predict how they'll act.

My dad does it whenever he gets stuck in a story. Sometimes he asks me to interview him, and he answers as if he's the character he's working on to get a better feel for their personality and motives. It helps him with his writing and me with my interview skills (which clearly still need work). My mom only has to do this in extreme cases, like when there's a custody dispute and one of the parents takes the kid and runs. Then she has to go full-on *Criminal Minds* and track them down.

So here's what I've learned about Gaby: I know she doesn't trust her mom but remains loyal to her family. I know she's a good asset to the investigation since she can introduce me to the important people in Eli's life without raising any suspicions. And based on how she handled the cover story for Eli's absence, she's a decent actress and liar. Now I know the roles she and her sister hold in the family—the angel and the rebel. But who is she really? I can't tell. Yet.

"Even if you don't like Winston, I have to talk to the guy. If she broke up with him for someone else, maybe they had an argument about the new boy. He could potentially tell me who he is or where she met him. And if Winston was salty about their breakup, maybe he had something to do with her leaving. This early in an investigation, every little detail counts."

Gaby sighs. "Fine. You want me to introduce you two or something? He knows I don't like him, though, so I'm not sure if I'd actually be helping."

"Maybe it's best if he doesn't know that we know each other, then. He's part of the school newspaper, so I can go there and try to get close to him. Just need to find out when they meet."

"Works for me," Gaby says as Jana and Eunice enter the caf.

She waves at them to get their attention, and they make their way over to us, both girls sitting on the same side as Gaby, ready for their tarot readings.

"I haven't been in here in forever," Eunice says, wrinkling her nose at our trays. "I guess they haven't changed the menu since I was a freshman. I remember eating most of my lunches out of the vending machines. I can't believe you eat here by choice."

I roll my eyes. "Do you want a reading or not?"

I'm usually a little more polite to my clients since repeat customers allow me to stay in business, but I'm in no mood to defend my socioeconomic status and subsequent dining choices. Though now that I study the three girls in front of me, I can tell that "free lunch" is not part of their vocabulary. I don't care about fashion, but my mom's taught me how to recognize wealth when I see it.

And, sure, I could use some of my tarot money to go out to eat instead, but the lure of fixing up my car is way stronger than the pull of fast food and acquaintances to eat it with. Growing up, I watched old detective shows with my dad and fell in love with the black 1994 Chrysler LeBaron convertible that Veronica Mars drove. I thought all my dreams came true when my grandparents spotted the car in a friend's garage and bought it for me.

It was super cheap since it needed over three thousand dollars' worth of repairs, which I've slowly been paying off for the past year. I only need nine hundred dollars more, and I'm that much closer to my mom acknowledging that I'm fit to work for her. That I'm independent and responsible enough to handle cases.

"Can I go first?" Jana asks. "My boyfriend has his heart set on going to Caltech, but my dream is to study food science at Cornell. I know we might not get into our top choices, but if we end up going to different colleges, is it worth doing long-distance, or should I cut my losses and start fresh?"

Must be nice, having choices like that. The college I go to will be the one that offers me the most financial aid. I'm sure my mom is hoping for the University of Chicago, not only because it's local but because it's prestigious enough to rub it in her family's faces. Even if I do make it in—and that's one giant "if"— I doubt they'll offer enough in scholarships to cover the full tuition. Let her dream, though.

I want a school that will keep my mom happy and let me live at home. My mom may talk a big game about wanting me to spread my wings and see what else is out there, but I know how much they need me around. Besides, since I'm an honors student, my grades are good, but they're not "full ride covering tuition, room and board, textbooks, and general living" good. At least Jana's not thinking about ditching her dream to follow her boyfriend to college. I would've made sure the cards told her not to give everything up for a guy.

I push aside my half-eaten lunch and wipe down the space in front of me before pulling my decks out of my backpack. I carefully unwrap the scarf around them and spread the scarf out on the table, placing the decks in the middle. I only have two decks right now, but choosing the right one can enhance the reading. I think for a moment before setting aside my old, beat-up Rider-Waite-Smith deck for the newer one.

"I'm going to do a three-card spread. While I shuffle, I want you to keep these three questions clear in your mind: What if I stay? What if I go? How do I decide?"

Jana eyes the deck. "Why those questions? Why not something more straightforward, like 'Should I stay with him?'"

"I don't like using yes/no questions or giving predictions. This isn't fortune-telling."

"Then what's the point?"

I bristle a little. "Tarot is more like advice. It's a way of looking deep inside yourself to see the truths you've been hiding from. It can also help you see things more objectively," I say, picking up the deck. "The cards don't lie, but they also don't tell the future. It's all in how you interpret them. Now, remember, those three questions should remain in your head."

I shuffle the deck a few times before laying it facedown again in front of her.

"Cut the deck in two or three piles and then stack them up again however you like."

Jana obeys, and when she's done, I pick up the cards and lay three facedown in front of her.

"The first card represents what could happen if you stay." I turn it over, revealing the Two of Chalices reversed. I'm careful to keep my face passive, but it makes sense.

"The next card represents what could happen if you leave." I turn it over, and the reversed Sun card greets us. Interesting.

"And, finally, how do you make a decision?" The Nine of Swords, also reversed. An entire inverted reading. It couldn't be clearer to me, but I always check to see how the cards resonate with the client before I share my interpretation.

"Do any of these cards in particular call out to you?" I ask.

Jana starts to reach out but pulls her hand back and glances at me questioningly.

I gesture to the cards. "Go ahead. Feel free to pick them up if you want to study them closer. Just know that the meaning changes depending on if the card is upright or reversed. These cards are reversed."

Jana takes her time, inspecting each card several times, but the one she keeps going back to is the Two of Chalices. "What does this mean? The picture is calling to me, but if it's upside-down, that's not good, is it?"

I'm using the new deck Junior and Nicole bought me for my birthday, the Star Spinner Tarot. Something about the beautiful fairy tale–inspired imagery makes it perfect for love readings. The card has shades of pink and yellow, and in the center are two mermaids facing each other, their hands on the other's hips, tails and flowing hair intertwined. In between them is a pink heart. Considering Jana wants me to give her relationship advice, I'm not surprised this is the card she's drawn to.

"The Two of Cups—or, in this case, Chalices—represents a healthy, balanced relationship. Because it's reversed here, it implies that your current relationship is unbalanced—one of you is giving more than you're getting, basically. And if you choose to stay in the relationship, you need to take a closer look at your partner and reevaluate your priorities to get yourselves back in balance."

Gaby and Eli's friends stare at me.

"What?"

"That is . . . excellent advice. Like, that's exactly how I'm feeling," Jana says. "Lately, it's like all I do is give. Listen to *his* problems, help with *his* homework, write him notes and texts that he never answers, and, like, where is that consideration for me? I have problems too. My life isn't always easy. And yet . . ."

She trails off, and I wait a moment to see if she has anything else to say, but it seems like she's done. "Well, glad it resonates with you."

I want to ask why they're all ogling me as if I literally have a third eye in the middle of my forehead, but I shrug it off and talk about the next card. "The Sun is meant to be a joyous card. You know, full of light and warmth and potential. Growth, new opportunities, all that good stuff. But, again, it's reversed. So if you break up with your boyfriend, it might seem like a great new beginning, but if you're not careful, you might end up like Icarus."

Jana scrunches up her face. "And what does that mean?"

"If you think you're hot shit when you're single, you might girlboss too close to the sun," Gaby explains. "Sound about right, Danika?"

I laugh. "That's exactly right. In the myth, Icarus was too ambitious. He literally flew too close to the sun and ended up falling to his death as a result. Your pride can bring you down if you're not careful."

"So both choices come with risks? Then how do I know what to do?"

I point to the Nine of Swords. "This decision has been weighing on you for some time. You want to do the right thing, you want to make the choice where no one gets hurt, and you constantly blame yourself for feelings you can't control. I'm guessing you haven't talked to him about this yet?"

She shakes her head. "I care about him. I don't want him to think that I don't believe in us by bringing it up."

"This card is telling you that you've been in your head too long. You've got to talk. He's in the relationship too. He deserves to have a say in this."

Jana is silent for a moment. "I'll think about it."

I've done my part—it's up to her to listen to the cards or not. I'm used to people ignoring my advice, but as long as they pay me, I couldn't care less. Which reminds me . . .

"Twenty bucks, please. I only take cash."

"You don't have Venmo or anything?"

"No paper trails. Cash only." I also don't have a checking account, but "no paper trails" sounds cooler.

Jana rolls her eyes and digs through her backpack to find

her wallet. I usually collect payment up front since more than one client has stormed off after hearing what I had to say. People don't like it when you don't tell them what they want to hear, but I refuse to lie during my readings. Tarot is supposed to make you honest. I respect the cards too much to twist the meanings for easy money. And as much as I need the cash, the purpose of this reading is to collect information and get close to Eli's friends. I can relax my rules if it's for the investigation.

After she pays up, I turn to Gaby and Eunice. "Either of you want a reading? I'm nice and warmed up now."

But they both shake their heads.

"Don't get me wrong. I can tell you're legit. But I feel like I should think carefully about the questions I want answered first," Eunice says.

Gaby agrees. "I want you to read for me, but I need to make sure I'm ready for the cards' advice."

"I get it." I pack up the cards and wrap the scarf around my decks before returning them to my bag. Jana thanks me, and she signals to Eunice that it's time to head out.

Once they're gone, Gaby says, "You know, you're different when you're reading the cards. Like, you sound super mature. And you've got this aura around you. It's really cool. You're good at this, huh?"

"Yep."

She laughs. "Okay, confidence! Most people would be like, 'Eh, I'm all right, I guess.' And you're like, 'Damn right.'"

I shrug. "I *am* good at this. I know it. My clients know it. Why the need for false modesty?"

"No, you're right. Own your power. I was surprised. In a nice way."

The bell rings, and Gaby and I get up to bus our trays and go to our next classes. Before we split up, she takes a moment to look me up and down and grins.

"I wasn't sure if going to you was the right move, but I'm glad I did. Can't wait for the next surprise you've got for me."

THE CASE FILES OF DANIKA DIZON

NOTES:

- Delgado family cooked up cover story to explain Eli's absence—out of town, watching over sick aunt.
- Delgado matriarch is vindictive; do not get on her bad side.
- Preliminary search of Eli's social media (TikTok, Instagram) reveals little, other than a sudden lack of photos of Winston Chang after January. Suspicion that they broke up confirmed. Source: Eunice and Jana.
- Eli has a part-time job. Source: Eunice and Jana.
- Potential secret boyfriend. Source: Eunice and Jana.
- Gaby doesn't like Winston. Look into this more?

NEXT STEPS:

1. Infiltrate school newspaper to get close to Winston Chang.
2. Find out which volunteer club Eli was a member of.
3. Locate Eli's place of work.
4. Investigate possibility of secret boyfriend.

CHAPTER SIX

I RUN INTO MY HOMEROOM TEACHER AT THE END of the day, so I take the opportunity to ask him about the newspaper club. He tells me they meet every Wednesday at three in Room 303. Perfect. Time to formulate my plan.

I'm supposed to go straight home after school every day to take care of my brother and help at the front desk of the agency, so if I want to stay late tomorrow to check out that school newspaper meeting, I have to ask for permission first. I'm about to ask Gaby if she can drop me off at the agency when I get a call from my dad.

"Can you pick up some apple juice on your way home? You don't need to go to the office, so come straight here. Your mom is going to be out late most of the week, so she wants to eat together today."

"I needed to ask you both something anyway, so that's perfect. See you soon."

After reminding me what juice brand Daniel believes is superior, my dad hangs up. Gaby has to stay after school to work on a project with a classmate, so I hop on the bus to run my errands before heading home. After the long ride, I greet Veronica by tapping her hood. "Soon."

When my mom's on a case, she has no set schedule, and it's not unusual for me not to see her for days at a time, either because she gets in late and leaves early or because she doesn't come home at all. That's typically only if she's tailing a difficult suspect, and she tries not to take on cases like that because of Daniel, but it does happen on occasion. Anyway, I'm glad she'll be home for dinner since she's the decision-maker in our house, so it's up to her whether I should join the newspaper.

My dad and Daniel are busy in the kitchen, and my mom's watching the news in the living room when I get home. I kick off my shoes, put the juice in the fridge, and hand my mom her favorite bag of shrimp chips before joining her on the couch. I'm about to ask her what her plans are later when she shushes me, her eyes glued to the TV screen.

"There are still no leads in the murder of Walter Abbot, the attorney and noted philanthropist who was found dead in his Gold Coast–area home almost three weeks ago. The police believe he was the victim of a burglary gone wrong and ask for the public's assistance in tracking down the perpetrators. If you think you can help, please call the tip line at 555-4356. The Abbot estate has promised a reward. Next in the news . . ."

My mom switches off the TV, shaking her head. "I knew Walter Abbot. A friend of mine worked with him on a couple cases, and he was always kind to me. Such a shame."

I figure now's not the right time to ask about joining the newspaper, so I go to help my dad with dinner. Once the table is set and my mom has her glass of red wine firmly in hand, I tell them my plan to get close to Eli's ex-boyfriend, Winston, by (temporarily) becoming a member of the school newspaper. I didn't think my parents would give me a hard time—it's for the case, after all—but I didn't expect they'd get so weirdly excited about it either.

"The school paper! That will look so good on your college applications, anak!" my mom says, taking a sip of her drink before joining us at the table. I can't imagine it pairing well with the fried fish and pinakbet we're having for dinner, but I also know that that single glass of wine she allows herself is an important daily ritual for her.

"Journalism, eh?" my dad says while cutting up the food on Daniel's plate. "Maybe we have another writer in the house! You're already so good at helping me research and combing through newspaper archives for inspiration for books; you'd be a natural at this. Though I'm sure the stories you cover will be a little less grisly than the ones you work with me on. Still, I'm happy to brainstorm topics and give you some feedback on your articles if you need it."

My dad writes a long-running mystery series about a Filipino American male chef in Chicago who keeps getting caught up in random murders that he's forced to solve for some reason or other. The books are equal parts dark and comedic, but my dad prides himself on getting the details right. Once he realized I was serious about becoming a PI like my mom, he taught me the basics of investigation and asked me to be his research assistant as part of my training. So far, I've helped solve a ton of fictional cases, but that's not enough to prove myself to my mom. I *need* to find Eli.

"Daddy, you know I don't like ampalaya!" Daniel catches my

dad trying to cut up the bitter melon into tiny pieces to trick my brother into eating it.

"Ah, you caught me!" My dad ruffles Daniel's hair. "I'll get you next time, Gadget!"

My brother laughs but refuses to touch his plate as long as the offending vegetable is on it.

"Here, let's trade," I say. "Give me your ampalaya, and you can have my kalabasa or sweet potato. You have to eat one piece of ampalaya, though."

He lights up. "Kalabasa, please! Thanks, Ate."

I take his bitter melon and fork over my delicious orange squash and add a couple sweet potato pieces for good measure. I'm not a fan of ampalaya either, but if you add enough bagoong, the fermented shrimp paste covers up the yucky flavor. And this way, I get Daniel to eat more veggies without complaining.

I drizzle patis and calamansi over my fish before taking a bite and chase it with a large spoonful of rice before responding to my parents. "It's not like I plan on staying on the paper. I need a reason to talk to Eli's ex-boyfriend, and this is the easiest way."

"What if he's not there tomorrow? What if you don't get a chance to talk to him? What if you do talk to him, and he doesn't give you anything?" My mom fires off question after question at me. "When talking to people, especially potential suspects, you can't expect them to simply hand over the information you need. These things take time, especially if you don't want to draw attention to yourself or the case you're working on. College applications aside, working on the school paper gives you access to the right people. It's not strange for you to be asking questions if it's for an article. Be prepared to play a long game."

I was thinking that the more I hung around Winston, the more chances I would have to slip up and clue him in on what I'm doing, but she's got a point. Guess that's why she's the professional.

I tell her so, and she says, "Things happen. You're new to this. Right now, your priorities are to learn what you can from Eli's ex. Find out whether Eli really does have a secret boyfriend and job. Normally, I wouldn't have a problem handling the second part on my own, but the Delgados have placed an annoying number of restrictions on who I'm allowed to talk to. We're going to have to be creative if we want to discover anything without upsetting them."

My mom always tries her best to stay professional when talking about her clients, even when complaining about their special requests. I can tell she was doing her best not to bad-mouth the Delgados in front of me and Daniel, but it was a STRUGGLE. I wonder if she has, like, a private investigator buddy she can be petty with. I may not see Junior and Nicole as often as I should, but our group chat stays busy with the stuff we wish we could say to people.

"Anyway, I wanted to let you know, since I won't be able to help out at the agency on Wednesdays, because that's when the paper meets. But I should make it home in time for Tita Baby's lessons."

"Why don't you invite the girl's sister, Gaby? It would be good for you two to spend time together. Perhaps in doing so, you'll be able to figure out what they're hiding from us," my mom advises.

I make a face. "She's already taking me to school every morning. And we had lunch together today. Won't it seem like I'm coming on too strong if I invite her to our family's Kali classes too?"

My dad raises an eyebrow. "'Coming on too strong'? Is a martial arts class your idea of a date?"

"Ugh, I didn't mean it like that!"

My dad laughs, but my mom gives him a side-eye that shuts him up quick. "I know you two are joking, but I hope I don't have to remind you that you should never date your clients. It's extremely unethical."

"Mommy, when have I ever dated anyone? You think I'm going to suddenly jump into a relationship with a client? You should know me better than that."

I get she's watching out for me, but I'm offended that she thinks I need the warning. I'm a professional, like her. And I've finally gotten the chance I've wanted for so long. I can't mess up.

"I'll invite her tomorrow, but only because you specifically told me I should be friends with her for the case. I know how to behave with my sources."

My mom cracks a smile at that. "I'm sure you do, anak. I trust you. But remember that you've always got eyes on you."

And as if she didn't say some really ominous shit, she turns her attention back to her plate, and my family resumes eating dinner like the conversation never happened.

Typical night in the Dizon household.

CHAPTER SEVEN

want to join now?"

Guess I shouldn't have worried about if I'd get a chance to talk to Winston Chang considering he's the one giving me this intense interrogation. I knew my timing was questionable since there's less than two months of school left, but I didn't think it'd be that big of a deal.

"I have zero extracurriculars, and my parents are worried it'll hurt my chances when I start applying to colleges," I say. "My dad's a writer, so he suggested I try out the school paper."

"Your dad's a journalist? Does he work for the *Sun-Times* or the *Tribune*?"

"No, he—"

"Oh, is he with one of the independents? *Block Club Chicago* is doing great work," Mr. Belzek, the club advisor, cuts in.

Winston nods his head, seemingly impressed until I say, "No, he's a mystery writer. His books are—"

"Fiction," Winston says, interrupting me. "How would being related to a fiction writer help you with journalism?"

Mr. Belzek doesn't say anything, but I can tell he agrees.

How does constantly interrupting the person you're interviewing help YOU with journalism? I want to say, but my parents have warned me more than once to watch my mouth if I want to get results, so I simply say, "Good writing is good writing. I'm observant, take good notes, and know how to organize the facts into an interesting read. Storytelling is in my blood, and articles are their own kind of story."

"The school has a wonderful literary magazine," Mr. Belzek says helpfully. "If you want to follow in your father's footsteps, that is. The *Lane Tech Champion* is for students serious about journalism. But if you're wanting to try your hand at writing articles, then—"

"I am!" I say, grasping the opportunity before it gets away from me.

To be honest, I thought school clubs only involved you walking into the room, signing in, and hanging out, with maybe an agenda item or two discussed. At least, that's what my dad said it was like back when he attended this school. I guess it's changed in the last twentysomething years. Whatever. I refuse to fall at this first hurdle.

"What kind of stories are you hoping to write?" Winston asks. "We've already got the major sections covered. By actual journalism students."

"As a newbie, I'm happy to simply shadow someone who's been doing this for a while or to collaborate on something," I say, starting to realize I was completely wrong about how the school newspaper operated. "I'm here for the experience, not for the bylines."

"Is that so? Would you be willing to assist me?" Winston grins at me, and suddenly I see why Gaby thinks he's a creep.

Don't get me wrong, he's cute. Kinda hot, actually, if I'm being real. His yearbook photos do not do him justice (not to mention that the images that "honor student" and "golf team" bring to mind really don't do it for me either). But there's something off about his smile. It's . . . calculating. Like he's sizing me up so he can figure out how he can use me. If we were in an anime, he'd be the megane character, pushing up his glasses right before delivering a devastating line.

"Um, sure? I mean, I want to observe so I can figure out my niche. You're the head editor, right?" He told me so as soon as I walked in, wanting to know why I wanted to work on "his" paper. "Who better to learn from than you?"

"Perfect. I've been wanting someone to dump all the boring research onto. You handle the stuff I hate doing these last few weeks of school, and I'll show you everything you need to know. Deal?"

My second full day on the job, and I'm already making deals with the devil.

I shake his hand. "Looking forward to working with you, Winston Chang."

WINSTON STARTS MENTORING BY HAVING ME TRACK the rising cost of admission to Illinois universities over the past ten years. Easy enough since I've already researched this all before.

Once, I created a whole PowerPoint when I was first trying to convince my mom that I didn't need to go to college and she should hire me full-time at the agency. I mean, my dad never finished college, and he's doing fine. My mom took off her slipper and pointed it at me when we got to that slide, though, so it didn't really have the impact I wanted.

As I sigh and jot down another boring statistic, some of the other members of the newspaper staff come up to talk to me. They stayed out of the way when Winston was around, but he left a few minutes ago to "chase down a lead."

"He stuck you with the college admissions article, huh?" A girl from my homeroom (I think her name's Sarah?) peers over my shoulder at my notes. "Probably thinks he can make the newbie do all the grunt work while he slaps his name on it, so he can focus on the real story he wants."

At my inquiring expression, she adds, "Mr. Belzek assigned this article to him, but everyone knows there's another story he's been obsessed with."

The other newspaper staff members take this opportunity to introduce themselves—there are quite a few of them, so I pull out my tablet to jot down names, what year they are, and any other identifying information they share that can help me later.

Mike, a junior and second-in-command for the newspaper, snorts. "Dude thinks he's gonna win a Pulitzer or some shit. Isn't he trying to get some breaking story on a corrupt alderman?"

Bethany, a sophomore girl, groans. "He's still on that? He was talking about it when I first joined last year."

Mike nods. "Right? He's graduating soon, so there's no

reason for him to be going so hard on this. Not for a high school paper. Who's even gonna read it? The only people who care about his articles are his girlfriend and Mr. Belzek. Or, I guess, just Mr. Belzek now, since Eli broke up with him."

Ohmigod, yes, finally, an in! Even with Winston right in front of me, there was never a good chance to bring up Eli. But if these people are ready to talk behind his back, then . . . Okay, Danika, play it cool. "So, Mr. Head Editor had a girlfriend, huh? Can't imagine what it'd be like to date Winston. He's so . . . you know."

Mike rolls his eyes. "Mr. and Mrs. Perfect. Though not so perfect together, I guess. I heard she dumped his ass for some college kid. Must've been some overlapping."

Sarah leans forward. "Ooh, an older man? Spill."

"I don't know Winston's ex all that well. Eli's bougie AF, so I never really had anything to say to her. But a friend of mine works with her and said she caught Eli making out with another one of their coworkers. Real bad-boy type, apparently." He grins. "Guess Eli got tired of being the good girl."

One of the seniors, Jessica, says, "The way her parents are, I'm surprised they let her take time away from studying to work. Not like she needs the money."

Mike shrugs. "They work at some ritzy country club, so I bet she was networking or something. Isn't that what people who own yachts do?"

The Delgados own a yacht? The dad doesn't strike me as a boat guy, but Mrs. Delgado definitely does. Or is Mike exaggerating? This is the third time someone has brought up Eli not needing the money. Being rich seems to be Eli's sole identity. It's one thing when her best friend comments on it, seeing as Eunice is presumably close to Eli and the Delgados. I don't know how close Jessica and Eli are, but Mike admitted he's barely talked to her. Is it common knowledge that she's loaded? Or is Eli the type of person to brag about how much money she's got?

Gaby doesn't talk money, but it's obvious her family's got way more than mine based on her brand-new Audi, how she dresses, and the little comments she makes. I know my mom said I could only investigate the school angle, but . . . something tells me that if Little Rich Girl ran away from her life, the lure of an unsuitable guy is the most likely reason. That's basically what happened with my parents. Pretty sure it was a motive in one of my dad's books too. Makes more sense than Winston scaring her off after the breakup, anyway. Her note said she was staying with a friend. Maybe she's shacking up with the secret boyfriend?

"Do you know the name of the country club? I've been searching for a decent part-time job that accepts high school students," I ask.

"Gimme a sec, let me ask my friend." Mike texts someone and, within a few seconds, says, "Chicago Glen Country Club. Good luck getting a job there, New Girl. It sounds fancy as hell."

I make a mental note to ask my mom how to handle this. If it's at a country club, I doubt I can waltz in and ask around about Eli's boyfriend, but my mom can figure out a way. I'll bring it up later at the Kali lesson. Gaby's coming, and this will be a good way to see if she's even heard of the club.

To be honest, I haven't ruled out the possibility that Gaby had a hand in her sister's disappearance. Not, like, she murdered her and is trying to cover it up by using me to throw people off her trail (though, again, not ruling anything out completely). But she could've helped Eli run away. I have a gut feeling there are some crucial details she's been omitting. Maybe she doesn't trust me, or maybe she thinks she's being loyal to her sister. Either way, I need to find a way to get her to open up more.

As I jot these notes in my tablet, Sarah peers closely at me, recognition finally lighting up her eyes. "Wait a minute! You're the tarot chick, right? I've seen you doing readings during homeroom."

I crack a smile. "I prefer Danika, but yeah. I do paid readings during homeroom and after school under Stairwell O."

"My girlfriend told me about you." Mike appraises me. "If you're as good as she says you are, your talents are being wasted working with Winston. Would you be interested in an advice column?"

As much as I want to get close to Winston, an advice column sounds way more fun than being Winston's lackey. It'd also be great to show to a college. And while I normally avoid advertising my tarot business so openly—I'm not supposed to be operating a business on school grounds, after all—I can't pass up this opportunity. Not if it'll help spread the word about my readings and get me the funds I need to fix up Veronica. If I've gotta move my tarot spot across the street because some school official finds out about me and throws a fit, then so be it.

But before I can accept Mike's offer, Buzzkill cuts in.

"You don't have the authority to add new columns to the newspaper, Mike." Winston stalks over, and I curse under my breath. I have no idea when he got back and hope he didn't hear us talking about Eli. I don't want to tip him off about my investigation.

"Bro, you're graduating. I'm the one in charge once you're gone. And—"

"Ugh, I shudder to think what the *Champion* will become with you at the helm."

"—I'm not going to be like you, ignoring what our members want. Students have been asking for an advice column, and this is the perfect time to test it out."

Mike and Winston get into a staring match that goes on way too long, and I'm half tempted to push their faces together and say, *"Now kiss."*

Before I let my meme impulses get the better of me, Winston sighs and turns to me. "Your gimmick is to use tarot cards to give advice. Right?"

"It's not a gimmick, it's—"

He waves off my retort. "Whatever, that's not important. Mike is correct that, next year, he is the one in charge of the *Champion.*"

"About time you—"

"But until then," Winston continues, cutting off Mike, "this is my paper. Before I let anyone on, you need to prove you belong here."

"So what? You want me to read for you to show my skills?" I shrug, reaching for my backpack for my decks. "I don't usually do free tarot consultations. Consider yourself lucky."

He snorts, a surprisingly undignified noise that cuts the tension. I pull out one of my decks and start shuffling.

"Do you have a question, or would you prefer a more general reading?"

Winston hesitates. "Do I have to ask the question out loud?"

No, but this is a good chance to get inside his head, see what kinds of things he worries about.

"You're the one making me audition for this role. How can I know the proper advice to give if I don't know what you're asking?"

"Fair enough." He eyes my hands, which move seamlessly from a bridge shuffle to cutting the deck and back again. "I want to know what I need to do to achieve my goal."

"What kind of goal?"

"None of your business."

I don't want to push too hard yet, so I wait to see if the cards can give me a nudge in the right direction. After I go through my routine, I lay three cards facedown in front of us.

"The first card represents your strengths." I flip it over to reveal the Moon. "The second is the obstacles in your way." The reversed Three of Coins. "And, finally, what actions you can take." The Fool.

Interesting. Two of the three cards are Major Arcana, which signal significant events or decisions. They also tell me a lot about his inner self.

I tap the Moon card. "I never would've guessed it, but you're a dreamer. You're someone who's in touch with his intuition, though you're careful not to make hasty decisions because you know not to trust surface-level things. Your subconscious will guide you to the correct decision as long as you don't let your fears and anxieties rule you.

"This is much less surprising." I hold up the reversed Three of Coins. "You are not a great team player. Whatever it is you're working on, either you have a different vision than everyone else, or you're not listening to or respecting other people's opinions. Either way, this disharmony is preventing you from moving forward. Based on the Fool card in the third position, I think you need to go back to the beginning. Remember why you made this your goal in the first place. And stop analyzing everything to death. For this to work, you need to take a leap of faith."

Winston stares down at the cards, finally picking one up to study more closely. "The Fool, huh? The card of opportunity and new beginnings."

"You know tarot?"

He shrugs and sets the card back down. "My favorite video game has tarot cards in it. I know the basics."

"You're full of surprises, aren't you?"

He grins at me. Not a smirk, not a calculated smile, but a full-on, genuine grin. "So are you. Welcome to the *Champion*. I have high hopes for you."

Bestie Group Chat

> **Danika:** Whats it mean when you meet someone whos super interesting but you can't trust?

Nicole: That just sounds like dating to me

You seducing people for your case? What's it called

A honeypot? Honey trap?

Junior: Bro

Nicole: Not ur bro

Junior: Sis

Nicole: Yes?

Junior: You are so unserious

Nicole: I don't wanna hear that from you

Danika: Read

Nicole: Oh so its ok for you to leave us on read?

I see how it is

CHAPTER EIGHT

"ELI RECOMMENDED THIS CLUB TO YOU? THAT'S surprising considering she's never actually participated in any of our programs. I didn't think she cared about our mission."

Gaby somehow figured out which club her sister had joined, so the two of us are checking out a Chi-Care meeting to see if they know anything about Eli's recent activities. Luckily, not only does the current secretary keep meticulous notes, including binders of previous years' sign-in sheets, but she's also one of my tarot regulars. I really should know her name considering how many times I've read for her, but if clients choose not to share it, I don't bother asking. I signal to Gaby that I'll handle this and that she should go talk to the advisor.

She gives me a slight nod before saying, "Eli knows I need more stuff to put on my college applications, so maybe that's why? I'll ask Mr. Chen about it."

She heads over to the teacher, and I turn my attention back to my client. "What makes you think Eli wasn't interested in the club's objective? She seemed pretty into it when she told us to join."

My client glances over at Gaby before leaning close. "No

offense, but Eli does not give a single damn about promoting health equity in underserved neighborhoods. She comes here, signs in, messes around on her phone instead of helping us create resources and plan our projects, and then peaces out before the meeting is even over. I wasn't shocked when she stopped showing up recently. I don't even know why she bothered to come to begin with."

I see Gaby wrapping up her conversation with Mr. Chen and sending me a cue that we should leave.

"Thanks for your help."

"No problem. Also, why haven't you been at the stairwell lately?"

"I've had some family stuff come up, but I'll be there after your club finishes if you want a reading."

"Cool."

I wave before following Gaby to the hallway.

"All I got was a less-than-flattering description of how little volunteer spirit your sister has. I suppose it wasn't entirely useless. It matches up with how people have said Eli's been acting different, and it shows us she clearly had something else going on, but—"

I'm about to say more when a large group of students passes us in the hall, and I'm reminded that even though the school day is technically over, plenty of people hang around after, and it's not smart to speak so openly about the case.

I wait until they pass and the coast is clear before continuing. "This was a dead end, and my mom is looking into the country club angle herself. She wants me to contain my part of the investigation to the school. But right now, the only lead I can follow is Winston. I'll have to wait until I see him again at the next meeting."

"Is he even a lead, though? I still think you're wasting time talking to him. You're better off convincing your mom to let you check out the country club."

I cross my arms and gaze coolly into Gaby's eyes, a reminder that she's not in charge of this investigation. I am. She sighs when she sees I won't budge on this. "Whatever. I'm just super frustrated, you know? Every time I think we have something, it turns out to be a dead end."

I study her, clocking the tightness in her jaw as she clenches her teeth. I place my hands on her shoulders, which are so tense, they're practically under her ears. "Hey, deep breaths. In through your nose, out through your mouth."

As we breathe together, I can feel her relaxing under my touch and remember what my mom said about inviting Gaby to Kali. She can use the time to de-stress while I get to know her better for the investigation.

"My aunt teaches Filipino martial arts on Mondays, Wednesdays, and Fridays. Would you be interested? It might be good for you to do something physical, work out that frustration."

Gaby goes still under my hands before laughing and pulling away. "I could definitely use something physical to help me work out this frustration. I'd prefer other methods, but I guess a martial arts class will have to do."

"Cool. We can head there after school tomorrow. And you can leave without me today. My parents already know I'm gonna be late, and I'd like to fit in a couple readings."

Gaby's eyes light up. "Can I join you? It was so cool watching you read for Jana. Oh, that reminds me, she told me to thank you. She finally talked to her boyfriend, and they're going to give it until the end of summer before making a decision about their relationship. After seeing you work your magic, I'd love to learn more about tarot."

She's the first person to express interest in learning about tarot, so I'm tempted to have her join me, but I can't let her compromise my professional integrity.

"I don't think that's a good idea. These sessions are supposed to be private. The reading with Jana was different," I add. "Talking to her was part of the investigation, and she's the one who brought up getting a reading during lunch. If the client doesn't care, I don't care. But my regulars come to me for advice because they trust me and know I respect their privacy."

I'm up on my soapbox about this when the client I was talking to at the volunteer club peers around the corner.

"I hope I'm not interrupting, but you said you were free for readings now, right?"

"Of course." Gaby and my client follow me to the stairwell, and I sit down at my desk and gesture at the chair in front of it. Gaby continues to hover, so I ask, "Would it be okay if she observes? She knows to stay quiet about anything she hears."

My client turns her attention to Gaby, who gives her a winning smile. "Danika is teaching me tarot, so I'm like her apprentice. Is that cool?"

My client agrees without hesitation and blurts out her question. "I think I'm in love with my best friend, and I don't know if I should tell her. I don't wanna make it weird if she doesn't feel the same way. Plus, I don't even know if she's into girls; she's only ever talked about guys. What do I do?"

Oof, poor girl. This isn't the first time I've gotten a question like this, but I sympathize every time. After sending a silent prayer to the Friendship Gods to make sure that messiness never happens to me, Junior, and Nicole, I start shuffling. Two cards jump out of the deck, so I set them aside as clarifying cards before setting three others down in front of my client.

"The Ten of Wands. This is a burden you've been carrying for a while, and it's time for you to set it down. The Hierophant in the obstacles position hints that an authority figure or traditional value is holding you back. Maybe one of you is super religious, and that's a concern? Or you're worried about how your parents will react to the news? The reversed Moon is telling me that you're letting this fear and anxiety guide you. You need to block out all that outside noise and listen to what's inside. What's your intuition telling you to do?"

"I don't know!" the girl wails. "Nothing about this situation is clear to me! That's why I came to you."

I sigh, turning over the two clarifying cards. Sometimes when shuffling, a card or two will pop out of the deck, letting me know they demand to be part of the reading. Here's hoping they shed some light for this girl.

"The Hermit. It's solo soul-searching time. You need to be apart from your bestie for a while to clear your head and really think about the situation. There are a bunch of different options in front of you, many different ways to handle this, but don't be tempted to go down the instant gratification route. That's what this Seven of Cups is saying. If you really love her, you need to think long-term about what you want from the relationship. You need to make the smart choice, not the easy one."

My client groans. "It's never a simple yes or no with you, is it?"

"If it was a simple yes or no, you wouldn't need me."

"I'd hate you if you weren't always right." My client sets a twenty-dollar bill on the desk before getting up. "Thanks, Danika. I'll take some me time to think about this properly. And I hope you can make it to another club meeting. No pressure."

Gaby waits till she's out of earshot before saying, "I hope things work out for her. It takes a lot of courage to confess your feelings, especially when it can ruin your friendship."

"You speaking from experience?" I ask, gathering up my cards.

"Freshman year. I told my childhood friend that I liked him, and we started dating. I thought things were going well, only to catch him cheating on me with a girl from a different school. He blamed me, saying that I never made him feel needed. That I was too independent, had too many opinions." She rolls her eyes. "I've gotten similar complaints from other guys I've talked to. Good thing I'm pan, because I am *done* with men. What about you?"

"I've never dated anyone or had any serious crushes. Gender doesn't really matter to me, though."

"Good to know." I turn questioning eyes to her, but she avoids my gaze. "Thanks for letting me stay. I don't want to be too much of a pest, so I'll leave you alone now. See you at the usual time tomorrow morning? Oh, and do I need to bring anything special for the martial arts lesson?"

"Just some workout clothes to change into. Even your gym uniform will work if you don't have anything else." I think for a moment and add, "Bring an open mind too. Kali is a combat sport, but there's a spiritual element to it too. At least the way my aunt teaches it."

Gaby studies me. "Kali means a lot to you, doesn't it?"

"Like with tarot, Kali isn't simply a hobby to me. It's a way of life."

"A way of life," she repeats. "So the more I learn about tarot and Kali, the more I'll learn about what makes you tick, huh?"

"I guess?"

She grins at me. "Very good to know."

"WAIT, WHAT DO YOU MEAN YOU'VE NEVER HEARD of them? How is that even possible?" Gaby gawks at me as if my not knowing about her favorite band is a criminal offense.

"Girl, Danika doesn't know any current music unless there's been a classical cover of it. If it wasn't for me and Junior, she'd have the musical taste of an old man," Nicole says.

"She *does* have the musical taste of an old man," Junior says, heaping rice onto his plate. "We make sure her playlists are a little less sad."

"I'm not that bad! I just don't remember names or titles or

whatever. I listen to a mix of stuff. I like being eclectic," I say, hoping that helps my case.

I should've known nothing good would come of mixing my worlds. Junior and Nicole were, like, embarrassingly happy when I introduced Gaby to them before the Kali class started.

I wanted to stress that Gaby is a client, not my friend, but that seemed super rude to say in front of her. Plus, she might not want people to know about the investigation. Client confidentiality and all that.

When class ended, they practically dragged her to the back to stay for the group meal. Conversation somehow drifted to music, and Gaby and Nicole are currently screaming about a concert they went to for some K-pop group I'd never heard of but is apparently the hottest band in the world. Now, thanks to my jerk best friends, Gaby knows about my absolutely tragic music knowledge, and from the glint in her eye, she is going to tease me about it until the end of time.

"Don't be too mean to her; it's not her fault. Whenever we tried to play music that came out this century, her dad would go on and on, like, 'That's not real hip-hop!' and make us listen to one of his records," Joemar says as he and Andrew introduce themselves before sitting next to our group.

"Then he'd shush us and be like, 'Listen to the lyrics! Now that's a storyteller,' and then do some dad joke about how our music sounds to him," Andrew adds, reaching for the bottle of patis in the middle of the low table.

Their impressions are pretty spot-on, so the most I can do to defend my dad is mutter, "The eighties and nineties did have some bangers . . ." and shovel some food into my mouth before I make the situation any worse.

"So these classes are a family affair, huh? How did this all happen?" Gaby asks.

Andrew replies, "Our mom's a champion martial artist. Used to compete around the world. She met our dad at a tournament in the Philippines, and he moved to Chicago to be with her. They gave up competing when we were born and opened up a gym with a friend of theirs who's a professional boxer."

"Tito Nick, the boxing guy, and our parents started these after-school classes to make sure the neighborhood kids stayed out of trouble," Joemar adds. "They've been doing it since before we were born. And after our dad died a few years ago, we stepped in to assist, since it's not like our mom can afford a paid employee."

"Sure would be nice if she could, though," Andrew says, raising his voice as Tita Baby passes by us.

She whacks him on the back of the head before smiling and smoothing his hair back. "I hope these two jokers aren't bothering you, Gaby. Did you like the class?"

Gaby grins. "I loved it! Danika was right. I feel more relaxed. And there's this power you feel once you're in a flow. I was watching you demonstrate some moves, and it was weirdly beautiful. Like dancing."

Tita Baby nods. "There's definitely a rhythm to the movements. And like with dancing, you have to watch and respond to your partner's actions. You can also practice alone, and it becomes like meditation."

"One of my favorite things to do is find a quiet spot by the lake and get into a groove," I say. "It's a spiritual experience, you know?"

Gaby adds some scrambled eggs to her plate. "You have your own Kali sticks, right? Where did you get them?"

I say, "Gifts from Tita Baby. She has cheaper ones for the after-school kids to borrow, but the more serious students buy their own so they can practice outside of class."

"You know, I think it's really cool what your aunt's doing here."

Tita Baby smiles. "It's not much, but we have to do what we can to make a difference."

After my aunt leaves, Nicole turns her attention to my cousins.

"What are you guys studying, anyway? We didn't have a chance to catch up last time I was here," she says, smiling at the twins, who are in their university tees.

Junior and I look at each other and roll our eyes. She pretty much fell in love with my cousins at first sight and never misses an opportunity to flirt with them even though they have zero interest in her. Trust me, I already told them what I'd do if they ever laid a hand on her, and they were legit insulted that I thought they'd ever do something with an underage girl. They then let me know in no uncertain terms what they'd do if they ever caught me messing with a guy who was way too old for me. So yeah, we keep each other in check.

Both twins instinctively lean away from Nicole.

"Andrew's the brain, so he's in UIC's sports medicine

program," Joemar says. "I'm doing business management. Tito Nick and our mom have good intentions, but good intentions don't make a successful business. I want to make sure nothing bad ever happens to the gym."

"And *he's* going to want to travel and compete like our mom did. Which is why it's gonna be my job to patch him up and any of our students who go down that path," Andrew adds.

"You both plan on taking over the martial arts studio some-day?" Gaby asks.

Joemar grins. "That's up to my mom and Tito Nick. And Tito Nick has a daughter who runs the boxing program now that he's sick. But, yeah, hoping they'll pass it down to the two of us when the time comes."

Who knew my cousins were thinking so seriously about their futures? Like me, they want to take over their mom's busi-ness. But unlike me, they've actually thought about how they can best support the gym according to their strengths. What even are my strengths as a PI? Maybe my mom is right. Maybe going to college and learning new skills to apply to the business is the best way I can make sure the agency stays open. Not that I'll tell her that.

"You guys are stressing me out now," I say.

We're super close, but it's not like we've ever talked about col-lege before. I was too young to care. And our hangouts mainly consist of us making our way through a Costco box of popcorn while we watch martial arts movies or playing video games or whatever. Not exactly the stuff of deep conversation. We're not like Nicole and her sisters, who are constantly in each other's business and have no real secrets from each other. She says it's healthy, but I think it's 'cause none of them can help running their mouths. I love Nicole, but if you want something to stay a secret, you absolutely do NOT tell her.

That's why I have Junior. He's a vault. He's also an only child (his mom likes to tell people that after dealing with him, she didn't have the energy to even think about having another kid) and learned a long time ago that there's an advantage to being the one everyone tells their secrets to.

Joemar reaches over and tugs on my braid. "You got time to figure it out. Don't stress too much, and sooner or later, it'll come to you. Right now, you're better off watching out for what's in front of you, or you'll miss out. Like this!"

He snatches the last slice of Spam off my plate and shoves the whole thing in his mouth before running off so I can't retaliate.

Andrew laughs. "Food theft aside, he's got a point. Also, your dad is a great sounding board. He helped us out. I'm sure he's dying for you to open up to him more."

"You talked to my dad about school?" I know my cousins are pretty tight with my dad, but I didn't realize they went to him for, like, life advice.

"Not by choice. Our mom pretty much shoved us in front of him and said, 'You better talk to these fools because I am done with them,' then left us at your house one day."

We finish the rest of our dinner before he gets up to join Joemar on the other side of the room.

"Your family's pretty cool, Danika," Gaby says, watching Andrew help my aunt clean the tables while Joemar play-wrestles with Daniel. "But it's a lost cause, chica."

She directs this last bit to Nicole, who grins.

"Oh, I know. I'd never actually mess around with them; that's too much of a betrayal to my bestie. I think it's fun, though, and Danika *hates* it, which makes it even more fun."

I make sure Daniel and Tita Baby aren't looking and give her the middle finger. "The day Nicole stops flirting with every dude in the room is the day I know aliens are real, since they've clearly body swapped with her."

Gaby tilts her head. "She hasn't flirted with Junior."

"He doesn't count," Nicole and I say in unison.

Junior rolls his eyes up to the ceiling before turning his attention to Gaby. "You see the disrespect I put up with? It's fine; it's not like that between us. Besides, dating either of them would be a nightmare."

Nicole and I quickly launch into defense mode, because while we might not want to date him either, we sure as hell aren't letting that go.

"Why would it be a nightmare? They're both really cute," Gaby says, grinning at us. "And seem cool. Who wouldn't want to date them?"

Nicole does a little head toss, her crown of golden brown curls bouncing around her head as she gives Junior a face that clearly says, *See? This girl knows.*

I've never been called cute ("intimidating" is the word most people use to describe me), and my friends and cousins are constantly pointing out how NOT cool I am, so I don't really know how to respond to Gaby's comment.

Junior shakes his head. "Don't believe any of it. Nicole falls in and out of love faster than Netflix cancels shows. And Danika couldn't flirt if her life depended on it. Best friend I could ever ask for. Zero sex appeal."

He dodges the punch I throw at him. "What?! That's a good thing! If I was into you, that could fuck up the friendship. But as we've established, this"—he gestures between me and him—"ain't ever happening. So we're all stuck with each other."

"I'll remember that, bestie."

Tita Baby gives the signal that it's time to close up, so Junior and Nicole head over to say their goodbyes. I scan the room to make sure that nobody forgot anything, and my eyes suddenly meet Gaby's.

"What's up?" I ask.

"Nothing. Or, well, I guess I wanted to thank you for inviting me. You don't really seem to like having me pick you up or eating lunch together, so I thought you didn't like me."

Huh? "Oh! Sorry, no, it's not like that. I don't know. Was trying to keep a professional distance, I guess. I'm not supposed to get too close to my clients. It's nothing personal."

Gaby smiles, the obvious relief on her face surprising me. "Is that all? I know I'm being pushy about the ride thing, but it's the only time I can ask you questions about the investigation without anyone around. I want to stay involved and help find my sister, but it doesn't seem like you want my input."

I don't want anyone's input on the case since it's *my* case, but I don't tell her that. Instead I say, "I appreciate the rides. It makes me want to get my car fixed up even more. And you introducing me to Eli's friends and telling me more about her is super useful. But you know what'd be even better?"

"What?"

"If you and your family would be honest with me and my mom."

She studies me warily before sighing. "Fair enough. From now on, I'll be more up-front, even if my mom isn't. There's no point in staying quiet since you can see through me anyway."

Not true, but she doesn't need to know that.

"Anything you want to share now?"

"Eli's note. It didn't seem to have any clues, so my mom said not to bring it up, but I still have it. I can bring it to you tomorrow."

I jot down the info on my phone since my tablet is in my bag. "Is that it?"

She nods. "What else can I do?"

I think for a moment. "If you want to keep having lunch with me, don't be weird about eating in the cafeteria. Not everyone can afford to get takeout every day."

Her eyes widen, and I can tell that that fact had never occurred to her. "I was being a privileged asshole, wasn't I? Feel free to call me out whenever I do or say something like that again."

"I promise to let you know when you're being a bougie b."

Gaby throws her head back and laughs. "I like you, Danika Dizon."

"You're not so bad yourself, Gaby Delgado."

CHAPTER NINE

"THANKS FOR INVITING ME OVER, MR. AND MRS. Dizon. Everything looks amazing!"

It's Saturday night, and my parents convinced me to invite Gaby over for dinner. My mom and I are supposed to meet with the Delgados tomorrow, but there isn't much to report. My mom's hoping Gaby will give us something to move us even an inch forward.

"Call me Ben. And any friend of Danika's is welcome here. Now, don't be shy and dig in!" My dad gestures enthusiastically at the dishes covering the table. He usually only gets to cook for family now that Junior and Nicole don't come over as much. "Have you ever tried Filipino food? Anak, why don't you explain the different dishes?"

I point to the pot of soup in front of me. "This is shrimp sinigang, a sour soup made with tamarind. One of my faves. Next to it is tofu sisig, which is a little bit spicy, so watch out if you don't like chilis. We've also got chicken adobo, which is, like, THE Filipino dish, so if it's your first time eating Filipino food, you've gotta try it. And, finally, that dish in front of Daniel has picadillo, which is ground beef cooked with potatoes and tomato sauce and stuff."

"The picadillo is my favorite!" Daniel pipes up. "It's so yummy. Do you want some, Gaby?"

He tries to hand Gaby the serving plate but wobbles a bit under the weight of the dish. My mom swoops in to grab the platter before it ends up in Gaby's lap. "Careful, anak. If you want to pass something, let us know, okay?" She hands the dish to Gaby and adds, "There's also sautéed bok choy if you want some greens."

Gaby samples each dish. After a few bites, she says, "Ohmigod, this is so good! Do you eat like this every night?"

I laugh. "No, when it's just us, it's a little simpler. Food's still delicious, though. I told my dad you liked rice, so he made a bunch of proteins that go well with it. Well, I say that, but most Filipino food naturally goes well with white rice, so it's not like he had to try too hard."

My dad sighs and shakes his head. "I cook and cook for hours to impress your friend, and this is how you treat me? Your generation is heartless."

Gaby tsk-tsks me. "*I* appreciate your effort, Mr. Dizon. I mean, Ben. I can't remember the last time I had anything near this good. And how did you know I like rice?"

"You mentioned it in the car a few days ago," I say.

"And you remembered?"

I keep my eyes on my plate, afraid to let her know about the detailed notes I keep on everyone. "I've got a good memory. Not a big deal. Who's the cook in your family?"

She shrugs. "No one, really. Around middle school, my dad was promoted, and his hours got really long, so he couldn't make it home for dinner anymore. My mom didn't see the point in sit-down dinners without him, so Eli and I have been on our own since then. Lots of frozen meals and delivery at my house."

"That's so expensive!" my mom says at the same time that my dad says, "That's so unhealthy!"

My parents exchange glances before my dad says, "You're welcome here anytime. It won't always be as much as this, but it'll be a real meal."

Gaby's silent for a moment, and I worry that my nosy parents have gone too far and made her uncomfortable. But she just says, "Thanks," and helps herself to more rice.

My mom switches the subject to Eli, which is the real reason Gaby's here. "Sorry to bring this up now, but have you heard anything new about your sister?"

Gaby wipes her hands on her napkin and gets up to grab her backpack from the living room. "Here's the note she left behind. I know my mom lied about it, but she's not here and I thought it might help. I also found this in one of Eli's drawers."

She hands my mom the note and what looks like a name badge.

My mom reads the note quickly before passing it to me and studies the name badge. "Chicago Glen Country Club. Seems like your source at the newspaper was right, Danika. I was investigating a different angle the last couple days, so I didn't have time to follow up on your tip. I'm going to bring this up during our meeting with the Delgados tomorrow, see if I can get their permission to interview Eli's coworkers. Thanks, Gaby."

The note proves a lot less useful.

Need to be away for a while.
Staying with a friend.
Mom, I know how you are,
so I doubt you'll involve the
police, but just in case.
Don't look for me. I'll be fine.
—E

"That's it? This is the note your mom wanted to hide?" I say, scanning the creased notebook paper. "Assuming that she's telling the truth, we at least know she's not on the street or staying at a cheap motel or something."

"Based on my experience, it's likely that she is staying with a friend, but it's one that her parents wouldn't know about since that would risk them showing up at that person's house," my mom says. "Gaby, have your parents reached out to all her friends?"

Gaby makes a face. "Yeah, but as far as I know, my mom didn't say anything about Eli being missing. I think she made up a story about why she was calling. Something about her checking in with everyone because Eli's phone was going straight to voicemail, and she needed to tell her something important about our aunt."

"How long does your mom think she can go on pretending nothing's wrong?" I ask. "And why hide this note from us? There's nothing suspicious about it."

"My mom would rather take this to her grave than lose face in front of her family and friends. I guess my dad didn't have a lot of money when they first got together, and it caused problems between my mom and her parents. It's really important to her that everyone thinks her life is perfect. A runaway daughter says otherwise." Gaby stabs at a bok choy half. "As for why she'd lie about the note, I have no idea. There's something they're hiding from me too."

My dad says, "As parents, we don't want you to worry. You probably feel out of the loop, but there's a chance they have a good reason for keeping you in the dark."

Gaby doesn't respond to that. She fiddles with the name badge from Chicago Glen Country Club that she found.

I stare at it. "Do you really think she has a secret boyfriend?"

Gaby puts down the badge and glances at me, then my mom, sadly. "The old Eli? Absolutely not. At least, not without telling me. But she's changed."

My mom leans forward. "How so? And do you remember when she started acting differently?"

Gaby chews on her bottom lip. "Probably since last year. My parents were the first ones to notice. Complaining that Eli was being disrespectful and wondering why she was so angry. I kinda brushed it off as them overexaggerating, because being angry and disrespectful to our parents was my thing, not Eli's. Eli was always so careful to be the perfect oldest daughter, doing whatever to make our parents happy. But one day, I got home, and I heard her straight-up screaming at our parents."

"Did you hear what she was saying?" I ask.

"Just that they ruined her life, and she hated them. Then she ran out of the room. I didn't want to get caught eavesdropping, so I crept up to my room before my parents saw me." Gaby laughs before picking up her utensils again. "And people say I'm the dramatic one."

"Was she referencing a particular incident, or do you think she was being hyperbolic?" my mom asks.

"I honestly have no clue. I've never heard Eli raise her voice to anyone, let alone our parents. Once in a while, she'll complain about them, but then she's quick to reassure me that they act like that because they care about us. Though sometimes I wondered if she was trying to reassure me or herself." Gaby toys with a piece of chicken adobo. "She'd kill me for saying this, but she's exactly like our mom. She needs everyone to think she's so pretty and put together."

The more she speaks, the more I think that she has a good idea why Eli ran away. "Gaby, do you know why Eli left?"

She meets my eyes. "No. I promise, if I knew, I'd tell you. It's just . . ."

"Just what?"

"I'm scared for her. You know? I do want you to find her. But at the same time, this could be her way of finally breaking away from our parents and the huge expectations they put on her. That she puts on herself." Gaby shrugs, a self-deprecating smile tilting her lips. "I'm mad at her for making us worry like this. And I can't ignore the fact that maybe there was a reason she felt like she *had* to run away. That she's not as safe as she said she is in her note."

The table is quiet for a moment while everyone finishes the last of the food on their plates, likely processing the heavy emotion Gaby dropped on us.

My dad is the first to break the silence. "Would you like some sweets? My older sisters brought over an assortment of kakanin after I told them we were having company."

"Rice cakes," I explain after seeing Gaby's questioning eyes. "If you've ever tried mochi, it's a similar texture but with different flavors."

"I love mochi ice cream and sweets in general, so I'd love to try them all, if that's okay."

"Of course. Do you want coffee or ginger tea to drink? Or does water work? We're out of hot chocolate, unfortunately," my mom says, getting up to prepare our drinks while my dad sets out the sweets.

"Ginger tea sounds great, thank you. Do you make it yourself?"

My mom snorts as she gets out the instant salabat mix and the instant coffee. "I pour hot water from the electric kettle. That's as far as my barista skills go."

"My dad and I are on coffee duty when we're at the office," I explain. "Mommy cares about the caffeine and sugar hit more than the flavor. But my dad's surprisingly picky about coffee, and I guess I inherited his bougie taste. We rely on the salabat mix for convenience, but I make it from scratch during the winter when Daniel's cough gets bad. If you like it, I can give you the recipe. It's pretty easy."

My mom brings over our mugs and gestures to the array of kakanin in front of us. "Help yourself."

Gaby points to the sapin-sapin. "Hey, isn't that what that lunch lady gave you the other day?"

"Yeah, she knows it's my favorite. It has layers of ube, jack-fruit, and coconut."

"I definitely want to try that first."

"Eat this one, Gaby!" Daniel says, pointing to the glutinous rice that was wrapped in banana leaves and steamed. "Suman is really good if you dip it in sugar and coconut."

"What's that next to it?"

"Biko, my mom's favorite. Sticky rice cooked in coconut milk with coconut caramel on top. It's probably the sweetest out of the dishes here, so if you've got a sweet tooth, you might like it the most."

"And this is my go-to," my dad says, holding a small, steamed white rice cake. "The humble puto."

Gaby chokes on her tea. "I'm sorry, the what?"

I laugh. "Yeah, I learned the hard way that 'puto' means something very different in Spanish."

"Oh God. What happened?"

"In fifth grade, my school had an international day, and we were supposed to bring snacks from our family's background. So imagine me at ten years old at a Catholic school with mostly Latine students, holding up a bunch of rice cakes in front of the class and saying I brought puto. I almost got laughed out of the classroom."

My dad is cracking up so hard, he has to wipe a tear from his eye. "It honestly hadn't occurred to me. I wanted to make something easy to cook in a large batch that was a good representation of Filipino snacks. Though I probably wouldn't have warned her even if I had realized. The story makes me smile every time."

I roll my eyes. "My dad is all about turning bad experiences into interesting stories."

"Better to laugh than cry, right? Besides, I'm a writer. Can you blame me for appreciating a fun tale?"

We help ourselves to the kakanin on the table with Gaby again sampling a little bit of everything and declaring herself a huge fan. Once we're done, Daniel helps my parents clear the table and stack the dishes in the sink for me to wash.

"Bye, Gaby! Will you be at Kali practice on Monday?" Daniel asks.

"I wouldn't miss it. And thanks for your recommendations. Everything was delicious."

Daniel smiles, his whole face lighting up. "I know! You have to come over again so I can show you more."

Gaby smiles back. "I'd like that."

"Final homework check and then bath time, Daniel!" my dad says. "It was a pleasure having you join us, Gaby. Our home is open to you anytime you need it."

Gaby's eyes widen in surprise. Does she not go over to her friends' houses often? Who even are her friends anyway? I haven't met any of them at school.

"Thanks, Ben," she says.

My dad guides Daniel to his room, and my mom walks with us to the door to say bye before joining them. "I hope you don't mind, Gaby, but I have one more question for you."

"Yes?"

"That argument you overheard . . . do you remember when it took place?"

"I think it was around the end of the last school year? So maybe April or May?" Gaby smacks her forehead. "Duh. My sister really wanted to do a study abroad program in Europe, and I don't know why, but it fell through. I think my parents changed their minds and didn't want her going so far away? Now that I think about it, the timing makes sense."

My mom nods thoughtfully. "If anything else occurs to you, please don't hesitate to let me or Danika know. I promise, I'm doing whatever I can to find your sister."

Gaby blinks a few times as if holding back tears. "Thanks, Mrs. Dizon. For everything."

"If my husband insists that you call him Ben, I suppose you can call me Angelica." My mom smiles briefly before saying good night and leaves the two of us standing at the door.

"Sorry about the interrogation there."

Gaby shrugs. "I figured that was why you invited me to dinner. I know we're cool now, but it's not like I'm magically your new best friend. Why else would you and your mom insist on having me over?"

"I mean, you're not wrong, but it really was fun having you over. And not because of the investigation. I hope you had fun too."

She tugs the end of my braid. "We're cool, and you are also investigating my sister's disappearance. I get it."

"Oh. Great."

Awkward silence.

"Well—"

My dad suddenly pops up, startling us both. "Oops, sorry

to interrupt, but I forgot to give you this. Can't have you going home empty-handed."

He hands her an old takeout container filled with some of the leftovers from dinner and another containing dessert. "I thought this would be enough for your baon tomorrow. I made so much."

Gaby glances at me as she accepts the food, and I explain, "'Baon' literally means 'leftovers.' It's usually the food you pack for your lunch the next day."

She grins. "So we'll have matching lunches tomorrow? Too bad we don't have school, because I love this for us. Thanks, Ben."

She waves goodbye, and my dad and I watch her to make sure she drives away safely.

"Matching lunches, huh?"

"Daddy, don't you even start."

"I'm just saying . . ."

As I roll my eyes and make my way to my room, I find myself really looking forward to those leftovers tomorrow.

THE CASE FILES OF DANIKA DIZON

NAME: Mary Gabrielle "Gaby" Delgado
RELATION TO CASE: Eli Delgado's younger sister
DATE OF BIRTH: July 28, 20XX; 16 years old
GENDER IDENTITY/PRONOUNS: female; she/her
HEIGHT: 5 ft. 9 in.–5 ft. 10 in.
EYE COLOR: dark brown
HAIR COLOR: reddish brown/auburn
HAIR TYPE: naturally curly but constantly changes styles
SKIN COLOR: light brown; has freckles
BODY TYPE: average
ETHNIC/RACIAL BACKGROUND: biracial; Colombian and Irish American
OCCUPATION: student, junior in high school

NOTES:

- Sisters bear little resemblance to each other; Eli seems to take after her father while Gaby looks more like the mother.
- Appears to have strained relationship with mother, so she'd probably punch me if I told her she looks like her mom.
- Loves rice. Source: mentioned during car ride to school.
- Likes K-pop, Japanese punk, and "gay girl music" (her words). Source: conversation after Kali class.
- Member of the art club.
- Sisters not close, but no evidence of rivalry or ill will.
- Rebellious—how much is real, and how much is an act?

CHAPTER
TEN

"DANIKA, ARE YOU READY TO GIVE YOUR REPORT TO the Delgados?"

"Almost!"

I check myself over in the mirror, making sure that everything is absolutely perfect. Long, wavy black hair pulled back in a neat French braid. Mascara and tinted lip balm to make me appear more put together but not quite made-up. Freshly ironed white button-down tucked into my nice light blue jeans. I wanted to wear dressy black pants, but my mom told me I was giving server at a steak house. After a bit of pouting, she lent me her casual navy blazer and a pair of cute flats to match. I take a moment to polish the brass Lingling-o necklace my grandparents gave me for my seventh birthday. It doesn't quite match my outfit, but I never take it off, so the least I can do is make it nice and shiny. I usually don't wear earrings (too easy to get ripped out in a fight), but I put on the small silver hoops Nicole got me forever ago to complete the ensemble.

I head to the living room, where my dad is reminding my mom of everyone's schedule for today.

"I'm dropping Daniel off for his playdate and then heading

to the library to get some writing done. Do you need me to pick anything up?"

My mom checks her phone's calendar. "This meeting with the Delgados shouldn't take too long, so don't worry about us. Danika can help me run the rest of my errands. You focus on your book."

My dad takes in my appearance and gives me a thumbs-up. "Very professional. You are your mom's Mini-Me."

"I'm at least four inches taller than her."

"Hey, I'm tall for a Filipina!" my mom insists. She glances at her watch. "Let's go. We're going to be late. Have fun with your friend, anak."

After waving goodbye to Daniel and my dad, my mom and I hop in the car and make the ten-minute drive to the agency.

"How do you think this conversation is going to go?" I ask. "Usually you don't meet in person until you have something concrete to report."

My mom tilts her head back and forth but keeps her eyes on the road. "I have information worth sharing with them, but if I'm to move forward on the case, I need their permission to pursue this lead."

"It's so annoying that they won't let you do your job. Like, does she want to find her daughter or not? Hiding things only drags out the process."

My mom sighs. "You know that and I know that, but I have to respect my clients' wishes. Especially when the case involves someone who's underage."

"She's seventeen, not a baby."

"But she's also technically not a legal adult, so I have to defer to her parents. There's a balancing act to this work—doing what you think is right and doing what makes your client happy. A lot of times, I don't have to choose and can conduct my investigations however I want. And sometimes . . ." She trails off for a moment. "Well, you'll see. If the opportunity comes for you to work on more cases, you'll get a better idea of what the job is really like."

Okay, so she said "if" and not "when," but this is the most concrete my mother's ever been about my potentially becoming part of the agency. Ever since I was a little girl and found out what my mom did for a living, I thought she was the absolute coolest and wanted to be like her. No shade to my dad, but I don't want to just write about solving mysteries. I want to be the one out there actually doing it. The power, the confidence, and, above all, the extreme competence . . . I absolutely have to kill it on this case so she sees how much of an asset I am. Once she sees how valuable the information I gathered at school is, she'll be able to take on more cases involving young people, and I can be her in. I simply have to prove to her and the Delgados that I'm a professional. I glance at myself one last time in the window before we enter the agency.

Showtime.

"HOW DARE YOU. WE COME TO YOU FOR HELP, AND you give us this . . . this slander? Our daughter would never behave like that!" Mrs. Delgado's voice gets higher and higher until she's literally screaming the last part. Mr. Delgado puts a hand on her arm, but she shakes him off. "Who told you these lies?"

So . . . the meeting is not going well. My mom started off with the facts she's gathered, some of which I already knew from my own investigation, but once Mrs. Delgado heard that her perfect angel daughter is not who she thought she was, Denial Mode hit her hard.

She doesn't want to hear about Eli cutting school. Or Eli breaking up with her perfect, safe boyfriend for a shady college guy. She doesn't want to hear that Eli doesn't hang out with the honors crowd the way she used to, that Eli not only lied about going to the volunteer club to cover up her secret job but was often seen out with her crew from work, some of whom are from "the wrong side of the tracks." Mrs. Delgado's words, not mine. Extra insulting, 'cause to many people, *I* live on the wrong side of the tracks. So she's basically insulting my family to our faces, but she has no problem asking us for our labor? Props to my mom, who takes it all in stride.

"I can't reveal my source, but they were able to talk to several of Eli's friends and coworkers, and they IDed her new boyfriend. His name is Caleb Miller, nineteen years old. Works as a server at the Chicago Glen Country Club and is in his second year at UIC. He—"

"That's enough," Mrs. Delgado interrupts. "Eli is dating a wonderful young man named Winston Chang, and—"

"Like my mom already said, she broke up with him. I'm on the school newspaper with Winston, and not only does everyone there know about the breakup but there's already talk about her new boyfriend," I say. "A member of the newspaper staff told me where Eli works."

Mrs. Delgado swivels toward me. "And you! What are you doing inserting yourself into my daughter's case? I hired a qualified adult to find my missing daughter. Not some bored teenager who wants to play Nancy Drew and spread rumors about Eli!"

"I'm not spreading rumors. Gaby introduced me to some of Eli's friends, and—"

"Oh, I'll be having a chat with Gaby after this, don't you worry. I don't want you anywhere near her. Juan David," she says, grabbing Mr. Delgado's arm. "We're done here. And we will no longer be needing your services, Mrs. Dizon."

I freeze. "Are you firing my mom?"

Mrs. Delgado ignores me, directing her attention to my mother. "You may keep the deposit, of course, but that's all you're getting out of us. You are off the case, and if I hear that you're poking your nose into our business, I will file an official complaint."

Mr. Delgado finally speaks up. "There's no need for that. We're no longer paying for their services, so there's no reason for this to go any further. Am I right?"

"Of course," my mother says. "I need you to fill out this form making it official, though."

Mrs. Delgado reaches for the paper, but her husband stops her. "I've got it."

He skims the form, fills in the appropriate areas while blocking his wife from reading over his shoulder, and adds his signature at the bottom. "Thank you for all you've done."

Mrs. Delgado mutters something under her breath, but he throws a sharp glance her way, and she shuts up. Finally.

"I'm sorry we weren't able to complete this case in a satisfactory way," my mom says, handing me the paperwork to file away. "I hope Eli turns up soon."

Mr. Delgado nods at her, then me, and drags his wife out of the office before she says anything more.

There's a brief silence once they're gone, and then my mom claps her hands together as if she's dusting them off. "Well, that was unfortunate. Unsurprising, though," my mom says, injecting a cheeriness I'm not buying into her voice. "I do hope their daughter turns up safe. Annoying client or not, I wouldn't wish that pain on anyone."

"I'm sorry, Mommy."

"For what? You didn't do anything wrong."

"I was the one who introduced them to you. And then she got extra mad when I butted in. If I'd kept my mouth shut—"

"If you'd kept your mouth shut, we would've presented an incomplete report. You handled yourself perfectly from beginning to end. It's not your fault that the client didn't want to hear the truth. This isn't the first time I've been fired from a case, and it won't be the last. I am sorry that your first case was cut short."

My one chance to prove myself, and I end up getting fired. Fantastic.

"No point in moping around. Help me finish this paperwork, and then let's get out of here. I'll let your father know that we can get Daniel on our way home since we finished early."

She keeps up a light chatter as we take care of some paperwork, but my gloomy mood follows me the rest of the day. I accidentally burn the onions for the spaghetti and have to throw them out, clean the pan, and start over again. It's not until I've thrown myself down on my bed and grabbed my phone to bitch to Junior and Nicole that I notice all the unread texts and missed calls from Gaby. I'd set my phone to silent for the meeting with the Delgados and forgotten to turn the sound back on.

Gaby: My parents won't let me go w them

Make sure to fill me in later. Dinner? 🍜

My mom just called to scream at me about you

Wtf happened???

Gaby: MISSED CALL
Gaby: MISSED CALL

Gaby: PICK UP YOUR PHONE

Gaby: MISSED CALL

Something about seeing her name makes me feel sick to my stomach. Shame at being fired? Guilt at not being able to help her find her sister? Anxiety about the confrontation we're about to have? Probably all of the above.

And some sadness too. I can't deny it. It's only been a week, but I've actually been having fun with Gaby. She met my best friends, had dinner with my family, picked me up and dropped me off every day, even joined my aunt's Kali class. Guess that's over with.

I sigh and tap her name to call since I know a text isn't gonna cut it. She can't yell at me over text. Well, she can and has, but you know what I mean.

She picks up almost immediately, the worry evident in her voice. "Danika, are you okay?"

Her concern is so unexpected that I answer her honestly. "Not really. How about you? Sorry about . . . everything."

"No, I'm sorry. My parents fucking suck, and they had no right to talk to you and your mom like that."

"Did they tell you what happened?"

She scoffs. "Only because I made the mistake of asking. I wanted to come with, but they said it wasn't my business. Can you believe it? NOT MY BUSINESS? My sister is missing, and whatever you and your mom found out is not my business."

She starts shouting in Spanish, and while I don't really speak Spanish, you can't live in a neighborhood called Hermosa your entire life and have best friends who are Mexican and mixed African American and Puerto Rican without understanding that she's cursing her ass off.

"I didn't know you spoke Spanish."

Okay, not my best work, but she doesn't seem like she's gonna stop anytime soon, and I don't know what else to say.

Gaby cuts off partway through a particularly creative phrase that I think involves a goat and laughs. "Sorry about that. My dad made sure that Eli and I are fluent. My mom doesn't like it since she can't understand us and thinks we're disrespecting her whenever we speak Spanish in front of her. Which, like, of course we use Spanish to talk shit in front of her. That's the whole point of being able to speak another language."

"She didn't try to learn it?"

She snorts, and we leave it at that.

"Anyway, I'm glad you called me back. I thought you were ghosting because you were mad at me."

Again, the shock makes me answer more honestly than I want to. "Me? Mad at you? When I saw your missed calls and texts, I was terrified that you were going to cuss me out, then tell me you never wanted to speak to me again."

"Aww, were you actually sad about that?" she teases.

I don't say anything, but that in itself is an answer, isn't it?

She waits for me to respond, but when it's clear that I won't, she says, "Well, it doesn't matter what my mom says. You're not getting rid of me that easily."

I let out a bunch of super smooth "uh" and "umm" noises in response.

"Let's be real, I can't afford your mom's rates. But . . . can I hire you?"

"Me? You want to hire me as a detective?"

"No, to be my fake girlfriend. Of course as a detective. We haven't heard anything from Eli since she disappeared, and it's not like she's going to waltz back into the house in time for prom. My sister is out there, and I have no idea if she's okay. But you were making some real progress. And I trust you."

She trusts me? To find her sister? Who she thinks ran away partly because of my tarot reading? Here's where she lays on the guilt, I bet.

"I understand if you can't take this on. I know you're super busy with taking care of your brother and helping your mom and all that family stuff. So no pressure."

Huh. It'd be easier if she tried guilting me.

"Your mom told me to stay away from you."

"Ooh, doesn't that make this even cooler and more forbidden?" She laughs. "Also, my mom can go screw herself."

I fight back a grin and fail. "You know what? She absolutely can go screw herself. I'm in."

CHAPTER ELEVEN

"ARE YOU GOING TO TELL YOUR MOM ABOUT US?"

I choke on the iced Vietnamese coffee Gaby bought me from her favorite café. "Tell her WHAT about us?"

Gaby takes her eyes off the road briefly to hand me some napkins. "That we're still investigating my sister's case?"

I grab a bunch to clean myself up. "Oh, that. You should definitely work on your phrasing. And, yeah, there's no point in me hiding it from her, especially since I might need her advice. Besides, you may be big on lying"—she protests and reaches out to whack my arm, but I dodge her and continue— "but there's no fooling my mom. She's going to wonder why you're still hanging around, so it's best to be honest with her. She knows what your parents are like, and she legit wanted to find Eli. It's fine."

"So you're telling me that your mom wouldn't believe that we're *hanging out* hanging out?" She smirks, and I nearly choke again.

All this week, Gaby and I continue our usual ritual of her picking me up in the morning and dropping me off after school, with lunch and some investigating in between. There's little progress on the Eli front, but a whole lot of *platonic* hanging out with Gaby. Because I'm a professional.

She attends Kali classes regularly with me, blowing off a ton of steam, and joins us for dinner again on Thursday, where we admit to my mom that we're at a bit of a dead end until we can figure out a way to talk to people at the country club Eli was secretly working at. My mom thinks for a moment before picking up her phone (my dad has a "no phones at the table" rule, but it doesn't apply to Mom, apparently) and tapping out a message. She waits for a moment, but there's no immediate response, so she puts her phone down and continues the conversation as if nothing happened.

It's not until Gaby's already gone for the day and I'm busy jotting down notes for my first advice column that my mom knocks on my door and enters my room. "You and Gaby are going to your Kali lessons tomorrow, right?"

I set down my pen and stretch. "That's the plan. Why? Who were you messaging earlier?"

"I don't want to say anything in case they don't come through. Just make sure both of you go to the class tomorrow, okay?" She glances down at what I'm working on. "That for the newspaper?" When I say yes, she says, "I know you're only doing it for the investigation, but I hope you keep it up when this is all over. I think being with people outside of your family is good for you."

It's annoying AF that she's pushing me to hang out with people outside the family as if she's not the main reason I don't. It's like she doesn't even notice how much she's constantly asking of me. How little time I have for fun. But I can't think of a way to voice my opinion without being disrespectful, so I shrug. "I don't hate it, so we'll see."

She nods and tells me not to stay up too late. I try to work for a little longer after she leaves, but I can't concentrate because my mind is busy wondering why she's so insistent that Gaby and I go to Kali tomorrow.

It occupies my thoughts for most of the next day, and I only grow more curious when my mom texts me.

Mommy: Go straight to the studio.

Danika: ???

Mommy: You'll see.

I relay the message to Gaby.

"Why's your mom being so cryptic?"

"She doesn't really like explaining herself. She kinda expects you to just do what she says."

Gaby snorts. "Sounds like my mom."

Considering I've met her mom and I know how she feels about her, those are fighting words. I'm about to warn her that she doesn't want this smoke when she pulls into a spot in front of my aunt's studio. I decide to let the affront to my mom slide since I'm more interested in seeing what my mom has set up than defending her honor, but Gaby better never disrespect my mother like that again.

My cousins are waiting for us near the entrance with a tall Asian dude who seems vaguely familiar and is holding a big cardboard box full of . . .

"Puppies!" I let out a squeal and run over. "Can I pet them?"

"Sure." The mystery guy lowers the box slightly, and I hold out my hand for the dogs to sniff. One of them, a pudgy round ball of brown fur, nudges itself against my fingers, and I carefully pick up and snuggle the pup. Is this what my mom wanted me to hurry over here for? A bunch of puppies? I'm not mad at it. That doesn't sound like her, though, so I turn my attention to my cousins while still making it seem like I'm focused on the puppy in my arms.

Out of the corner of my eye, I see my cousins nudge each other before Joemar speaks up. "Danika, Gaby! Glad you could make it. I wanted to introduce you to Alex Lim."

Alex smiles down at us (not "down" as if he thinks he's better than us, but "down" because, like, he's probably the tallest Asian dude I've ever met) and shifts the box to one arm to stick out his hand. "Nice to meet you both. Your cousins told me a lot about you, Danika."

Andrew says, "He's on the same team as us in the PBA, and he also goes to school with you both. At our last game, he was trying to get our teammates to adopt these puppies he found abandoned on the side of the road."

"The Philippine Basketball Association," I explain to Gaby after seeing her head tilt at the unfamiliar acronym. "My cousins have been playing ball since they were kids."

"Me, my mom, and my sister aren't around enough to give

these cuties enough love." Alex gazes at the puppy nuzzled in my arms, his hand still out. "Your cousins said if I brought the puppies over today, they'd help find them good homes in return for a favor."

I know my cousins and the kinds of favors they ask for, so I ignore his outstretched hand. With more than a little apprehension, I ask, "What kind of favor?"

Alex grins at us. "Your cousins told me the two of you are looking for work. I'm a host at the Chicago Glen Country Club and can probably help you get a job there. They're hiring."

I stare at him for a second, barely comprehending what he's saying, and then my eyes slide over to my cousins standing behind him, who are signaling and mouthing silently to me like, *THE INVESTIGATION. DUH!*

I snap out of my stupor and glance at Gaby before belatedly sticking out my own hand to shake Alex's. "I don't know how helpful we'll be in getting these puppies adopted, but I'd absolutely love a job at the country club."

Do I have time for a job at a country club? No. But I'll make it work. Somehow.

"My dad's allergic to fur, otherwise I'd help you out," Gaby says. "But, yeah, I'd love a job there too."

"The dog you're holding is definitely getting adopted," Joemar says to me.

"By who?"

"By you."

I laugh. "Did you forget that I also have, like, zero time to raise a puppy?"

"Daniel is going to take one look at the dog and fall in love, and you know you never say no to him. Besides, we already asked your dad, and he said it was okay."

"Did you ask my mom?"

"Of course not. She'd just say no."

"You know she gets the final say."

"It's your job to convince her. You love acting like you got +3 Persuasion skills. Let's see you put them to work, cuzzo."

Joemar and Andrew prove themselves to be annoyingly correct. The second Daniel sees the dog in my arms, he beelines over and reverently pets the dog's fur. A quick glance at my dad, who dropped him off, and I know the dog's coming home with us. I pass the dog, who appears to be some kind of mix between a Shiba Inu and a corgi, to Daniel. He cradles the puppy carefully.

"What's her name?" Daniel asks after checking with Alex if the dog is a girl or boy.

Alex sets down the box with the other two puppies and stoops to Daniel's eye level. "She doesn't have a name yet. You're her human now, so it's your job to give her a name, okay?"

Daniel nods solemnly. "I'll think of a good one."

"I'm sure you will." Alex straightens up. "I've got the leash, dog bowl, and puppy kibble I've been using in the back seat of my car. Oh, and a snack from my mom."

He retrieves the items and hands them, as well as a paper bag with slight grease stains, over to my dad. "My mom works at a bakery in Chinatown, and she wanted to give this as thanks to whoever gives the dogs a home."

My dad laughs. "We're only taking one dog, but I'll gladly accept those treats."

"We found homes for the other two puppies already, so don't worry about it," Andrew says. "Now, what did your mom give us this time?"

My dad reaches into the bag and pulls out a fried sesame ball. "Oh, buchi! It's been a while since I've had this."

He holds the bag out to Gaby, who takes one, and he passes another to me once I've cleaned my hands with the wipes he carries. I break the buchi in half, exposing the sweet bean paste in the middle. "Here, Daniel. I know you love these."

But Daniel's eyes are going back and forth between the little brown dog curled up in a ball in his arms and the large sesame balls in our hands. "Buchi! The dog's name is Buchi!"

Buchi stirs in his arms after hearing her new name, and everyone else smiles down at her, happy that she approves. Meanwhile, I'm smiling discreetly at Alex, who has put me one step closer to finding Eli.

TITA BABY ARRIVES SOON AFTER THAT, AND SO DO Junior and Nicole. After introductions and squealing over the newest addition to the Dizon household, my dad takes Buchi home so we can focus on our Kali lessons. Alex heads out too, but not before getting my phone number and promising to contact me about an interview at his job.

I immediately drag my cousins into a corner to get the full story.

"We've actually known Alex for years. Like I said, he plays basketball with us as part of the PBA. He's a good dude," Joemar adds.

"Your mom messaged us the other night to see if we could get in contact with that missing girl's boyfriend since we go to the same school," Andrew explains. "UIC's huge and we're in different departments, so that was a no-go, but then she mentioned where that guy works. I remembered Alex had to miss a game recently because he got called in to cover an emergency shift at his job. I knew he worked at a country club, so I asked him the name of the place he works, and, yeah. Hell of a coincidence, huh?"

"Um, yeah," I say. "You think he really can get us jobs there?"

Joemar shrugs. "He seemed pretty confident about it. He's cocky as hell on the court, but he's pretty solid otherwise. He didn't make any promises, but he's also not the type to say something without being able to back it up."

Andrew glances over his shoulder at his mom, who's striding toward the front of the room. "Class is about to start. Let's talk about this more later."

After the lesson, I gather at a table for family meal with Gaby, Junior, Nicole, and my cousins. The food hasn't even made its way to us yet when Gaby bursts out with questions about Alex and his connections to the country club.

My cousins reassure her the same way they did me earlier. "It was really cool of you to ask him to get jobs for us. Thanks. How do we get in touch with him about that?"

"Oh, I gave him my number before he left," I say.

She whips around. "You gave him your number?"

I give her a weird look. "Well, yeah. How else would he let me know about the jobs?"

"When was this? It's interesting that he didn't ask for my number, no?"

"You were busy talking to my aunt, I think. He probably assumed I'd keep you updated." Something occurs to me. "Oh, sorry! Do you want his number too?"

I pull out my phone, and Nicole and Junior, who'd been eating silently next to us, both laugh. So do my cousins. The only one not laughing is Gaby, actually.

I glance at everyone. "What?"

"Nothing, babe. You keep being you," Nicole says, pulling me into a side hug and giving me an exaggerated kiss on the cheek.

I swat her away. "I'm surprised you didn't make a move on him, actually. He's definitely your type."

"And what's my type?"

"Tall and athletic. He's a basketball player, so he's got nice arms, which is totally your thing. Oh, and he's got dimples."

Nicole and Junior exchange glances and grin. "Sounds like you were the one checking him out, chica."

"Me?" I laugh. "You know I observe everyone closely. Don't you remember—" I start to say, and then remember Gaby's there and shut up.

"Remember what?" Nicole asks, but Junior clearly knows because he starts cracking up.

"Oh, that's right! I can't believe I forgot about that."

"Forgot what?"

"Her serial killer notebook."

Gaby's eyes widen. "Her what?"

I smack Junior on the arm. "He means my detective journal!" *That I still use.*

"Ohmigod, yes! The teachers were so freaked out, and—"

"Anyways, that's not important!" I interject. "The point is, I am very observant."

"Oh, no, you're not getting out of this," Gaby says. "What was in your detective journal that freaked everyone out?"

"Nothing!"

"Oh, come on, it wasn't that bad. You were misunderstood," Junior says, as if it was a simple childhood misunderstanding to laugh about and not, you know, a super traumatic thing that lost me all my friends and had teachers literally running the other way when they saw me.

Gaby studies my face. "If you don't want to talk about it, that's fine. We all got stuff we want to leave in the past."

Which I appreciate her saying, but I don't want it to seem like an even bigger deal than it already did.

"If you really think about it, it's totally natural that I had that notebook. You know, with my mom being a PI and my dad a mystery writer, right? Both of them talk about how important it is to people watch, so I kept a notebook of the things I noticed around me."

"That's it?"

I hesitate because, yeah, that's it, but also, it was kinda way more than that?

I glance over at Junior, who explains, "She kept detailed

notes on EVERYBODY. Students, teachers, parents. Full names, physical descriptions, notes about their families and any rumors she heard."

"Yeah, and one day, I think we were in sixth or seventh grade, a teacher found the notebook on the ground and opened it to see who it belonged to and flipped the fuck out when she saw what was inside."

"Why? I mean, it sounds a little extra, but it's just, like, Enola Holmes–type stuff, right?"

Junior turns to me. "Actually, why did Ms. Cassiere freak out? She even called a parent-teacher conference if I remember right."

I sigh. "Enola Holmes wishes she had my observation skills. Anyway, I guess because I also included inferences I made based on my notes. Like, I knew which teacher was having an affair with which parent. That one of the volunteers at the church was skimming money from the fundraisers. That one of the students was having, uh, home issues. Things like that."

Gaby's eyes widen. "That's incredible, no? And you were still in middle school?"

Here Nicole and Junior gaze at me sympathetically, as if finally realizing why I didn't want to talk about it.

"Turns out they were embarrassed that a kid was able to figure out their dirty business, and word got around that I was a creepy weirdo who liked spying on people." I smile as if it's not a big deal and I'm totally over it, which I am. "Junior and Nicole were the only friends who stuck by me. So, yeah. It's fine—it's not like I have time to hang out with people anymore, anyway. I already don't make enough time for these two."

"Oh, so you do know how you treat us," Nicole says, shoving me lightly. "I was starting to wonder if you were delusional."

"*Anyway,* let's hope Alex comes through," I say. "Eli's secret job and boyfriend are the only things we haven't investigated yet, so if we're going to get any clues as to where she went and why, that country club is our best bet."

"What if he can't get us in?" Gaby asks.

"Then we'll have to find someone who can."

Gaby makes a face but lets it go. "By the way, you guys didn't tell Alex why we want jobs at the country club, did you?"

My cousins shake their heads. "We told him you both needed money since you're on your own for college."

"Alex has a tough family situation, so he's sympathetic to stuff like that," Joemar adds. "The minute I told him that my poor, beloved cousin might have to give up on going to college since her family can't afford it, I knew he'd be in."

I laugh. "You played him."

"Like a violin." Joemar grins. "It's fine. It's kinda true, right? The best lies always have a grain of truth in them. And once you know how your target thinks and operates . . ." He pantomimes playing the violin. "Gets 'em every time."

I'm glad Alex and Gaby don't run in the same social circles, because he'd know that she's not in it for the money. Still, playing up your target's sympathies is an excellent move.

"You have a very devious mind," Gaby says, nodding at him approvingly.

Joemar bows. "Why, thank you."

Tita Baby calls for my cousins, and they both get up.

"Let us know if Alex doesn't contact you before the weekend is over. He's still your best bet on getting in, but we've got a couple other strings we can pull if we need to," Andrew says before heading over to his mom.

"I knew the twins were well connected, but damn. Maybe I should talk to them about finding me a job too," Nicole says, watching them walk away.

"You already have a job," Junior points out. "You complain about it every single day. Half of our group chat is us bitching about work."

He's been at a family friend's deli since he was fourteen.

"I complain about it every day, so clearly that means I need a better one," Nicole says. "One that pays as well and has a flexible schedule."

She works at a grocery store near us that actually takes care of its employees and is super accommodating. It even lets cashiers sit, which, like, no other grocery or retail type place I know of does. Decent pay and conditions aside, there's no way a job like that would satisfy Nicole's creative mind.

Gaby asks, "How do you all still have time for school and these lessons?"

Junior shrugs. "We all *need* jobs. Well, Nicole and I at least get paid. Danika's been working at her mom's agency basically her whole life, and for free at that."

Gaby glances at me, and I shrug. "It's not like we can afford to hire anybody. My mom pays my cousins for their help, but they're technically freelancers."

"Yeah, but—"

"Gaby, your privilege is showing."

She clamps her mouth shut. "Sorry. I can barely get by with the schoolwork and art projects I have now. I can't imagine taking on more stuff."

Nicole gives a little half smile. "It's amazing what you have time for when you don't really have a choice. I try to fit Kali in around my job and schoolwork so I don't burn out. But I can't let my grades slip if I want to make it to SAIC."

"Ohmigod, that's where I want to go!" Gaby bursts out. "Their metal shop is amazing."

The School of the Art Institute of Chicago is one of the best (and most expensive) art schools in the area. It's been Nicole's dream to study fashion design there since we were kids. Considering it's a big deal for someone in our area to make it to any college, let alone a prestigious one like that, I worry that she's getting her hopes up. But it's not like being a private investigator or author or professional martial artist is a typical, stable career path either, so if my family's taught me anything, it's to dream big and figure everything else out along the way.

"I knew you were into art, but I didn't know you were into metalworking or whatever it's called," I say to Gaby.

"My dad used to be really into building things and working with his hands. Fixing cars, making a playhouse for me and Eli, stuff like that. Our garage was his workshop, and he'd let me help him with small projects, but my mom hated it. Said it was too dangerous to have all that equipment around young kids. And then he started getting busy at his tech job and didn't have time for his hobby, so he eventually sold all the equipment to keep my mom happy," Gaby explains. "I don't have access to the materials anymore, so I mostly stick with painting and small sculpture work that I can do at school, but it's not the same. I wish we still had shop classes at Lane. They'd be so much fun."

"Must be nice knowing what you want to do," Junior says. "I'm just an average dude, so I'd settle for a job that doesn't suck and pays me enough to live comfortably."

"If the private detective thing doesn't work out, I'm pretty much in the same boat as Junior. My mom's agency is all I've ever known. If she loses it or if I can't prove myself . . ."

The future becomes entirely uncertain. And few things scare me more than uncertainty. I'm reminded of those early days as a kid, before the Dizon Detective Agency found its footing and my dad's books found a legit audience. There were days where we weren't sure when the next paycheck was coming. When our electricity would randomly get shut off because we couldn't pay the bill and would have to stay with my paternal grandparents or with one of my aunts. But little by little, word of mouth spread for both of my parents. When the tiny indie press that published my dad's books folded, he had enough of a following for a big publisher to take him on and pay him real money. We were all super happy for my dad, but while that was going on, my mom hustled her ass off to become one of the top private detectives handling family issues in Chicago.

That's part of the reason I admire my mom so much. Even when her life was entirely upended by her own parents, she knew who she was and what she stood for and was able to build a business where she relied only on herself.

Junior nudges me with his shoulder. "We've got plenty of time to figure out who we want to be."

"Thank you, O Wise One," I say jokingly, but I smile at him to let him know I'm not dismissing him. Because he's right.

I can only focus on the now.

CHAPTER
TWELVE

"I CAN'T BELIEVE IT. ALEX ACTUALLY CAME THROUGH,"
Gaby murmurs as she examines our plush surroundings. We're
sitting in the hallway outside the office of the general manager
for Chicago Glen Country Club, waiting for our individual
interviews. It's the Sunday after we met Alex, and he's already
arranged an interview for us with the club's manager.

"Why do you sound so shocked? My cousins said he'd handle it."

Gaby shrugs. "I guess I'm used to men letting me down, you
know?"

"As the great Ted Lasso said, 'If that's a joke, I love it. If not,
I cannot wait to unpack that with you.'"

That earns me a smile that's quickly replaced with a pan-
icked expression when the office door opens and an older white
woman pokes her head outside. "Mary Gabrielle Delgado? We're
ready for you."

Good luck, I mouth to her as she follows the woman inside
the office.

Ideally we'd both get jobs here to double the sleuthing,
so I cross my fingers that the positions available don't require

previous work experience. I at least can list my years at the detective agency, but as I pointed out a couple nights ago, Gaby's never actually needed a job.

I pass the time by finishing up the article I need to give Winston on Wednesday—he chose the questions from the anonymous submissions we received for my first advice column. By the time I reach the last question, the door opens again, and Gaby steps out, followed by the woman who first invited her in.

The woman smiles when she sees what I'm doing. "I can see that you're a hard worker!" She glances down at a clipboard. "Danika Dizon? We're ready for you."

"I'll wait for you out here," Gaby says. I try to read her face to see how it went, but a brief shrug lets me know that she has no idea.

I follow the woman, who introduces herself as Annette, the assistant to the general manager, Mrs. Jennifer Whittle. Mrs. Whittle is sitting behind her desk but stands up to introduce herself and shake my hand when we approach. "Nice to meet you, Danika. Let's jump right in, shall we?"

At my nod, she asks, "Your resume says you've been working for your mother's detective agency for years. If you already have a job, why are you now seeking a position at the Chicago Glen Country Club?"

"My goal is to someday take over my mother's agency," I explain. "However, that dream is a long way down the road. To prepare for that, it's best that I get experience working various jobs that expose me to people from all different walks of life. It's important to me that I don't stay in a comfortable little bubble."

"And you think the Chicago Glen Country Club will provide you with that experience?"

"Absolutely. Thanks to years of working the front desk of the agency, I know how to answer phones and emails in a professional way. I can speak politely and calmly to guests and defuse situations. Because of the confidential nature of my mother's work, I'm good at being discreet, should the occasion call for it. But I can also be clear and direct, if necessary," I say, reciting all the strong points that my father and I practiced. "I'm also quite strong and used to doing physical labor, if that's what the job entails. Heavy lifting, cleaning, recreational activities . . . I can do it all."

"Ah yes, I see in your hobbies section that you take martial arts classes," Mrs. Whittle says, scanning my resume. "We do have an opening in the kitchen that you would be well suited for, but it's almost all men back there. Would you be comfortable working in that kind of environment?"

I start to shrug and then remember my mom whacking my shoulders to encourage good posture and body language. "It wouldn't be a problem. I've been studying Kali almost my entire life, so I'm used to being in male-dominated environments."

And if Eli's new boyfriend, Caleb, is one of those men, even better.

Mrs. Whittle nods as if her mind's made up, but then Annette clears her throat. "Excuse me, Mrs. Whittle?"

Mrs. Whittle and I start as if we both forgot that her assistant was there. "Yes, Annette?"

"I agree that Danika would fit well with the kitchen staff," Annette says carefully. "However, I think it's more urgent that we fill the front desk associate position. Leah's already threatening to quit if we don't fill Eli's spot since she's been so swamped."

My ears perk up at Eli's name.

Mrs. Whittle sighs and rubs her temples. "I understand that, but so far I haven't found the right person for the job."

"I think Danika would be perfect—"

"I am not putting another high school student in that position; they are far too flaky. I made an exception for Eli, and you see where that left us? No offense, Danika."

There's an awkward pause, but now that we're on the subject of Eli, I can't let it end here.

"Um, you said the previous front desk worker was a high school student as well? Sorry if I'm being nosy, I'm just surprised someone so young was put in that kind of position. She must have been very capable."

Mrs. Whittle huffs. "In the beginning, Eli was absolutely perfect for the role. Polite, intelligent, and so attentive! Really made each member feel like she knew and cared about them. But then she up and quit with no prior warning! Didn't even have the courtesy to do it in person; I only found a signed resignation letter on my desk one day. She apologized for leaving without giving two weeks' notice, but still." She shakes her head. "I'm sorry, I know I shouldn't be talking about a former employee like this, but she really left us in the lurch."

"I can see why you'd be hesitant to hire another high school student," I start, "but I believe I have all the qualifications necessary to be a front desk associate, and it would be mutually beneficial for both of us."

Please give me this job so that I can get better at my real job!

Before, I didn't care what job I got as long as I had an in at the country club. But now, knowing that Eli's role is up for grabs and I can interact with all the people that she did and see the places she went makes me desperate for this position. I need to make this woman see she needs me as much as I need her.

"I want a job that lets me interact with lots of different people so I can learn more about the world, and you need someone to fill this position immediately. Why don't you let me take over the front desk role during the busy season, and once it's over, you can either keep me on or find someone you feel is a more permanent fit?"

Mrs. Whittle leans back in her very obviously expensive office chair and studies me. "Do you have a reliable mode of transportation?"

What she really wants to know is if I have a car or if I'll be relying on public transportation. But I've been taught not to elaborate on that point, so I just say, "Yes."

Not like I'm lying. If I get this job, I should be able to (finally!) afford the repairs on Veronica in a month.

She holds out her hand. "Welcome to the Chicago Glen Country Club, Danika. I think you'll do well here."

CHAPTER THIRTEEN

"WELCOME TO THE CHICAGO GLEN COUNTRY CLUB. My name is Danika, and I'm the front desk associate this evening. How may I help you?"

I'm only into the second hour of my shift, and I've repeated that same introduction so many times, I almost wish I could record myself and hit play whenever someone new walks in. Not that the country club is bustling or anything like that—they've got nothing on a coffee shop in the morning or even a halfway decent brunch place on a Sunday.

The Chicago Glen Country Club *is* exclusive, though. They wouldn't want something as pedestrian as a packed room, since that would mean letting anyone in. But apparently it's a super popular golf destination, and with the busy season about to start, things are going to get real hectic real fast. It seems the guests want to wring out every last minute they can on their super expensive, horrible-for-the-environment hobby. And after going a few rounds (That's what it's called in golf, right? Rounds?), what better way to cap off the evening than with a horribly overpriced meal?

Well, overpriced in my opinion, anyway. For all I know, the food here is god-tier and worth those extra $$$. But for someone like me, who thinks Panera Bread is a splurge (I wish I could quit you, broccoli cheddar bread bowl . . .), I can't imagine any steak being worth that price tag. But it's not like I can say that when my job is to inform the guests of our daily specials while making dining reservations.

My responsibilities include handling all reservations, greeting the members and their guests when they come in, running errands, answering phones and emails, and basically being the human version of an FAQ section for the club.

Not gonna lie, it actually is pretty fun, especially as someone who likes to people watch. Most conversations are as mundane as you'd expect, but every now and then, I overhear a nugget like "If Mallory gets one more facelift, I swear the woman will be able to blink her lips." Savage, but I give a quick glance at who they were talking about, and they're not wrong.

Or "I tried that thousand-dollar steak in Miami, and, you know, it was a fine show, but I wish my husband had chosen a better song to accompany it." I had to Google WTF she was talking about during my break and, honestly, wow. Money really is wasted on the rich.

But my favorite bit of gossip that day is from a couple of women who are chattering away while I register them for the club's wine tasting event that weekend: "Don't look, but Vanessa Andrews is wearing fake diamonds. I bet she thought no one would notice that she swapped out the real things for those fakes, but she can't fool me. I bet she sold the real ones because she's having money problems."

My mom's given me a pretty good education on how to separate high-end products from cheap fakes—not as detective training, mind you, but because she considers it an important life lesson for anyone who loves luxury goods. I don't care about that stuff, but I managed to put this knowledge to good use during one of her old fraud cases. However, I doubt even she'd be able to figure out whether that Vanessa woman is wearing fake gems. That they could not only spot the difference but come up with a logical reason for the swap is impressive. These women are no joke, and I feel a grudging respect for their skills, even if this is how they choose to wield them.

As I fill out their registration forms, I hope they'll continue to make noteworthy observations, but then they start talking about some new prototype golf club that one of the partners has, and unless that's code for some sex thing I don't know about (which, to be fair, is very possible), this new topic is way less interesting, so I finish up their registration and move on to helping the next guest.

My position requires me to get to know anyone who comes in and out, the club layout, and the general way the club operates. Eli's alleged boyfriend is one of the servers, and I ask Alex to introduce me to the ones working that day during our shared break. Before I started this job, my mom shared the file she made on Caleb Miller and included a grainy photo of his student ID. So I know quite a bit about him, from surface level stuff like his appearance (blond hair, blue eyes), school (UIC), and major (computer science), down to where he grew up (Naperville), his high school sweetheart (Margot Rivera), and how many traffic violations he's received (three).

Alex is one of the hosts for the dining room, so he knows the servers pretty well, and I can tell they respect him despite the age difference—the servers at this club are all college-aged or older since they need to be able to serve alcohol. They're also all ridiculously good-looking, almost unnaturally so, as if they were the cast of some paranormal CW show.

The two men and three women greet me warmly, but none of them are the guy I'm here for. Until . . .

"Hey, where's Caleb? I thought he was on the schedule for today," Alex says.

"He called in. Said something came up but promised he'd be here on Saturday for the wine tasting event," one of the men says.

"He better be," a female server mutters. "He's been super flaky ever since Eli quit."

"Can you blame him? Mrs. Whittle's been giving him crap about it as if it's his fault."

"Maybe it is his fault. Maybe he shouldn't have been dating a high school student, and then she'd still be here," one of the women points out.

One of the guys appears uncomfortable. "I mean, she's eighteen, right? Not like he's doing anything illegal."

The woman says, "She's *seventeen*," at the same time the other guy says, "Not that, anyway."

I am DYING to know what that second guy means, but Alex glances at me and says, "Not to be that guy, but I don't think you should trash-talk one of your coworkers in front of the new girl. Kind of sends the wrong signal, don't you think?"

I glare at him. "The new girl has a name."

He smiles. "Sorry. Please don't say things that will make Danika, the lovely new girl, not want to work here. Okay?"

The woman grins at me. "Sorry about that."

"Yeah, please ignore us. Caleb's a good dude, and the front desk is totally not cursed. You'll be fine," the guy who defended Caleb says.

"Wait, what?"

"Oops, dinner's starting soon. Later!"

And they all rush back to their positions in the dining room with Alex refusing to meet my eyes.

"Alex?"

"Yes?" he says, busying himself with the reservation list I brought him.

"Why did they just say that my position is cursed?"

"No clue."

"Alex?"

"Yes?"

"Do you want me to tell my cousins that you're withholding important information from me? Information that might compromise my safety?"

"Don't you dare!"

For a guy who's got a good six inches or so on my cousins (Joemar, Andrew, and I are the same height), he looks hilariously frightened of them. As he should be.

"So then, are you going to tell me what they're talking about?"

He sighs. "The last two front desk associates quit without warning, maybe a month or two apart. Eli at least left a note. Emily was a no call, no show and disappeared one day."

"Disappeared? Are you serious? And somehow—"

"No, wait, I don't mean disappeared in, like, a breaking-news type of way. I meant more like she ghosted. I thought we were cool, but when some of us reached out to her, there was no answer. I think she blocked our numbers."

"And what about Eli?"

"What about her?"

"You don't think it's weird that she left too?"

"Kinda but not really. I mean, her aunt's sick, right? It sucks, but at least there was a reason, unlike—"

"Wait, how do you know about her aunt?"

He gives me a questioning look. "Was it a secret? Gaby told Mrs. Whittle during her interview, and word got out."

"Oh. That makes sense."

I don't know what Alex sees in my expression, but suddenly his eyes get soft, and he reaches toward me. "Danik—"

"Danika!" Leah, the other woman working the front desk with me, hurries toward us. "There you are!"

I glance at the time on my phone. "Oh, sorry. My break isn't over yet, is it?"

"It is now. I need you to . . ." And as she leads me away, listing the number of tasks that apparently need to be taken care of ASAP, I can feel Alex's gaze following me.

"SO HOW WAS IT?"

Gaby got a job as a caddy and arranged it with Mrs. Whittle that we work the same shifts so she can drive us back and forth "to save the planet, not because Danika doesn't have her own car."

She lights up. "One of the guests was complaining to his

friend about how his wife keeps losing the jewelry he buys her. She claims it must've been stolen, but he doesn't buy it."

"Why not?"

"He told his friend that she's always losing stuff, and he bets it's just an excuse so that he'll buy her new jewelry. Plus, nothing else is missing from their house."

"Hmm . . ."

Gaby deflates. "Yeah, you're right. I doubt anyone would break into someone's house for a couple of bracelets and a ring, even if it was a rose gold Van Cleef & Arpels."

A rose gold ring?

"Eli was wearing a rose gold ring when she came to me for the reading. I noticed it because her nails were a mess. And the ring looked expensive, so it stood out."

"But why would she wear a stolen ring at work when she knew she could run into that guest at any time?"

"Maybe she didn't know it was stolen."

Gaby's about to reply when my phone starts buzzing. "Sorry, someone's texting me."

Alex: You and Gaby free after work on Saturday

Danika: I think so. Whats up

Alex: We always have welcome parties for new staff

That day work for you

I check with Gaby. "What do you think?"

I wait for her to say something, and when she doesn't, I continue, "We need to get to know as much of the staff as possible to find clues about Eli. Plus, Caleb is supposed to work that day, so he might be around for the party too. Should I tell him we're both down? Oh wait, we should probably ask our parents first."

That finally gets a reaction out of her as she bursts into laughter. "Oh my God, do you seriously ask your parents for permission to go to parties? Still?"

"I, uh, don't really go to parties. But, I mean, I have to let them know where I am. I can't come home all late and have them worrying about me, you know?"

"That's very sweet."

I don't think she's trying to patronize me, but she sure as hell sounds like it. "So what? Your parents don't care where you go?"

"Pretty much." She glances over at me. "Like you couldn't tell from those times you met them? My family is nothing like yours, Danika. They don't worry about me. They only pay attention if I'm doing something that might embarrass them."

Now it's my turn to possibly be patronizing without meaning to. "I'm sorry, Gaby. I didn't mean—"

"Whatever. I accepted it a long time ago. Most people I know's families are similar to mine. You're the odd one out. In a good way, I mean. You're lucky."

My mom would scoff at the thought. She doesn't believe in luck. After all, she was born into a wealthy family and chose to leave her privilege behind. *Hard work,* she'd say. *That's what got our family to where we are.*

But isn't it luck that working at her father's law firm led her to befriending one of the private investigators that the firm hired? That that friend reached out after my mom was disowned and helped her become a certified PI? Luck that my parents met and fell in love at all, despite the odds against them? I don't know. I want to be more logical like my mom, but now that Gaby has me really thinking about my family and our circumstances, I can't help being a little emotional.

"Yeah. I guess I am pretty lucky."

CHAPTER
FOURTEEN

"DANIKA, GABY, HEY!"

Gaby and I both turn to see Alex grinning and making his way across the hall. We're near the cafeteria, and considering that it's fifth period lunch and people are trying to get inside, his attempts to cut through the pack are what I imagine it must be like watching salmon swim upstream.

I smile up at him when he finally reaches us. "Hey. You also going to lunch?"

"Yeah, me and my boy Felix are going to eat out on the lawn. You want to join?" He gestures behind him to a guy who's studying me and Gaby with interest. Not like creepy interest, but more like a "Who are these girls talking to my friend?" kind of thing.

I glance at Gaby, who shrugs. Since I brought lunch for both of us at Daniel's insistence, it's not like we have to eat in the cafeteria. And I was telling her the other day that it would be good to get close to Alex since he has access to people and details about the club that we don't.

"Sure, why not? It's actually nice outside, so might as well enjoy it while we can."

April in Chicago can mean either gorgeous, sunny weather or a straight-up blizzard, with not much in between, but today is hoodie weather, my absolute fave. We make our way to the school's spacious front lawn, and I'm about to sit on the grass when Alex says, "Wait."

He pulls a blanket from his duffel bag and sets it down before gesturing for me and Gaby to sit. "I think we should all fit."

Gaby plops down without hesitation, but I take my shoes off before sitting cross-legged on the blanket next to her.

"You travel with a blanket for, what? Impromptu picnics?" Gaby asks, watching as he pulls a battered lunchbox from his bag as well.

He laughs. "Kinda? I mean, when the weather is nice, Felix and I always eat outside since I bring lunch for both of us. He doesn't like sitting on the grass, so I started carrying this blanket around so His Highness wouldn't have to worry about grass stains."

"Well, excuse me for caring about my appearance," Felix says dryly. "You could put a little more effort into your clothes too, you know."

"What's wrong with his clothes?" I ask.

Alex is dressed in a simple gray T-shirt, jeans, and gym shoes. He might not be as stylish as Felix, who's wearing a Fear of God hoodie (a brand that my cousins are obsessed with but will never be able to afford) with some equally-expensive-looking black jeans and spotless Jordans, or Gaby in her thrifted artsy vintage ensemble (I thought thrift stores were for buying cheap clothes, but Nicole told me that the one Gaby shops at is $$$), but his clothes are clean, have no holes, and fit him okay. Better than okay, really.

Both Gaby and Felix turn to me to check if I'm joking, then simultaneously glance at my outfit.

I reflexively look down. "What?"

Today I've got on my exercise leggings and a tank top with my dad's old heavy gray flannel shirt over it. My gym shoes are a little beat-up since I haven't bought a new pair in years, but they're still perfectly fine. I'm not winning any beauty contests, but it's not that bad . . . Is it? Nicole's been bugging me to change up my style—or, you know, actually get one—for years now, but I thought she was being her usual fashionista self.

It must be pretty dire if a client and some dude I met two seconds ago are staring at me like I'm a toddler who's dressed themselves for the very first time.

"Danika and I have similar styles. You know, um, athleisure," Alex says.

"Yeah, but you take it a bit too far. You wore basketball shorts year-round until I bought you those damn jeans for your birthday."

Alex shrugs. "Shorts are more comfortable. I do like these jeans, though, so thanks."

Felix shakes his head sadly. "All that height is wasted on you."

Gaby laughs. "He's not very aware, is he? It's kind of refreshing."

Alex flushes a deep red. "Are we gonna eat, or are you guys gonna spend the whole lunch period going on about me?"

"You are fine; your clothes are the problem," Felix says, then changes the subject. "So, what's on the menu today?"

"Leftover stir-fry and rice. I tried using ground turkey instead of the usual pork to be a bit healthier, but my family didn't exactly love it, so there's a lot," he says, pulling out a huge Tupperware full to the brim with food.

I grab the containers with my and Gaby's lunches and hand her the I Can't Believe It's Not Butter! tub. Alarm and confusion sweep over her face until she opens it and sees the Filipino spaghetti.

"It's sweeter than the spaghetti you're probably used to, but I think you'll like it. Unless you don't like hot dogs, but I'll gladly eat those for you."

Gaby accepts the fork I hand her and takes a small test bite before grinning. "When you said sweet spaghetti, I got a little nervous, but this is great! If I don't see him later, tell your dad thanks for the food."

"Your dad's the cook in the family?" Alex asks after swallowing the giant spoonful he shoved in his mouth.

"Yeah. I can make simple stuff, but my mom doesn't cook at all," I say, twirling spaghetti on my fork. "How about you?"

He shrugs. "We take turns, but it usually falls to me because my mom and sister are exhausted by the time they get home. I try to make stuff with lots of protein and vegetables to help me stay in shape, but they don't always appreciate it."

"That's because you care more about macros or whatever than flavor," Felix says, dousing his stir-fry with the soy sauce packets and hot sauce Alex gave him. He takes a bite, then nods, satisfied. "Turkey as a substitute is always a mistake, but this isn't bad. You just need to season it more."

"Does Alex always make you lunch?" Gaby asks Felix.

"Pretty much. No one in my family cooks, and he got sick of watching me eat fast food and instant noodles every day. He's a good guy," Felix adds, grinning at me for some reason.

"At least staff meal means you get a decent dinner when you're at work. You'd probably get sick of my cooking real fast if I had to make you lunch and dinner. Felix works at the country club too. He's part of the kitchen staff," Alex says, directing that last bit toward me and Gaby. To Felix, he adds, "They started the other day."

"Oh, so you're the new girls he was talking about! Why didn't you mention that sooner, man?" Felix says, smacking him on the shoulder. "You're definitely coming to the welcome party on Saturday, right?"

"Yeah, of course," I say.

He grins. "Good. It'd be kinda messed up if the guests of honor weren't there. Don't expect anything too special, though. It'll mostly be us drinking cheap beer at someone's apartment, but it's a good time."

"I won't be drinking since I have to drive, but who doesn't love a good party?" Gaby says, scraping the last of the spaghetti from the container. "Won't you be tired? If you're kitchen staff, you probably have to help with the event."

"The kitchen'll be busy for sure. But we've prepped for a bunch of these events before, so we're used to it." He takes a few sips from his water bottle before handing Alex back his Tupperware. "My next class is on the fourth floor, and I got stuff to do, so I'mma head out. Good meeting you two."

I check the time on my phone. "We've got some time, but my next class is pretty far too. I should get going soon."

But I find it hard to get up with my tummy full of good food and the sun beaming down on us, so instead I lie down, using my backpack as a pillow, and let the warmth wash over me. I must doze off for a minute, because the next thing I know, Alex is shaking me awake, and I open my eyes to see Gaby snapping her sketchbook shut.

"Time to go, Sleeping Beauty," she says. She holds out a hand and helps me up.

"You work tomorrow, right?" Alex asks as we trudge back to the building. "Want to ride together?"

Before I can answer, Gaby says, "Thanks, but I always drive us."

"I worked my schedule so that I can stay after school to do my tarot readings before my shift starts, anyway. Thanks, though."

"Oh, that's cool! I didn't know you read tarot. You'll have to tell me about that sometime. And I don't mind waiting if you want to head to work early, Gaby," Alex offers.

She shakes her head. "I've got stuff I need to finish up in the art room, anyway."

"Oh, cool. Well, I guess I'll see you two later."

I expect him to turn and leave, but he stands there eyeing us like he has more to say. I tilt my head and wait for him to speak, but he just bites his lip before waving and walking away.

I watch him for a moment, then turn to Gaby to say something, but I catch her staring at me. "What's up?"

"There's something off about Alex. I don't trust him."

"Why? He seems like a really nice guy."

"Yeah, TOO nice. Like, he was literally holding a box of puppies when we met him. He cooks for his mom, sister, and best friend every day. He was able to get us jobs without breaking a sweat. He's totally okay with the way you dress."

"You're saying all this like those are bad things, and, also, ouch on that last one."

"I'm just saying, nobody's that perfect. Plus, he works at the same place Eli did and is friendly with her boyfriend. Suspicious much?"

I was going to brush off her comments as paranoia, but she does have a point. To dismiss possibilities without even looking into them is bad detective work. I trust my cousins, so I'm sure Alex is exactly who he seems to be, but it couldn't hurt to keep an eye on him. The point of getting a job at the country club was to find clues and suspects, after all.

"We'll need to spend more time with him to see what he knows, but we should keep our guards up. And since Felix is his best friend and also works at the club, that's another possible source."

Gaby beams, satisfied. "Sounds good. Anyway, you're going to see Winston later, right? Have you figured out a way to ask about my sister yet?"

"I have to quit the newspaper since it's way too much on top of everything, but first, I'll bring up the new job and where I'm working and see if he reacts."

Gaby glances at her watch. "We better get going. Good luck with Winston. I'll meet you at our usual spot."

The rest of the day passes quickly, and soon I'm dealing with Winston Chang. After telling him I'm leaving, he spends a few minutes of the meeting berating me for being flaky and wasting his time. I'm only able to shut him up by thrusting the article I finished and printed out the night before into his hands.

"You spent zero time helping me, I finished the advice column like I promised, and we're at the end of the school year, so I don't wanna hear it."

He pauses to skim the piece, then stops to read it more closely. "You may be flaky, but this is actually really good. Sympathetic but no sugarcoating, with a touch of humor," Winston says, looking so impressed, it doesn't feel like a compliment. Like, how low was the bar he'd set for me?

"Listen, I'm sorry to be leaving, but I only said I'd shadow, and I just got a new job. Making money for my family is more important than beefing up my college applications."

"Oh, that's tough. Sorry, then, I get it," he says, showing that he actually does understand human empathy. "Where are you working?"

I was hoping you'd ask that.

"I'm the front desk associate for the Chicago Glen Country Club," I say, drawing out my job title and place of employment to see if he recognizes either of them from his time with Eli.

Sure enough, there's a spark of recognition, but not the one I was going for.

"That's cool. I go there sometimes with the golf team for special matches. They let us practice there sometimes too. It's a great place."

"Chicago Glen Country Club?" Mike, the guy who gave me the name of the club last time I was here, chimes in. "Isn't that where your ex works?"

"Eli?" Winston's eyebrows shoot up in surprise. "That's news to me. She must've started after we broke up. Though, maybe that's how she met him . . ."

He says that last part quietly, almost to himself, but I jump on it.

"Met who?"

"We broke up because she cheated on me with some college guy. I always wondered how they even met, but if she has a job, that's probably where. Don't know why she bothered hiding the fact that she was working, but if she was doing dirt, it makes sense." Winston smiles wryly. "Better off without her, anyway."

"And I work with this girl?" I ask.

He shrugs. "I guess. Her name's Eli Delgado. If you haven't met her already, you probably will soon. She's the type to plan welcome parties and team-building activities and whatnot, so look forward to that."

"I think she's still out of town taking care of her aunt," Mike says. He glances at Winston. "No one's heard a peep about her coming back."

Winston tilts his head. "Guess that's why I haven't seen her around lately."

Hmm, is that reaction genuine? I mean, even I knew about the sick aunt story outside of the case, and I didn't date Eli for three years. If he is involved with Eli's disappearance, it would make sense for him to cover his tracks and go along with the lie the Delgados cooked up. Does he benefit from lying about that, or did he really not know?

The bell rings, and Mike goes to grab his stuff and leave with the rest of the staff, but Winston stays behind to clean up, and I help him.

"Considering she cheated on you, the breakup must've been bad if you didn't even know about her going out of town," I say to Winston.

He shakes his head. "It was one of those things, you know? We'd been together forever, and I thought that was how it would always be. But when we ended it earlier this year, I realized it was for the best. We're both going away for college, might as well start fresh, you know?"

There's no animosity in his tone or expression, and what he's saying makes sense. I decide to move him down the priority list.

I'm late meeting Gaby, but now that he's finally talking to me, I can't pass up this opportunity to see what else he knows. I try to keep this line of conversation going. "You're being really mature about it."

He shrugs. "I may not want to see her with her new boyfriend, but I do want her to be okay. We weren't really in love near the end. We were more like best friends."

Our area now clean, the two of us leave the newspaper classroom and start walking down the hallway together.

"Come on. You're not even a little pissed that she moved on so quickly?"

"I'm annoyed about how it all happened, but I'm not mad that we're not together anymore." He gives a self-deprecating laugh. "Though it would've been nice if she'd told me instead of having one of my friends show me a picture of her with the new guy. That sucked. But it's fine. My prom date is way hotter than her."

I roll my eyes. "Sometimes you impress me with how mature you are, and sometimes you remind me you're a typical dude."

"You are so weird. I say one nice thing about your writing, and suddenly you think you know me."

I'm several strides ahead of him before I notice he's stopped walking. "Winston? What's up?"

I follow his gaze and see Gaby waiting for me near the exit. "Gaby! Just finished newspaper."

She was staring at her phone but glances up when she hears my voice. Her smile starts to slide off her face when she notices Winston, but she quickly fixes her expression. "Hey, Danika! And Winston. It's been a while."

I glance over at Winston to see his reaction, and he clearly isn't a fan. "What's wrong?"

"Nothing. I didn't know you two knew each other. Gaby's actually my ex-girlfriend's sister."

"Really? We're in the same year and work together, so she usually gives me a ride."

Gaby checks the time on her phone. "Speaking of, we better head out if we don't want to be late. Nice seeing you again, Winston."

He nods at her. "You too. I hope your aunt pulls through."

She thanks him before hooking her arm through mine and practically dragging me out of the building. I barely have enough time to say goodbye to Winston before we're outside, power walking to her car.

"Um, what's with the fast and furious exit? I finally got him to talk to me. And we don't even have work today; we're going to Kali, and Tita Baby knows we're gonna be late."

"Oh, sorry. I used that as an excuse since it was awkward seeing him again."

"Are you going to tell me what happened between you? Because there's obviously something more that you're not saying."

She's walking so fast, we've already reached her car. She slides wordlessly into the driver's side, and I get into the passenger's seat, figuring she's going to keep quiet about whatever I just witnessed.

She takes a deep breath before turning to me, her eyes resigned. "We got really drunk and made out at a party during spring break."

"Excuse me?"

"It was after he and Eli broke up! I'd never do that to my sister. But, well, we were drunk, and we got into an argument about something un-Eli-related, and then suddenly we were making out."

I wait for her to say more, and when she doesn't, I ask, "Then what's with the animosity? I get it being awkward, but it seems like way more than that."

"The next day, I texted him to meet up. He thought we were going to continue fooling around. I told him it was a mistake, and we needed to forget it. Some not-so-cool things were said, stuff you can't really take back. So, yeah. That's our story."

"Does your sister know?"

"No."

"Do you think Winston has anything to do with Eli running away?"

She hesitates before shaking her head. "They've been broken up for months. I know I lied about being suspicious of him, but I don't actually see him deciding to take revenge, especially since he's paranoid about anything interfering with his college plans."

Something occurs to me. "Wait. Didn't you tell me that you had no idea that Eli and Winston broke up? But you clearly did if you were making out with her ex at a party."

"At that time, I didn't want you talking to Winston and finding out what we did." Gaby squeezes her eyes shut, but I'm glaring so hard at her, she must feel it. "I feel so guilty about it. Even if they weren't together, it's like I betrayed my sister. And I didn't want you thinking any less of me. But I promised you I wouldn't lie anymore, so there. You happy?"

The moment I think I understand Gaby and that we're getting closer, she pulls something like this. I guess this is why we're supposed to have clear personal boundaries with our clients.

Now it's my turn to avoid her eyes. I put on my seat belt and turn my attention outside the window. "We better get going. We're already late for our Kali lesson."

"Danika . . ."

I'm trying so hard not to judge her, to keep an open mind like my parents taught me, but I can't help but side-eye her a bit. How could she do something like that to her sister? Is this why she's trying so hard to find Eli? Does she think it'll make herself feel better? Make things right?

I hear the click of her seat belt, and she drives us to my aunt's studio in silence, the weight of her guilt and my disappointment so oppressive that I don't think either of us could talk if we wanted to.

DEAR DANIKA

A special guest advice column featuring Lane Tech's resident tarot card reader

Q1: My best friend is making lots of bad decisions lately, and I'm worried she's going to ruin her life. She used to have a solid 3.5 GPA and was a starting member of the [REDACTED] team, working hard for a scholarship. But now she's always cutting class, her grades have dropped, and I think she got kicked off the team, but she won't tell me what's going on. It's like she doesn't care about anything anymore. How can I help her?

—Concerned BFF

Dear Concerned BFF,

First, I suggest you keep an open mind. She could be dealing with mental health issues and need help, but it might be difficult if she feels like she's being judged. It's also possible that the things she used to care about, such as academic success, are not as important anymore, and she has new interests that you're just not seeing.

The Page of Chalices implies that your BFF needs to explore a different side of herself, allow herself to dream impossible dreams, and become more in tune with her emotions. You both need to be open and honest with each other—right now, it's not cold, hard logic that's needed but trust and understanding.

Q2: My family moved to Chicago for my dad's job, and I transferred to this school halfway through the school year. I'm finding it hard to make friends. I don't want to go the entire summer without anyone to talk to. What should I do?

—Lonely

Dear Lonely,

That's a difficult position to be in, and I'm sorry you feel this way. I'm not going to say, "Just talk to people!" because if it was that easy, you wouldn't have written to me. However, the reversed High Priestess does hint that you're being too swayed by outside voices and aren't really listening to your inner self and what you need. Are you afraid of being rejected and end up holding yourself back without meaning to? Do you have interests you want to explore but think you might be judged for them? Take some quiet time to journal and figure out what you want—your intuition might guide you to the person(s) you've been looking for.

Q3: How do I tell someone I'm not interested without hurting their feelings? This girl in one of my classes asked me to prom, and TBH, I'm not really into her. But I've been rejected before, and it suuuucks. I don't wanna be that person, so what do I do?

—*Not a Jerk*

Dear Not a Jerk,

Sometimes it's easy to just go with the flow to avoid conflict, but you're emotionally mature enough to know what you want and what you don't while still being mindful of others. Good on you. That said, rejection is a part of life, and most of us will have to experience it again and again. The best way to handle this situation is to speak from the heart. The Ten of Chalices hints that this might actually be the beginning of a new and wonderful relationship. BUT I urge you to trust your emotions and let your feelings guide you. You do a disservice to yourself and to that girl if you're not being honest about what your heart wants.

Well, that's it for me! This is my one and only advice column, but if you ever need to talk, come find me. IYKYK.

—*Danika Dizon*

CHAPTER FIFTEEN

"SO YOU GONNA TELL US WHAT'S UP, OR ARE WE just gonna pretend everything's cool?" Junior asks before he shovels a mound of veggie fried rice into his mouth.

Gaby didn't bother staying for family meal, though she at least said goodbye to me at the end of the lesson. That, plus the stilted conversation we had with Junior and Nicole before class started, must've tipped him off.

"There's nothing to say," I lie, jabbing my spoon into the mound of corned beef on my plate. "Or nothing I can say. It involves the case, and you know I'm not allowed to talk about it."

"Girl, get creative," Nicole says. "How much of it is confidential because of your work, and how much of it is actually personal?"

Junior and Nicole know the case involves Gaby's sister since she told them, but they don't know any details.

"None of it's personal. My mom's always stressed how important boundaries are, so I've been careful about that, especially since we're spending so much time together lately."

"Then that's the problem," Junior says with an understanding nod. "You and Gaby are getting close, which means your relationship is changing, and those boundaries aren't so clear anymore. That's what's messing you up."

"No, that is NOT the problem. Stop talking like you know me," I say, even though nobody in the world knows me as well as Junior. "The issue is that she lied to me *again*. I thought I could trust her, but I can't, and that makes the case that much harder."

"How serious was this lie?" he asks.

I know he won't stop prying, so I try to talk around it. "The thing she lied about probably isn't that important, but it involves someone who could be crucial to the investigation. And if she hadn't lied, I wouldn't have wasted so much time on that person. Or, at least, I might've tried a different tactic. Not having all the info from the beginning makes it hard to form a strategy. And I don't get why she'd lie about something that was supposedly meaningless."

Nicole asks, "Is the thing she lied about personal?"

I think for a moment. "The act itself was personal, but it also affects the investigation."

"How personal are we talking?"

I don't answer.

"Let me put it another way," Nicole says. "After she admitted whatever it was she lied about, did it change the way you saw her?"

"Kind of? I mean, I'm more upset about the lying, honestly. As for what she did, I think I was more confused and disappointed than anything."

"There's your answer," she says.

"What?"

"She lied to you because she didn't want you to think badly about her."

"She said that, yeah. But what does that matter? It's not like I'm gonna drop the case or not work as hard because of that."

"Lord, give me strength," Nicole says, rolling her eyes up to the ceiling. "How are you so smart and so good at figuring out people but so terrible when it comes to yourself?"

"Let's not get into that right now; she's not ready," Junior says. "The point is, Gaby didn't lie because she loves being messy. Well, I get the feeling that she actually does love being messy, but this isn't that. I think your opinion matters to her, and she was right to be scared of your reaction since you're a by-the-book kind of person."

"But we barely knew each other when this potential suspect first came up. And it's not like I'm super judgmental or anything, right?"

My best friends pause long enough that I can't help but cringe.

"Not judgmental in the way that you're thinking," Junior is quick to clarify. "More like you're constantly analyzing people. Sometimes I see you staring at someone, and it's like you're dissecting them to try and figure out what makes them tick. Almost like you're studying a subject, not trying to get to know a human being. Does that make sense?"

Nicole jumps in. "He's making it sound creepier than it is. You're constantly reading people and careful to control the situation to keep things smooth and simple. It's hard to know what you're really thinking sometimes. Remember that time when we were all trying to figure out what to do for the talent show in fifth grade? All the girls in our group—moi included—were talking over each other, but you took notes on what everyone was saying and used that to come up with a compromise that made everyone happy. Without ever sharing your own opinion. It's kinda always like that with you."

I focus on emptying my plate.

Junior and Nicole also turn their attention to their food, but I see them sneaking glances at me out of the corner of my eye, and I can't help but smile.

"I'm not mad, so stop eyeing me like that. You've given me a lot to think about, that's all." I sigh. "And I'll smooth things over with Gaby. Maybe she was embarrassed and wasn't trying to be difficult," I realize.

Nicole leans in. "Please spill already! What did she do?"

"I ain't saying nothing."

"Don't be like that! It's gotta be juicy for you to be acting like this."

I gaze at Nicole and realize she's the perfect person to give me insight into sister relationships. I'm having a hard time understanding how Gaby could betray her sister with some dude she doesn't even like, but maybe Nicole would get it.

"Would you ever mess around with one of your sisters' ex-boyfriends?"

"Oh damn, it's like that?" Nicole laughs. "I gotta call up Gaby to go shopping someday, because I need the full story."

"That would actually help a lot, but you didn't answer my question."

"We've had crushes on the same guy before, and more than once, one of us has dated a dude that another sister rejected, but an ex . . . That's so messy."

"Told you Gaby screams messy queen," Junior interjects.

Nicole continues, "Eh, it's hard to imagine a guy being worth the drama. Unless you don't like your sister, and you're doing it to piss her all the way off. Are Gaby and her sister tight?"

"It's not like they hate each other. They don't really talk anymore, though. And her sister was the one to break it off with that guy for some new boy."

"So she says. Now I think you might be right that Gaby's trying to cover shit up," Nicole says, leaning close. "Smooth things over with her, get on her good side, but don't get too attached. Just because she says she doesn't hate her sister doesn't mean it's true."

Nicole's right. I set those client boundaries for a reason, and I need to reestablish them. That'll get me back on track.

"Thanks, Nicole. That helps a lot."

"Of course it does. I give excellent advice. I'll try to hang out with her sometime and see if I can get a read on her. She's got great style, so a shopping trip will be fun." At my raised eyebrow, she adds, "What? I said you should be careful around her; that has nothing to do with me. Who am I supposed to talk fashion with? You and Junior?"

"Ruthless," Junior says. "Anyway, it's better to let her think she's one of us if you're trying to get her to open up or admit to anything."

"Keep your friends close and your enemies closer, huh?" I grin. "I can handle that."

"I PROMISED MY FRIENDS THAT I WOULD START EAT-ing lunch with them again, but I'll still meet you at the usual spot for work. Is that cool?" Gaby asks as she hands me my go-to iced Vietnamese coffee after I slide into her passenger seat the next morning.

I study her expression as I accept the drink, but her huge sunglasses cover her eyes, and it's hard for me to gauge anything. I shouldn't be surprised she's putting distance between us after what went down yesterday, but somehow, I am. I thought I'd be the one to establish our boundaries. Whatever, it all works out.

"Yeah, sure. If I'm late, it's probably because I'm in the mid-dle of a reading, but I'll try to give you a heads-up."

Gaby nods, then turns up the music, and I find myself bob-bing my head along to her favorite K-pop group as we head to school in silence. If one thing has come of our situationship, it's that I now know too much about pop music.

The day passes quickly, and my old lunch crew (three girls in my next-period AP Environmental Science class) expresses sur-prise and happiness when I slide my tray onto our usual table and sit down.

"I thought you'd ditched us forever! Your girlfriend isn't here today?" Marie, a girl I've been friendly with since freshman year, asks. "Or did you break up already?"

I choke on my water and have a coughing fit. "Girlfriend? I'm not dating anyone. What gave you that idea?"

Marie shrugs. "Usually when someone suddenly stops hanging

out with their old group and is constantly seen hanging around someone new, it's because they started dating. If you're not all partnered up, why have you been MIA?"

The two other girls at the table also turn their attention toward me. Their laser focus is making me sweat, and I struggle to come up with a decent explanation for my absence. I remember what Nicole said last night, about how I'm good at reading rooms and smoothing out conflict but not great at expressing my own opinions. To be fair, how can I do that when the main reason I left is confidential, and the other reason is that I didn't think they'd notice or care if I hung out with someone else?

Don't get me wrong. I think these girls like me just fine, and the feeling is mutual. I always enjoy my time with them. But it's not like we talk anytime other than class or lunch. I don't see them outside of school, and even though we have a group chat, I'm not all that active in it. To be honest, I muted it a while ago. I guess I'd gotten so used to chilling in the periphery, observing people but not getting close to them, that I expected everyone to think of me the way I thought of them.

The silence must've gone on for too long as I was thinking all this, because one of the other girls finally says, "Hey, it's not a big deal. Did you finish Ms. Choi's assignment? It's taking me forever doing all that research she wants."

"I totally forgot about that!" I groan, burying my face in my hands. "I was finishing up a column for the newspaper, and I started a new job, and there was some family stuff, and—"

"Oh wow, you've got a lot going on," Marie says. "I'm guessing some of that is why you haven't been around?"

I grasp at that excuse like a lifeline. "Yes! That girl I've been eating lunch with, Gaby, we work together. Since I don't have a working car yet, she's been giving me rides, and so we started hanging out. A lot's happened these past few weeks. Sorry if I've been a bad friend."

Marie glances at the other two. "You always seem like you're a million miles away, worrying about things you never tell us about. Even though we're always sharing our problems with you."

My shoulders tense toward my ears, and I force myself to relax. Haven't Junior and Nicole said the same thing? "I prefer listening."

"Yeah, but the only time you pay attention to us is when we're complaining about our problems. Any other topic, you're spacing out, but when it's time to give advice, you're there."

"Yikes. You're probably trying to vent, and I'm here acting like I can solve all your problems. I swear I don't have a savior complex." I cringe as I say that because, let's be honest, I totally do. "I'm just so used to being the go-to person for advice from my tarot clients that I didn't know I was acting that way with you all. My bad."

"Well, now you know." Marie dips a limp fry into a mix of ketchup and mayo. "Anyway, we can take the heat off you. Tell us more about this new job."

"I work at the front desk for the Chicago Glen Country Club," I say, eager to move on.

"How do you like it?" one of the other girls asks.

"Hard to say since I'm new. But some of the younger staff are throwing me and Gaby a welcome party on Saturday, so that should be cool."

We spend the rest of lunch chatting about my new job and

the assignment for our shared class, and when the bell rings and we bus our trays and walk to class together, I'm reminded of how easy it is being with them. After spending all my time with Gaby these past couple weeks, where I've constantly been on guard, assessing what she's saying since every conversation is part of the investigation . . . it's nice to engage in some mindless chatter for once. I even unmute our group chat.

This lighter vibe carries through the rest of the afternoon, and when I'm in my spot under the stairwell doing a tarot reading for one of my regulars, I can't help but feel like I'm back where I belong.

Today's client is going through a friendship breakup, and my heart goes out to her. Maybe it's because I've never been in a romantic relationship, but I always feel a little detached during my love readings. But I know what it's like to lose a friend, and this client wants to know if there's any way to save the friendship.

I shuffle and go through the regular ritual as I set up a three-card reading, focusing on the past, present, and future of their relationship.

"All reversed. Interesting. This first card here, the Seven of Swords, shows what your relationship was like in the past. There was a betrayal, probably on your part, and you thought you got away with it, but your friend saw through it. That leads to the present with the Knight of Chalices. It's a sign that you need a reality check and that it's time to do some self-reflection. You think you're in touch with your emotions and you know what's going on, but you don't. Might also hint that you're acting out because things aren't going your way."

This reading is a little harsh, so I glance up at my client to see if she's following along, and she gives me a sad smile. "It's okay. Finish the reading."

I turn my attention to the last card. "The World. You say you want to try to save this relationship, but really what you're seeking is closure. You're still emotionally attached to your friend because it's comfortable and what you've always known, but deep down, you know that you and your friend aren't the same people anymore and that you both have to move on."

Her face falls. "I was afraid of that. Is there really no way . . . ?"

"You need to let go." I say it as firmly and kindly as I can, but I know what comes next is up to her. "I'm sorry. I hope that helps."

My client takes a deep breath, and I hear it catch as if she's fighting back tears, but when she peers up at me, she gives me a genuine smile. "It does. Thanks, Danika. I knew I could count on you to be real with me."

After she pays me the standard twenty bucks and leaves, I glance at my watch. Almost time to meet Gaby. I'm leaning over, arranging things in my backpack when I hear a familiar voice.

"Wait. You've got time for one more, right?"

I slowly straighten up and meet Gaby's eyes. "You want a reading?"

She nods.

"I thought you didn't want a reading from me until you thought of a good-enough question," I say.

That day I read for Eli's friend during lunch, I got the sense that Gaby hadn't taken the cards seriously before then. And that she didn't want me turning my all-seeing eye on her.

"I'm ready."

I gesture for her to take a seat and lay out my scarf and cards again. "What's your question?"

"How do I gain your trust?"

I stiffen. "Are you asking me, or are you asking the cards?"

"Both."

"Well, let's see what the cards say."

In my head, I flip through the possible three-card spreads I can do for this question. Should I approach this more like an action-oriented question and read for the situation, obstacles, and possible outcomes? Is this technically a relationship question, like the one for my previous client? Or is it more of an internal, self-discovery type of question?

I decide to combine the various types and lay out three cards facedown in front of me. "The first card is what will help you achieve your goal, the second is what holds you back, and the third is your untapped potential."

I turn over the first card and can't hold back a bitter smile. "The reversed Ten of Swords. You recognize that you handled things poorly, but you're too afraid to do the work and confront the fact that you need to change. Once you realize what you need to let go of, you'll be able to break the cycle of guilt and fear and start fresh."

Gaby bites her lip and nods, motioning for me to continue. I flip the next card. "The reversed Fool card. Damn, the cards are really letting you have it. Anyway, this card is telling you to check your stubborn, childish side. Take responsibility for your mistakes. And that, yes, new things can be scary, but don't let that fear and anxiety hold you back. Don't be afraid of growth."

"Are you sure that's the cards, or is that what you think?"

I shrug. "The cards don't lie, and neither do I. Not when it counts. Anyway, the last card."

The upright Six of Chalices. That's unexpected. "This card symbolizes nostalgia. Looking back at past happiness, remembering that sense of joy and innocence and freedom you had as a child. It also indicates a step forward in relationships. The Five of Chalices is about turbulent waters and volatile emotions, but Six shows that you've moved past those problems and are ready to cooperate and do what it takes to establish harmony."

"So . . . there's still hope, is what you're saying."

"For this friendship? That depends on you. And that's both me and the cards saying it."

Gaby deflates. "Yeah. Of course. Thanks."

"No problem."

She watches me gather up my things, and when I sling my backpack over my shoulders, she says, "I don't have cash on me right now, but I can treat you to dinner sometime."

"During our break later? Sure."

"No, I meant . . . Never mind. Let's go. We're going to be late for work."

Gaby practically sprints toward the exit, and I hurry after her, wondering how I can know so much about her yet still have no clue what's going on in her head.

CHAPTER SIXTEEN

"CHEERS TO DANIKA AND GABY! WELCOME TO THE team," Ricky, one of the kitchen staff and tonight's host, says, holding up a Solo cup full of cheap wine as everyone cheers and clinks their cups together.

I take a sip and try to hide my expression at the super sweet taste, but the person next to me laughs and reaches out for my cup. "Not a drinker?"

"Not really," I admit. There was that time Junior, Nicole, and I got sick after drinking an entire pack of wine coolers together, and sometimes we have a few sips of beer from Junior's "cool" uncle, but that's it.

"Caleb and some of the staff are coming over with the good stuff after the wine tasting, but right now all we got is MD 20/20 and beer."

I perk up after hearing Caleb's name and take another sip to not seem too eager. "This is fine. Better than beer, anyway." I gulp down more of the drink. Somehow, the more I have, the more delicious it tastes. "Who's Caleb, by the way? I don't think I've met him yet."

Despite my best efforts.

"He's my roommate and one of the servers at the club. All that stuff over there is his, so make sure you don't touch it," Ricky says, gesturing toward some bulky objects covered in black plastic sheets at the far end of the room that's been blocked off. I guess so drunk partygoers don't accidentally spill anything on his stuff.

"That's cool; you both live and work together. Did you know each other before the club?"

"We're both studying computer science at UIC and have a bunch of classes together. My uncle owns this building, so the rent on this place isn't bad, but it's Chicago. I still needed a job and a roommate to afford it. I knew Caleb was also searching for a place, and he said if I was willing to pay most of the rent, he'd be my roommate and hook me up with a job too."

I survey the space, which has an open kitchen and a large living room. Definitely a good spot for hosting parties. Down the hall is the bathroom, and I see an additional three rooms as well as a staircase leading who knows where. Not only is the building close to their university, but their apartment is huge, and everything in it seems relatively new. The neighborhood isn't great, but it's not terrible either. And considering how many students are stuck with crappy housing, this looks way more expensive than the average student can afford. His uncle must be giving them a great deal.

"He's the one that got you a job at the club? That's nice of him, but this place must be hella expensive. You okay being stuck paying most of the rent?"

Ricky notices my empty cup and holds up a bottle of MD

20/20 (ooh, Electric Melon) to see if I want more. When I nod, he refills our cups. "He's not home much, so it's almost like I got the place to myself. The only time it gets annoying is when he brings Eli over. You've probably heard about her and the front desk curse. I haven't seen her around lately, so maybe they finally broke up."

I raise my eyebrows. "I'm guessing you're not an Eli fan?"

He shrugs. "She's fine. But those two are either super lovey-dovey or fighting; nothing in between. And with how thin these walls are, both those modes are a problem, you feel me?"

I know my cheeks are turning red at what he's implying, which is so embarrassing, because what am I, a child? I try to play it off like it's the alcohol making me go red and laugh. "Yeah, I get it. Um, you got any bottled water? I think I'm drinking too fast."

He waves his hand toward the fridge. "Help yourself. The night is young, so you might want to take it easy, new girl."

"Thanks." I excuse myself to grab a water bottle and pour out my half-full cup. I join a couple of my coworkers on the couch to chat, and I sip my water as I get to know everyone. I'm not sure how much time passes, but I'm pretty much sober and grabbing another water bottle from the fridge when I hear Ricky call out, "Caleb! It's about time, man. We're almost out of drinks."

Caleb? I eye the tall, well-built white guy joining us in the kitchen with interest. The gossipy newspaper members described him as a bad boy, so I was totally picturing scruffy facial hair and a bunch of tattoos and piercings or whatever. Leather jacket and a motorcycle. I have no idea why my vision of a bad boy is a cliché Hollywood stereotype, especially with the kinds of guys I know from my neighborhood, but here we are. Since I made a similar assumption about Winston, I decide it's time to stop watching cheesy nineties and aughts movies with my dad, since they're clearly affecting my impressionable mind.

There's nothing in Caleb's clothes or general appearance that makes you think this dude isn't some squeaky-clean nice guy, which makes sense since he's a server at Chicago Glen and the country club has a certain image to uphold.

It's in the way that he carries himself, the boldness in his eyes, the confidence when he speaks, the way his smile curls across his face all slow and sensual, that makes me think, *Oh yeah, this guy is trouble.* He's not even my type, and I'm ready to make some absolutely terrible decisions. Good thing Nicole's not here, because that girl would either be egging me on or throwing herself at him while Junior and I did our best to hold her back. What can I say? White boy's got rizz.

Focus, Danika! This guy is taken (?) and the most likely suspect in Eli's disappearance. If he's not the reason she ran, he probably knows where she is.

I snap back to attention as Ricky says, "Hey, Danika, this is Caleb. Caleb, this is Danika, one of our guests of honor. She's not a big drinker, so what would you recommend for a newbie?"

Caleb sets down the bottles he's carrying and studies me. "Do you have a preference between red and white?"

I'm pretty sure white is sweeter, but it's red wine that my mom drinks every evening. "Red."

"Bold choice for someone who doesn't drink," he says, a

suggestive smile curling the edges of his lips. "Let's take baby steps. I'll make you a simple wine cocktail."

He fills a cup with ice and pours in a mix of half red wine and half Coca-Cola before handing it over to me.

"Are you messing with me?" I ask, staring at the dark liquid in the cup. "There's no way that's good."

He laughs. "It's called a kalimotxo. It's pretty popular in Spain and a great way to use up cheap red wine, but it works well with the good stuff too. I promise."

I squint at him, not quite convinced, but take a sip anyway. It's sweet and tart with the tiniest hint of bitterness from the red wine, and I take another sip. And another.

Caleb's watching me the whole time, his eyes dancing with an emotion that I don't recognize or trust. "Nice, huh? Love this stuff. Little bit classy, little bit trashy. Like me."

I snort into my cup and start coughing. The picture of beauty and grace. "Don't make me laugh while I'm drinking! But you're right."

He taps his plastic cup against mine. "Cheers. And welcome to the team. How you liking it so far?"

I take another swig while I think over my answer. What's the best way to get on his good side? Based on his file, he probably doesn't like suck-ups, so no need for me to gush about how happy I am to be part of the "family," as Mrs. Whittle likes to call us.

Ultimately I decide to go with "honest but innocent." I bet guys like Caleb are into the naive type—makes them easier to manipulate.

"It's kind of a lot, but I'm having fun. People have been really nice to me . . . Well, the staff, anyway."

Like I predicted, his eyebrows scrunch up at that last part. "The staff . . . meaning the club members haven't been nice to you?"

I force a laugh. "They're all right."

"You can be real with me," he says, grinning. "I'm not gonna report you to Mrs. Whittle or anything like that. I'm not a snitch. I like keeping an eye on the new kids."

My face twitches at him referring to me as a kid, but I shrug it off. "My friends warned me that customers are the hardest part of any service job. Most of the members have been decent."

Which is true. I expected most of them to turn their noses up at me or be super rude, but for every entitled jerk there was someone who took the time to thank me or even compliment me by name to Mrs. Whittle.

"The jerks are easier to remember, though, I'm sure."

True. "Have you worked the front desk before?"

"Nah, but I knew the girl who had the position before you. I heard all kinds of stuff. Plus, I'm a server. In the dining room, I'm either invisible or a punching bag for those people. Don't sweat it. And don't bottle it up. The problem isn't you; it's them."

I'm touched until I realize he finally gave me an opening. "What was the girl before me like? I heard she quit suddenly and left management scrambling. Which, you know, worked out for me! But someone made some joke about the position being cursed, so I'm curious."

"Cursed, huh? Maybe." Caleb's quiet for a moment. "Eli's

smart. Ambitious. She was really great at her job. And she seemed happy. But I guess I was wrong."

"You know her pretty well?"

"I thought I did." Caleb drains his cup. "I need a refill. Nice talking to you, Danika. Enjoy the rest of the party."

He goes back by the kitchen island, where the drinks are laid out, and grabs a full bottle before disappearing down the hall. I debate following him, maybe apologize for upsetting him and see if he'll open up to me again, but Felix comes over to me and slings his arm around my shoulders.

"Bad idea, newbie. Caleb's a cool guy but too much to handle for a girl like you."

I quirk an eyebrow. "A girl like me? Meaning?"

He grins. "A good girl. Super smart. Hard worker. Tight with your family. Probably have a curfew. And don't get mad, but I bet you have no experience with guys. Did I nail it?"

Well, all right. I'm not used to someone reading me so quickly. That's my job.

I don't want to admit to it (I've got my pride), so I try to brush him off. "You think you know me after having lunch together one time?"

"I'm an excellent judge of character. And that one lunch was enough for me to figure you out. You're like Alex." Felix's eyes sweep over me appreciatively. "You clean up nicer than him, though. That's for sure."

Working at the country club requires a certain standard of appearance, so I've been paying more attention to my looks lately. My hair is the same since Mrs. Whittle approves of my neat French braid, but Gaby has been helping me with my makeup, and Nicole's been in charge of my general grooming. When she heard I was going to a party tonight, she showed up at my house the night before to thread my eyebrows, and she and Gaby combed through my family's closets to put together a decent outfit to change into after work.

I always thought stuff like this was too much of a bother—I can spend hours putting together a thousand-piece puzzle or guiding Daniel through his Kali practice or even figuring out the perfect argument to pull an essay together. But fashion? That's the one area I have no interest in, so I'm surprised at how good I feel in this outfit—loose vintage Nike track pants, a black crop top, and a cropped cardigan. The pants are my dad's, the top mine, and the cardigan belongs to my mom, but I never would've thought to put them together. My dad said I looked like I was cosplaying as Sporty Spice (whatever the hell that means), but my mom, Nicole, and Gaby booed him. For some reason, those three seemed super happy with my style evolution.

"Considering how terrible you thought I looked a few days ago, I must've really stepped it up."

He laughs. "I did not say you looked terrible; don't even do me like that. I just, you know, see a diamond in the rough or whatever."

I'm play shoving him when Alex joins us. "Danika, is this clown bothering you?"

"Your knight in shining armor has arrived." Felix smirks at his best friend. "What are you gonna do if I am bothering her? Duel me for her hand?"

"Do I need to?"

Felix shakes his head. "Nah." He claps his hand on Alex's shoulder and grins at him. "I was only telling Danika that I like her new look. She looks pretty tonight, right?"

Alex tilts his head in confusion. "Danika's always pretty."

Felix's grin gets bigger. "Of course she is. I meant her style is different."

Alex studies me for a moment. "You look really nice. Especially the . . ."

He gestures toward his ears, and I realize he means my new earrings. "Oh, thanks. Gaby made them for me. Aren't they great? She made this bracelet too."

When Gaby realized the only accessories I own are my Lingling-o necklace, the small hoops Nicole gave me, and my mom's old watch, she brought over a bunch of jewelry that she'd made to see which pieces suited me. I tried to turn down the gifts, but she said it'd be a waste since she already made them, and I'd be doing her a favor taking some off her hands so she can clear some space in her room.

I touch the dangly earrings made of hammered bits of metal. "I usually don't wear earrings since they'd get in the way during a fight, but Gaby said big earrings are perfect for me since I always wear my hair pulled back."

Alex nods. "She's right."

"You're not gonna comment on the fact that her first thought was that earrings get in the way during a fight?" Felix asks.

"A legit concern," Alex replies.

Felix inspects the matching cuff I'm wearing. "That is really cool, though. And the fact that she made it means it's one of a kind. Do you think Gaby would make some pieces for me?"

"And why would I do that?" Gaby pops up at that moment with a cup in each hand. "Try this, D. It's a sweet sparkling red. Might be easier to drink than the stuff you tried earlier."

"D?" I ask as I take a sip. "Hey, this is really good! How did you know I'd like it?"

She smiles at me. "I'm learning you."

"And how would you describe her taste exactly?" Felix asks, a glint in his eye that I absolutely do not trust, but Gaby doesn't take the bait.

"You never answered me. Why should I bother making you accessories? What's in it for me?"

"Other than my eternal gratitude?"

"I've got enough junk in my life, thanks."

"So cold! Let's see, what would someone like you want . . ." Felix taps his chin in a very dramatic thinking pose. "I know someone who owns a machine shop. I can get you all kinds of materials. Maybe even access to some of the hardware if you can prove that you won't chop off a finger and get his place shut down."

Gaby's eyes gleam, and I can tell she's trying hard not to show how badly she wants this. "Depending on the types of materials and tools you can get me, we might be able to work something out."

"Girl, don't act like you can bargain like us," Felix says, gesturing to me, him, and Alex. "You think you can hide the fact you come from money? That you're trying to mimic the way

Danika talks so you can fit in with the help? You got money, but I got what you need. Take it or leave it; it don't hurt me none."

Gaby reels as if Felix's words were a physical blow, and the shock and hurt she lets slip into her expression makes me want to fight him. But before I can do something that'll definitely get me thrown out of my own party, Alex smacks the back of Felix's head. Hard.

"Dude, what the fuck?"

"Apologize."

"For what? I'm right."

"For acting like an asshole. She didn't do anything to deserve that."

Either Felix recognizes the truth in what Alex said, or he doesn't want to fight his much bigger and stronger friend, but he turns toward Gaby. I unconsciously move in front of her, and the tension in Felix's face eases.

"Chill. You don't have to protect her from me. I'm about to apologize."

Gaby moves to my side and crosses her arms, seemingly unimpressed. "Save it. I don't need your fake apology or machine shop. Let's go, Danika. We've got work tomorrow."

As we cross the room to say goodbye to some of our coworkers, I hear Alex behind me hiss, "Dude, that's Eli's sister. You know her family situation. Why would you say something like that?"

I turn around and see Felix's eyes widen. "I didn't know. Why didn't you warn me? I'll talk to her tomorrow, okay? I'll fix it."

I can't hear Alex's response because I'm hurrying after Gaby. I thank Ricky for inviting us before shutting the apartment door behind me. I immediately want to know what Alex meant about the Delgados' "family situation." Does he know why Eli ran away?

I glance at Gaby, wondering if I should say something, but she simply pumps up the volume on her radio. Okay, message received.

For the rest of the ride, I stare out the window and plan my next move.

CHAPTER SEVENTEEN

GABY'S FOUL MOOD CARRIES OVER TO THE NEXT morning, evidenced by her blasting her music loud enough to let me know that conversation is off the table. But she still got me a large iced Vietnamese coffee, so I know her mood has nothing to do with me. *Not my problem,* I tell myself, sucking down my super sweet, hyper-caffeinated drink to get me ready for the day. Alex texted me a million times last night apologizing for his friend, but I let him know that he and I are cool. If Felix wants to remedy this, he can do so himself.

The workday flies by since Sunday is the busiest day at our club (big family day, apparently), and by the time I clock out, I'm exhausted. Hopefully, Gaby's in a better mood. If not, I won't exactly be upset by her new "no talking in the car" rule since it'll take a hell of a lot to keep me from passing out. As excited as I am to show off Veronica, being a passenger princess has its benefits.

Gaby's already waiting for me at the entrance, her expression and stance giving off strong "don't talk to me" vibes. Caleb either doesn't notice or is unbothered because he strides past to talk to her, and I hurry after him see what he wants.

"Gaby, right? I heard you're Eli's little sister."

She scowls. "We're less than a year apart. I'm not a child."

He smiles. "I didn't say you were, but I'll keep that in mind. Anyway, I wanted to introduce myself since we didn't get to talk at the party last night. I'm Caleb. Eli and I . . ."

"You're her boyfriend, right? Or is it ex-boyfriend now?"

His smile drops, and he steps closer to her. "Did she say something to you? She hasn't been answering my calls or texts. I don't know what I did wrong."

"Hey, you're blocking the entrance." One of the caddies addresses Caleb and Gaby, who move out of the way, and they stay quiet until several of our coworkers say their goodbyes and head out.

Caleb finally notices me standing nearby. "Hey, Danika. You good?"

"I'm her ride," Gaby says, moving next to me. "And if you want to ask about my sister, we should move somewhere else."

"We can meet at my apartment. It's where we had the welcome party," he says. "Ricky told me he'd be back late, so we'd have privacy."

Gaby looks at me, probably wondering what the best move is. It's obviously dangerous for us to go to some random dude's apartment, especially if he's the reason Eli's missing. On the other hand, the questions I want to ask are not really something we can talk about in public, and I want to check out Caleb's place to see if I can find any clues since I couldn't do that at the party. Not that I'm expecting to find Eli locked up in his basement or wherever you hide people in apartments, but I'm seriously lacking information on Eli and her secret life. This might be the best chance we have to find out what she's been up to.

"We have to run an errand real quick, and we'll meet you there," I say.

We all exchange numbers, and he heads out first. Once Gaby and I are in her car, she asks, "Is this smart?"

"Not really, but sometimes you need to take a calculated risk to get the information you need. Don't worry; I'll text my cousins to let them know what's up. Knowing them, they'll probably be waiting outside Caleb's apartment in case we need help. And if they don't hear from me after a certain amount of time, they know it's time to bring in reinforcements."

"You mean the cops?"

"No, my mom."

★ ★ ★

Cousin Group Chat

Danika: Gaby and I are going to Caleb's apt

I send them the address.

Danika: I'll let you know if I need backup

You know what to do

Joemar:

With the plan confirmed, Gaby and I head up to Caleb's apartment. We already saw the shared space at the party, but he lets us into his room so we'll have privacy in case Ricky comes home early. While his bedroom is small, it's surprisingly clean and organized with little touches that make the room feel down-right cozy.

"No offense, but this isn't quite what I thought your room would look like," I say, taking in the hanging plants and herb garden on the windowsill bringing color and life to one side of the bedroom and the fuzzy blanket and plush pillows covering up the shabbiness of the obviously hand-me-down bed. Every-thing in the room appears to be secondhand, though well pre-served, except for the shiny new DJ equipment in one corner of the room. Of course he's a DJ. If I didn't know before, I sure do now: Caleb Miller is a textbook F-boy.

"Hmm? Oh, you mean this?" He sweeps his arm as if to encompass everything I've observed and points to a wall cov-ered in framed photos. "That's all Eli. I don't care about deco-rating and she loves it, so I let her do whatever. It made her happy."

Gaby studies the photos, a mix of landscapes and candid shots, each one vibrant and full of life in a way I can't quite explain. "These are so good. You're into photography?"

Caleb makes a weird face. "Eli took those. You can't tell?"

"*My* sister? I didn't even know she was into photography . . ."

"Really? She told me you were artsy, so I figured this was a thing you two shared."

"No, the closest she got was when my parents signed her up

for violin lessons in grade school. Didn't last long, though. She's more book smart."

"Yeah, she told me she hated violin. And chess. And all the other activities that little rich kids are supposed to like. She said the only reason she could deal with working at a country club was because it wasn't the one her mom's friends all went to, so at least she didn't have to pretend in front of them." He lets out a short laugh. "I was kinda hoping that I was another reason she was happy to work at the club, but she quit without saying anything, so what do I know?"

"You seem to know her a hell of a lot better than I do," Gaby replies.

Caleb doesn't say anything, just points to a photo on the lower right of the area where the photos are hanging. A colorful mosaic of wildflowers stretches across a wall next to a train station, the image vibrant and striking against the expanse of gray.

Gaby gasps. "Is that my mural by the Austin Green Line stop? She didn't tell me she went to see it. I figured no one in my family cared."

"I can't speak for your parents, though Eli's told me plenty about them, and most of it ain't nice. But from what little she's said about you, I can tell she cares."

Gaby snorts. "She's got a funny way of showing it. She ignored me as soon as she started high school, and now I find out she has a whole secret life?"

"Secret life? What do you mean?" Caleb keeps his tone light and curious, but since his focus is on Gaby, he probably doesn't notice how closely I'm observing him. And I know I'm not imagining things. The moment Gaby mentioned Eli's secret life, he seemed scared.

I don't know if she saw it too, but she starts pushing him. "Well, you, first and foremost. I had no idea she got a new boyfriend. An older boyfriend, from her equally secret job."

"Hey, I'm only a couple years older than her, and our relationship is totally legal. I'm not some creep."

He's right about the age thing, but whether he's a creep remains to be seen.

"How'd you two meet? You're not in the same department at the club," I ask.

"Same way I met you two. It's like a tradition to hold welcome parties for the newbies, and the staff gets together regularly to blow off steam. Not the higher-ups, of course. Mostly the kitchen staff and anyone our age who's cool." Caleb changes the subject. "So how's Eli doing? She hasn't said anything about me, has she?"

"I didn't know you existed, remember?"

He winces. "You know I thought we were good? Better than good, actually. Then I go into work one day and find out she quit out of nowhere. And now she won't answer my calls or messages, and I just . . . I wanna know what I did wrong."

"What you did wrong?"

"I mean, I must've done something, right? For her to quit so she doesn't have to see me at work? I know how badly she needs the money, so it doesn't make sense unless I'm the problem."

Gaby's voice gets sharp. "Wait, what do you mean she needs the money? For what?"

Caleb jerks back. "Hold up. You don't know? I figured you started working at the club because of your parents too."

"My parents? What the hell are you talking about?"

"Um, I'm probably not the best person to tell you. You should ask Eli about it."

"I don't want to ask Eli. I'm asking you!"

"Fair, it's not Eli's job to cover for your parents. They're the ones you need to talk to."

"I don't WANT to talk to them. I want you—"

Gaby's about to explode, but I can't have her pushing Caleb away yet, so I interrupt. "Gaby, this sounds like family business. Maybe he shouldn't get involved."

"Sounds like he's already involved," Gaby mutters, but I can tell she sees my point.

"So we're cool?" Caleb asks, eyeing Gaby as if he's worried she's either gonna swing on him or burst into tears. Or both.

"You tell us. The way you're talking makes it seem like you might've hurt her in some way, and that very much makes us not cool," I say.

His eyebrows shoot up. "I'm not, like, the greatest boyfriend, but I would never lay a hand on her if that's what you're implying."

"Okay, but you must've done something, because you sound guilty as hell when you talk about her."

He studies me. "If I tell you why I *think* she's avoiding me, will you arrange a meeting between us?"

"And why would we do that?"

"If she doesn't want to be with me anymore, then whatever, but she at least owes me an explanation. Do you know how messed up it is that she ghosted me?"

In a small way, I feel for him. It must mess with your head for you to think you're in love and then suddenly you never hear from your partner again. But I've been at my mom's agency for years. I've seen the kinds of cases she works, the clients she gets. As a female PI, she receives a lot of sensitive cases regarding women. Because of that, I know if you're in a relationship where your partner suddenly ghosts you, there's often a solid reason, and that reason is usually you.

"Dude, it sucks, but there's probably an explanation for her icing you out. Like, I don't know, maybe she doesn't feel safe being around you?"

I'm pushing it. I know I am. But I want to get past the smooth, sweet facade and have him show us who he is inside. Because if he isn't the reason that Eli ran away, he must be at least partly responsible. I mean, look at his place. Why else would she cut off all contact with someone she was *clearly* planning on moving in with?

"Excuse me?" Caleb's voice is calm, but I can see the veins popping in his neck from the effort.

I gesture around. "The plants, the framed photos, the little soft touches around the place . . . she was nesting. You only started dating a few months ago, but it was serious enough for you to let her decorate. Does she have a few drawers here?"

"I don't know what you're talking about."

"I can see a woman's cardigan draped over that chair," I say pointing. "So either you were cheating and some other girl left that here, or that belongs to Eli."

"It's Eli's," Gaby confirms. "I recognize that cutesy heart print."

"You have a roommate and your bedroom's small, so it's not like you can hide much here. But I bet if we go to the bathroom, we'll find an extra toothbrush and some of her bath-and-body stuff."

Gaby moves toward the only open door in the apartment, which must house the bathroom, and Caleb follows her.

"Hey, stop that! You can't go through people's stuff."

Gaby ignores him and calls out, "You're right! This is the bodywash Eli uses. And this caddy has her face cleanser and a bunch of other stuff I know she buys."

Caleb yanks her out of the bathroom and slams the door shut. "What's this about? Why are you two acting like I've done something? I thought you didn't know anything about me?"

I glance at Gaby, who shakes her head and says, "Before she quit, she started acting weird, and she wouldn't say what's wrong. I thought talking to you would help me figure it out. I'm worried about her."

His expression softens. "I'm worried too. But on God, I never hurt her. I just want to see her. That's all."

Or, you know, lure her out of her hiding place since you know why she ran, and you want to cover it up. That's all.

He must read the skepticism on our faces because he adds, "Listen, Gaby. Talk to your parents about your financial situation. Once you do, let me know. I might be able to explain why your sister's been acting weird. She'll probably get pissed at me, but if you know, you might be able to help."

"Cryptic much?" I ask.

"If I tell you now, you won't believe me. I know you won't. Either that or you'll try to beat my ass. I'd rather you have all the facts before you do."

I'm about to argue back when my phone starts buzzing.

Cousin Group Chat

Joemar: Cuzzo! You good? You been in there awhile

Andrew: You better answer quick bc he's ready to bust down dude's door

Joemar: He ain't wrong

You got 1 minute to answer before this becomes a fight

Danika: I'm fine! Just finishing up

No violence

Joemar: You never let me have no fun

Danika: You can keep an eye on him after we leave

He def knows more than he's letting on

Andrew: Fine but you owe us

I turn to Gaby. "I don't think we're going to get any more info out of him until you talk to your parents, so let's get out of here."

She glares at Caleb but agrees. "Once I talk to them, you better be ready to tell me everything you know."

Now that we're no longer pressing him, he seems to have regained his confidence. "Or else what? You've got ways of making me talk?"

I grin. "My family runs a detective agency, so, yeah. If you don't want us digging into you and finding out your dirty secrets, I'd cooperate."

He's gotta be involved in some shady stuff. How else can a college kid on the kitchen staff at a country club afford that DJ setup when everything else in his room is obviously a hand-me-down or a curbside pickup? I know Ricky is covering the majority of the rent, but that's still way above Caleb's pay grade.

I know I'm right when he turns pale at my threat. Whenever I read that expression in a book, I wondered what that would look like, since how could a white person get whiter? Like, was it a turn of phrase or something that actually happened? Turns out a white person can indeed get paler, because his face drains completely of color (like, not a hint of redness in his lips and cheeks, real sickly looking), and he looks like he's about to throw up.

But he plays it off. "Yeah? That's pretty cool. Anyway, don't forget to hit me up once you talk to your parents, Gaby."

He's trying to act like everything's fine, but something's off. His eyes are flicking around his room as if casing the place. Is he planning on making a run for it now that he knows about my family?

"Hey, is it cool if we give Eli her sweater back?" I ask.

He startles as if I've interrupted his train of thought. "What? Oh yeah, yeah. Take it; it's not like I need it."

He obviously wants us out, so as Gaby and I head down the stairs, I text my cousins to warn them that we may have a runner. I can see them in their shared car outside Caleb's apartment, and I give them a nod as I get into Gaby's car.

"I think I spooked him, so we better move fast. You okay with talking to your parents?"

Gaby shrugs. "Not like I got a choice, right?"

Then she turns up her music and drives me home in silence as I wonder if the Delgado parents hold the piece to the puzzle that'll finally start making things click into place.

CHAPTER EIGHTEEN

"DANIKA, I'M OUTSIDE. CAN YOU LET ME IN?"

After Gaby dropped me off, she told me she was going to confront her parents. Considering it's been less than two hours and now there's this surprise visit, I'm guessing it didn't go too well.

I open the door and have a few seconds to clock Gaby's red eyes and duffel bag at her side before she pushes past me into the house.

"I'm sorry I didn't call you ahead of time, but I had to get out of that house and didn't have anywhere else to go."

Luckily, my parents are out with Daniel right now for some kid's birthday party, because we are moments away from a meltdown. Gaby takes off her shoes, and I have her sit on the couch while I get us something to drink. She needs to calm down (and would murder me if I actually said that), so anything with caffeine is out.

"We've got passion fruit honey tea, salabat, and this nice herbal tea my mom uses to relax. I can make any of those hot or cold. Just let me know."

"Salabat is that ginger tea I had before, right?" When I say yes, she asks, "Can you show me how to make it from scratch? You said you know how."

I gesture for her to follow me to the kitchen and get to work. As I bash up the sliced ginger, I say, "I was worried about you."

She doesn't respond, and I slide the ginger into a medium saucepan and fill it with water. I keep my eyes on my task and away from her, sensing that she's not interested in scrutiny or judgment.

"You're always welcome here; you know that. But what do you mean you have nowhere else to go? I've seen you at school. You have a ton of friends."

Not that you've ever introduced me to any of them.

"None I can talk to about this."

"What do you mean?"

"I've got my childhood friends who come from money. They'll understand the whole 'my parents are the fucking worst' part but nothing else. And there's, like, an unspoken rule when it comes to talking about money. Rude to flaunt it around the scholarship kids, crass to bring it up around the rich ones." She watches me add a cinnamon stick and pinch of cayenne to the pot before setting it on the stove at medium-high heat. "As for my high school friends, those are my art people. They don't know about my family, and I want to keep it that way."

I give the now-boiling mixture a stir and lower the heat to a simmer. "So I'm the only one you've got since I don't come from either of those worlds."

She gives me a lopsided smile. "Basically. You're the only person I know I can really be myself around. Like, my whole self, not the different sides I show to different groups. It's like I can take full breaths when I'm around you. Does that make sense?"

I meet her eyes, and it feels impossible to take a full breath with her gaze on me like this. Still, I nod my head at her, because I think I understand. Thanks to the case, I already know so much of her family's dirt that she doesn't feel the need to put up a front. And given what her family's going through, she probably sees me and my family as a safe space. Honestly, I'm touched she feels that way. But I also feel like there's something deeper going on, something I can't quite decipher about our relationship.

"Is that why you've never introduced me to any of your friends at school?"

She flinches. "I didn't want them to find out about Eli. I promise it has nothing to do with you."

The moment I flick my gaze away from hers toward the sala-bat on the stove, I can feel the invisible thread woven between us snap. Whatever was brewing in that moment is gone, and I find it hard to resume eye contact. I turn off the heat and busy myself by pulling out mugs, honey, and bottled calamansi juice. I ladle out the ginger tea and tell Gaby to adjust hers to her taste. She watches what I do and follows suit, then we make our way back to the couch, still not looking at each other. She's calmed down at least.

I wedge myself into my favorite corner of the couch and take a sip, the spicy brew coursing down my throat and burning away the awkwardness in the air. "Do you want to talk about what happened? Or would you rather watch a movie or play video games or something?"

Gaby smirks, wrapping her hands around her mug. "I'm

surprised it took you that long to ask. You have a lot of patience. And self-control. If I were you, I would've made you spill the second I opened the door."

I wrap my hands around my own mug, comfortable enough to face her again. "I was tempted. But you came here because you need help, not an interrogation. You don't have to talk until you're ready to. Until then, I'm totally ready to kick your ass at *Mario Kart.*"

She laughs so hard, the sudden movement jostles her mug, and she spills salabat on herself. I grab a dish towel from the kitchen, and as I help her clean up, I can feel her eyes on me once again. "God, you're so—"

The sound of the front door opening interrupts us. Buchi runs in, barking excitedly, and she's followed by my parents and brother.

"Gaby! To what do we owe the pleasure?" my dad asks as my family comes in. Daniel stoops down to clean Buchi's paws with the wipes near the door before the two of them hurry over to me and Gaby.

Out of the corner of my eye, I see Gaby tense up, so I step in. "She needs help with some stuff, so she asked to sleep over tonight. That's okay, right?"

Before my dad can give his enthusiastic approval, my mom cuts him off. "That depends. Do her parents know she's here?"

I glance over at her, and she shakes her head. "I told them I was staying at a friend's house, but I didn't say which one. It's not like I snuck out, though. They know I'm not coming home tonight."

My mom studies Gaby for a moment. "If you tell us why you

won't go home, you're free to spend the night, and I won't bother calling your parents. If not, I'm afraid I'll have to insist on you getting their permission."

"I'm not a child," Gaby mutters. "I don't need to ask their permission for anything."

"By law you are," my mother counters. "And if you're staying under my roof, with my family, I need to know what's going on. The choice is yours."

Gaby slams her mug on the coffee table. "If you don't want me here, then fine. There are other places I can go."

She stands up and grabs her duffel bag, but before she can move toward the door, I grab her wrist to stop her.

"I get that you have family problems, but you do not talk to my mom like that."

"She's the one being—"

"You don't want to finish that sentence." I tighten the grip on her wrist. "I don't want to fight with you in front of my little brother, but I will if you continue disrespecting my mom like that."

Her gaze flicks over to Daniel, who's clutching Buchi to his chest and peeking out behind my father, watching us with wide, scared eyes, and I feel the fight leaving her body. I loosen my hold on her enough that she can pull away if she really wants, but firm enough for her to know that I want her to stay. "Gaby, chill. We only want to help."

I glance at my mom, who rolls her eyes and says, "If you're going to insist that you're not a child, I suggest not sulking like one."

"I think we all need a time-out," my dad says. "Gaby, are you hungry?"

Gaby, seemingly thrown off by the sudden question, answers honestly. "Uh, yeah."

"I am too. So why don't I whip up a quick dinner, and after we've eaten, we can finish this conversation *respectfully*. I find people's moods and minds tend to be much clearer after a good meal."

"Thank you. And, um, sorry for the outburst."

With another look at my mom, my dad disappears into the kitchen, and my mother sighs and rubs her temples. "Right. Daniel, let's finish your homework before dinner."

My little brother hid behind my dad during the confrontation, but with the tension (mostly) gone, he wedges himself next to Gaby on the couch. "We just got home! I want to play with Gaby."

"There's plenty of time to play after dinner. She's spending the night," I say, eyeing my mother.

I never go against my mom, but in this case, she's being too forceful. Gaby was disrespectful, but I handled that. My mom should understand complicated family situations better than anyone. Why she's being so strict when it comes to Gaby, I have no idea.

"Your Ate's right," my mom says. "The sooner you get your homework out of the way, the sooner you can have fun."

"Your sister promised to kick my butt at *Mario Kart*, but I think we can take her," Gaby says to Daniel. "Do a good job on your homework and we can challenge her after we eat, okay?"

His face lights up, and he grabs our mom's hand. "Let's go, Mommy!"

He drags her to his room, Buchi following at his heels, and the silence that follows is a little awkward.

"My mom's not usually like that. I didn't expect her to go full narc on you."

"It's cool. I deserved it. This is her house, after all. And I think I know why she acted like that."

"Really? Why—"

"Let's go help your dad. I'm starving, and I should probably pull my weight around here since you're letting me stay."

"You don't have to—"

But she leaves before I finish my sentence, and I stand there wondering how the roles have reversed—she's the one who won't meet my eyes.

"I CAN'T BELIEVE YOU MADE SO MUCH FOOD. DIDN'T you just come from a party?"

I stare at the table bearing three different types of torta, stir-fried vegetables, nilaga, and a massive amount of rice. Sure, the nilaga was left over from the previous night, we always have rice, and torta are basically Filipino omelets so they're quick to make, but it still seems like a ridiculous amount of food for a regular dinner. And didn't they just eat?

My dad makes a *psh* noise with his lips. "Only pizza and cake, and barely enough for everyone. What kind of party is that? No wonder your mom's so grumpy."

My mom rolls her eyes to the ceiling. "Yes, I'm the grumpy one. Not the person who spent the entire drive back complaining that he couldn't take home leftovers."

My dad believes every celebration requires an abundance of food and that a party ain't a party unless everyone leaves with a plate, a belief he shares with the chef main character from his mystery series. I guess that's another reason for the current feast. I can always tell when my dad's avoiding a deadline, because he'll spend extra time in the kitchen, claiming it's "research."

Meanwhile, Daniel explains what each dish is to Gaby, who is nodding genuinely and asking questions.

"Which one's your favorite?"

"Ate Danika likes the potato torta, but I like the one with meat. The one Mommy and Daddy like is the same as mine, but it's also got yucky eggplant." Daniel tilts his head, thinking for a moment. "Well, I think it's yucky. Maybe you like eggplant, so, sorry. And the soup is really yummy too, but it's hard to eat with the bones."

"I'll make sure to try everything." Gaby piles her plate with rice before adding some vegetables plus small slivers of all the torta. After tasting each, she turns to my dad. "I wasn't expecting much from omelets, but they go so good with rice! Have you ever thought about opening a restaurant?"

My dad beams at her. "Eggs and rice are the best comfort food, aren't they? And a restaurant is way too much work for too little profit. I already have to deal with that as a writer. I appreciate it, though. Make sure to try the nilaga. I know you're not big on meat, but at least try the broth and vegetables. I think you'll like it."

The rest of the meal passes by in casual chitchat, but when my mom places Gaby's mug of salabat in front of her, she finally addresses the elephant in the room.

"Are you ready to talk?" she asks Gaby.

Gaby glances at Daniel, whose head swivels back and forth between her and our mom.

"I'm gonna go finish my homework. Call me when it's time to play games, okay?" he says before picking up his mug of hot chocolate and heading to his room with Buchi.

Gaby watches him leave, a softness in her eyes. "He's a great kid. Surprisingly thoughtful and observant for his age too."

I puff my chest out. "Damn right he is."

Everyone's quiet for a beat, and then Gaby says, "My family's in a lot of debt. Caleb was right."

"Caleb? Caleb Miller? What did he say to you?" my mom asks.

Gaby explains the interaction we had with him earlier. My parents look PISSED that we went to Caleb's apartment alone, but they stay quiet until Gaby finishes her story.

"I confronted my parents. My dad was happy that he didn't have to hide anything anymore, but my mom was very upset."

I ask, "What happened?"

"Apparently my dad got laid off two Christmases ago. But he didn't want me and Eli to worry, and he and my mom didn't want to make a big deal about it right before the holidays. My parents throw a huge Christmas Eve party every year and I guess kept it up to save face in front of their family and friends. I had no idea. I mean, he still went out every day as if he was going to work. He says he has a new job now, but it pays way less than his old one."

"How did Eli find out?"

"My dad thought he'd find a job right away, but the search was harder than he thought. When he couldn't find anything by the end of the last school year, he canceled her study abroad trip. Apparently Eli tried to use some of her college funds to pay for it, but she found out our parents had drained the account to cover the bills."

A bitter smile spreads across Gaby's face as she turns to my parents. "They drained mine too. We were already in a lot of debt because of our house and all the cars and fancy parties and whatnot. My mom's receptionist job and the unemployment checks weren't enough to cover everything. The bank wants to take away our house because we're so behind. My dad's thinking of filing for bankruptcy, but my mom would die of embarrassment if that happened. So basically I might be moving out of that house sooner than I thought. And better hope I get a scholarship or grant or something, or I can kiss college goodbye too."

Gaby's tone is flippant, as if it's no big deal that her parents lied to her and her sister and pretty much ruined their lives. Or at least their immediate futures. But no matter how good an actress she is, I see through her jaded "tough girl" facade, as does my mom.

"I'm sorry that your parents' poor decisions have hurt you and your sister. And that your mother is being so difficult." My mom hesitates, then places her hand on Gaby's. "You're allowed to be angry. And not just about the money. They've betrayed your trust. That is not okay."

Gaby gazes down at my mother's hand on hers and bursts into tears. "Oh my God, sorry. So sorry. I never cry. I don't know what's wrong with me."

My mom and I both stare at each other, eyes wide and having a frantic, silent conversation:

Did I make her cry? Oh God, I made your friend cry. What do we do?

I don't know! Should I pat her back? Do people like that? Mommy, how do we handle this?!

My dad let me and my mom steer the conversation up to this point, but our ineptitude at handling human emotion makes him step in. "You don't have to apologize for your feelings, Gaby. They are real, and they are valid, and there's nothing wrong with crying. Release them and then tell us what you need."

Gaby sobs even harder after that, and I get up to grab a box of tissues. I try handing them to her, but she just hugs me and cries even more. My mom and I do our "deer in headlights" expressions again, but soon Gaby's warmth seeps into me, and my arms unconsciously tighten around her, and she squeezes me back. She tucks her head down into my shoulder, and I rest my head against hers until I can feel her breathing slow down and her tears finally stop. I don't pull away until she reaches out for a tissue and blows her nose.

"Oh God, I needed that." She sees my tearstained top and turns red. "Sorry about your shirt."

I shrug. "It's going in the wash anyway. No worries."

My dad gets up. "We appreciate you sharing that news with us, Gaby. I'm sure it wasn't easy."

My mom chimes in, "There's probably more we should talk about, especially since your family's situation is likely related to your sister's disappearance. But for now I suggest you both change into your pj's and set up that game for Daniel. He's been waiting for you two."

We do as she suggests, and the very heavy, emotional night quickly shifts to lots of laughter (and quite a bit of screeching after a blue shell takes me out).

CHAPTER
NINETEEN

ON MONDAY AFTERNOON, AS GABY AND I ARE ON the way to the martial arts studio, I get a call from Joemar.

"Alex is missing basketball practice tonight because he has to cover for Caleb at work. Want me and Andrew to stop by his place for a chat? You might be right, and he's getting ready to run."

"Tita Baby will need one of you to help with class today, so how about Gaby and I meet up with you now? Andrew can help your mom and let her know we'll be late. You can ride with us in case we need backup with Caleb."

"Good choice. I am the more intimidating twin," he says. "We're both still on campus, so I'll have Andrew drop me off in front of Caleb's place, where I can keep an eye on it till you arrive. No idea if he's actually there, though."

I relay the plan to Gaby, and I let Joemar know we'll see him soon. It's only fifteen to twenty minutes to UIC and Caleb's apartment is right off campus, so we get there in no time. Joemar's leaning against a lamppost across the street from Caleb's apartment, being conspicuous and threatening as all hell.

"Way to stand out, man," I say as Gaby and I approach him.

"This isn't a stakeout, and I'm not trying to hide. Hell, I want him to know I'm here. Make him think twice about running. Or at least put enough pressure on him to make him wanna talk. Either way, this is your show, ladies. I'm only here as backup."

Joemar gestures for us to go ahead of him, and we cross the street toward Caleb's apartment. On the way over, I texted Caleb to let him know that Gaby did what he asked and now we need to talk to him about Eli. He didn't respond, but that doesn't stop us from buzzing his apartment doorbell now. No answer there either.

Not a minute later, though, a delivery guy appears. He presses the button for a different apartment and gets buzzed in right away, and we wait a beat before following him inside and heading up to Caleb and Ricky's place.

I'm tempted to pound on the door, force Caleb to acknowledge us, but sounding like the cops are banging down his door probably isn't the right move. I knock and wait for him to approach. Nothing. Knock again. Again, nothing. Finally, I call him and hear his phone ringing in his apartment. He's inside.

"Caleb, open up! I know you're in there."

Silence.

"Dude, we heard your phone. Gaby and I need to talk to you. We have some news about Eli."

Gaby grabs my arm and gives me a warning look, but I wave her off and mouth, *I'm bluffing, chill.* She lets me go as Caleb opens the door.

"What's going on with Eli?" he asks as soon as he sees us. Then he spots Joemar standing behind us and tries to slam the door closed, but I shoulder it open, and we force our way in.

"Don't mind my cousin; he's with us because it's apparently

not safe for two young girls to be alone in a man's apartment," I say, surveying the space. Open boxes are scattered around the room along with several garbage bags full of clothes. "You didn't tell us you were moving. A little sudden, isn't it?"

"Oh, uh, Ricky's uncle raised the rent, and I can't afford to live here anymore." Caleb's eyes dart around the room as if plotting an escape. Joemar's standing in front of the door, arms crossed, and Gaby and I are flanking him. "Hey, can you back up? You got me feeling claustrophobic. Now, what's up with Eli?"

I relax my stance but don't actually move away from him. I want him to feel pressured but not cornered. "First things first. You said you had something to tell us once Gaby talked to her parents. She did that, and I'm sure we can all agree they majorly suck. What does that have to do with you and Eli?"

Caleb eyes Joemar again. He's taller than my cousin and has a decent body, but Joemar is a solid dude. Not only has he done martial arts and basketball his entire life, but Joemar has an edge to him that his brother doesn't, which is why I chose him for this particular assignment.

"I'm really not comfortable talking about this with him here."

"Well, I'm not comfortable leaving two underage girls in the apartment of some shady college boy who has no problem dating high school girls, so you know what? Indulge us anyway," Joemar says.

On God, I think Caleb is about to swing on my cousin, and I tense up in case it comes down to a fight, but he seems to think better of it. "Prick," he mutters. "Look, no cops, okay? Can you at least promise me that?"

"Dude, we're not freakin' narcs. We're not trying to get Eli in trouble. We want to know what's going on with her since she's not doing too well," I say, by which I mean she's missing and no one has heard from her to know how well she's actually doing.

Caleb's "tough guy" persona melts as genuine concern for Eli surfaces. "Is she sick? Is that why she suddenly disappeared?"

"What do you mean, disappeared?" Gaby asks sharply.

Good catch, I think. Maybe the concern only *seems* genuine. Maybe he knows Eli did a runner, and that's why he's trying to get more info on her.

"Um, she dropped off the face of the earth. I'm not the only one whose calls and messages she's not answering. She's ignoring everyone from work."

"She's only ignoring the people from work?" I ask.

He shrugs. "I've never met her other friends, so I have no clue."

"When's the last time you talked to her?"

"The last time I saw her was the beginning of the month. She worked her usual Monday shift, but instead of waiting for me after work, she bounced. And then I didn't see her or hear from her again."

"Let me see your phone."

"Bro, that is an invasion of privacy—"

"Just the most recent texts to Eli. I want to confirm that you're telling the truth."

He grumbles, but after a moment he shows me his WhatsApp chat history with Eli. The last time she responded to him was Monday, April 1. The day before she got a reading from me.

I whisper that fact to Gaby, who claps her hands together

loudly. "Caleb. My family is broke, and that's why my sister got a job. Right? So what else is there?"

"Well, it's not exactly ABOUT your sister. I mean, she's involved, but I don't know if that's related to anything. I wanted to help you out since you're in the same boat she is." Caleb glances at me. "You're in Eli's old position, so you might be able to help too. I know you don't have money like that either."

Rude but accurate.

"We've got a thing going at the country club. You know how all the guests are rich assholes while most of the employees are struggling enough that we have to work multiple jobs to get by?"

The disparity has always been obvious to me, along with the fact that the majority of the Black or Brown faces you see at the club are only there because they're in uniform. So I get what he's saying but not what he's getting at.

"Yeah, yeah, the wealth gap between the social classes, eat the rich, et cetera. Not that I don't agree with you, but what's that got to do with Eli?" I ask.

He hesitates before blurting out a random question. "Have you ever seen that old movie *The Bling Ring*?"

"Yeah, my dad loves Emma Watson. Again, what does that have to do with . . ." I trail off as the pieces click into place. Eli's disappearance. Caleb's intense DJ setup. "You're stealing from our club members? Breaking into their houses?! How? There's no way that people who live here aren't locking their doors."

"Well, it started small. Mostly stealing people's credit card information and stuff like that. We couldn't take anything while members were at the club because they'd suspect right away that it was one of us." Caleb starts talking faster. "But one of us started thinking big. They would have people 'borrow' the keys from our targets and press them into molds so the boss could make copies from the impressions. That way we could return the keys to the owners without them realizing anything. We wait for a day when we know they'll be out of the house, and a couple of us get in and out real quick with any cash or jewelry or whatever we can find. Rich people always have insurance for things like this, so it's like a victimless crime."

My head is spinning at the audacity, but I'm also more than a little impressed that someone thought this up.

"What happens if you get caught? Either by the owners or on a security video or something?" Joemar asks.

"I don't really know, to be honest. I've never had to deal with it. We're told to report in if we have any problems."

"Report to who?"

"No clue. We get burner phones, instructions, and our cut of the take in our lockers at work from whoever's in charge. But whoever the boss is, they're not the one doing the recruiting. They have us scout employees who either are in a decent position to get info, need the money, or both. And if we have a good feeling about them, we see if they're interested in joining."

"Oh my God, you're like a multilevel pyramid scheme," I say. "Bro, you are literally recruiting people to commit breaking and entering."

"'Scheme' is such a harsh word. Think of it like we're all Robin Hood. Nothing wrong with stealing from the rich to give to the poor, right?"

I pointedly stare at the expensive-ass DJ equipment he hasn't packed up yet.

Caleb's eyes follow mine. "That's an investment in my future. You can't get started in the music industry without proper equipment, and who's got the money for that? I sure as hell don't. Or I didn't before I was recruited."

He's gonna keep fighting me on this, so I focus on the other shady aspect of the situation. "But why do you need to keep roping employees in? This doesn't seem like something that needs a large group working it. In fact, the more people, the more likely you'll get caught."

"It's not a large group, but different people got different skills, you know? And we can't only target people at our club, or it starts getting real suspicious. We need people who either can chat up our members to see who else might make a good target or have direct access to membership information. Like you, Danika," Caleb says. "We haven't needed anyone new since Eli joined, but with her gone, the boss needs a replacement."

"And now you want us," I say, "to take part in something WILDLY illegal, an arrangement that doesn't sound like you can leave whenever you feel like it."

Caleb shakes his head. "Man, that's the best part. You can walk away, no hard feelings or nothing."

"Just like that?" Gaby asks.

"Just like that," Caleb repeats. "The boss said it's, like, mutually assured destruction. No one can say anything without getting themselves in trouble. And since nobody knows who the boss is, there's no point in trying to blow up the whole thing. All they ask is that you find someone to replace you."

Joemar rolls his eyes. "Let me guess: You gotta hit a certain quota each month, whether that be dollars or clients, or you get kicked to the curb. Maybe even get charged a fee for not holding up your end of the bargain?"

"I mean, that's fair, right? The boss is the one arranging everything, getting the keys made, doing the research, gathering all the info. And even though they're usually not the one breaking in, they handle the sales, so it's not like they're sitting around safe while we do all the work. It's a huge risk, so there's, like, a minimum buy-in."

"Do you get a special bonus or commission for each successful thief you bring in?" Joemar asks. "You got Eli involved in the scam, didn't you?"

Caleb's face hardens. "Hey, she came to me. She figured out I was making money on the side and said she wanted in. No, *needed* in because of her parents. She understood what she was doing."

"And no one's gotten hurt? Not a single person's gotten fired or physically harmed or had the cops called on them?" I ask.

He shakes his head. "Not that I know of. Trust me, if something like that happened, the collective would hear about it. Like I said, it's not a large group. That's one of the reasons why people are so curious about what's going on with Eli. With her and Alberto gone, we gotta either slow down operations or take on new recruits."

Alberto?

Why does that name sound so familiar?

I mean, there are probably, like, a million Albertos in Chicago, but still, I can't shake the feeling.

"Who's Alberto?"

Caleb gives me an "aww, shit" look.

"Alberto was a member of the kitchen staff. He died in an accident a few weeks ago."

"He died?!" Gaby asks.

"Accident? What kind of accident?" I add.

Joemar steps to Caleb. "Bro, you're honestly trying to get my cousin to join your gang of criminals when someone died recently?"

Caleb holds his hands up. "Wait, wait. It really was an accident! He was carrying a box full of heavy kitchen supplies down to the storage area when he fell down the stairs."

"The accident happened at the club?" I ask. "I haven't heard anything about this."

"Of course not. Mrs. Whittle wants to keep it all hush-hush, says it gives the club a bad image. We got a fund going for his family to help with funeral costs, but we had to keep quiet."

"Dude, that's so messed up," I say.

"Management doesn't give a damn about us. All they care about is the club's image. So what if a member of 'the help' dies while working their minimum wage job? Chicago Glen has a reputation to uphold." Caleb shrugs. "I figured that was why Eli left at first. She and Alberto weren't close, but she knew him. They went to school together. But then she didn't come back and started blocking us, and now I don't know what to think."

They went to school together? Then it clicks. "Alberto's the senior they had that memorial for!"

"Yes! I forgot about him since I didn't know the guy and was

so focused on . . . you know. Do you think they're connected?"
Gaby asks.

"What's connected?" Caleb asks. "Alberto dying and Eli
leaving? I mean, the accident had nothing to do with her. But
maybe it made her think about her own mortality or something
since they're the same age, you know?"

"You think Eli quit her job and blocked everyone from work
because she's now afraid of dying?" I ask, dubious as hell.

He shrugs. "Everyone's got their own way of coping. When
you're in high school, you think you're gonna live forever, right?
Having that illusion shattered must mess you up, especially when
you're sensitive like Eli."

Gaby scoffs. "Sensitive? You've gotta be joking. My sister is
the most logical, emotionally constipated person I know. Well,
other than our mom."

"What? Eli is so in touch with how everyone around her is
feeling. What did she call herself . . . an empath? Or something
like that? That's why I fell for her."

"How did you two get together anyway? You're not really her
type." Gaby doesn't even bother to say, "No offense."

Caleb laughs. "Your sister acts so prim and proper that you
can't help but wanna mess with her, right?"

Gaby doesn't deny it.

"I knew it was a mistake to approach her the way I usually do, but I had to try, right? Her welcome party was a couple
weeks after she started at the club. I tried talking her up, and
she rejected me so fast, it was more humbling than humiliating.
But then she said, 'You don't have to put on that act around me,

you know? Try being yourself, and maybe I'll give you a shot.'"
He clutches his chest as if Cupid shot him in the heart. "She saw
right through me. More than that, she saw ME. No girl ever
thought there was more to me than what was on the surface. No
girl ever made me want to be better, if I'm honest."

"But Eli did?"

"She did. She might be the best thing that's ever happened
to me." He laughs. "Guess it's not the same for her, though. Tell
her I'm sorry. For whatever it is I did that made her think she
couldn't talk to me. And that I won't wait around for her if she
doesn't want me to."

"What if she does?"

"She's got my number. It's not like I'm in a hurry to get with
anyone else. I got my own stuff to focus on."

"Yeah? Is that why you're suddenly fleeing your apartment?"
I ask, bringing the subject back around.

"I swear I'm not skipping town. I still gotta work to pay for
school, you know? But Ricky's uncle really is raising the rent, and
when you mentioned your family's detective agency, I thought
it might be a good idea for me to move somewhere you don't
know."

"But you said you still plan on going to work, so I'll see you
there anyway. What's the point in moving?"

He musses up the back of his hair. "Yeah, fair, but all I could
think before was that you were going to find out about the burglaries and then narc on me. I had to get out."

"But we'd be able to find you at work," I repeat, truly not
understanding his thought process.

"Okay, I get it. I wanted out of here anyway." Caleb looks at one of the open boxes, and I recognize the photos on top as the ones from his bedroom wall. The ones that Eli took. "If she's not coming back, I don't really want to stay in a place we were supposed to share together. Corny but true."

Gaby goes over to the box of photos and stares at them for a moment before turning to Caleb. "Caleb, can you swear that this scam you got my sister involved in isn't going to cause her any problems?"

He thinks for a moment before responding. "She was never directly involved in the robberies. She only collected information about patrons while at the front desk, then passed it on to figure out the next best target. I can't promise anything, though. Maybe Eli got a guilty conscience over what she was doing, but there's no way she got hurt."

He truly seems to believe that. Not that it means anything. He could be a really good liar, super dense, or both. Still, we've got more than enough out of him, so I gesture to Gaby and Joemar that it's time to leave.

"You swear you're not gonna narc on us? And you'll tell Eli what I said?"

If I report the burglary ring before we figure out how it's connected to Eli's disappearance, it may do more harm than good. My aunt taught me about active stillness in Kali—a warrior must have patience and know the right time to strike. This skill is as important for a detective as it is for a fighter. My gut tells me it's not time to make a move yet.

I pull Gaby aside to tell her this, and she agrees, saying to

Caleb, "I won't say anything about what you told us unless you give me a reason to. Leave Eli alone. You've done enough damage. I won't stop her if she wants to contact you, but we're sure as hell not going to encourage it either."

Before we leave, I have to confirm one last thing.

"You gave Eli that ring, didn't you? The rose gold flower one."

His eyes widen. "One of the members I was serving took it off at the table to put on some hand lotion and forgot to put it back on, so I pocketed it when no one was looking. It was meant to be a promise between me and Eli, but I should've known it'd never work out."

He turns away from us. "She deserved better than some stolen ring."

Back in her car, Gaby asks, "Do you think Caleb was telling the truth?"

I glance in the back at Joemar. He's been in the field longer since he and Andrew help my mom out with stuff like this.

"I believe everything he said is the truth as he sees it," he says.

I think that over before asking, "You don't think he's lying to us, but you also think there's more to this scam and with Eli than he realizes?"

He nods. "I mean, come on. A kid who's part of the group dies in an alleged accident, and then another member up and quits with no notice right after? I'll accept that maybe Eli is naive, but she knows she's committing crimes. If she truly wanted out for no nefarious reason, all she had to do was find a replacement.

Or pay some sort of fee? Why suddenly disappear and risk pissing off the big boss?"

"Maybe Eli didn't want to get another coworker into that mess? Or what if she couldn't afford the fee?"

"Joemar's got a point, though," Gaby says. "I know liars, and while Caleb has probably deceived plenty of people, I don't think he was trying to lie to us. He's in over his head."

We're all quiet for a moment before something occurs to me. "The curse."

"The *what*?" Gaby and Joemar ask at the same time.

"Eli and the girl before her, both of them worked the front desk, and both of them ghosted. Caleb mentioned that position being useful since Eli was able to access member information and pass it along to the others." The more I say it out loud, the more it makes sense. "What if that girl was also part of Bling Ring 2.0 and disappeared for the same reasons as Eli? I'll ask Alex about her, see if I can find a connection. He said her name was Emily. Wish I had a way to look up her old employee files."

"Let me and Andrew handle that," Joemar says. "We've known Alex for years, and he won't think it's weird if we frame it like we heard rumors about your workplace and we're worried about you."

"You sure? I don't want to tip him off about the investigation."

"Nah, he trusts us."

"Awesome, I'll let you two handle that part so Gaby and I can focus on Caleb and the current Chicago Glen staff."

Gaby pulls in front of my aunt's studio, and Joemar gets out after thanking her for the ride.

"You're not coming in for family meal?" I ask. She hasn't turned off the car.

"Not hungry. Besides, after talking to Caleb, I think I want to search Eli's room again. There's gotta be something I'm missing. I'm gonna check her social media again too. See if maybe I can figure out the passwords or something."

"All right, I'll see you tomorrow. Good work today."

She finally smiles. "Yeah, you too. Thanks again for agreeing to help. When I hired you, I had no idea we'd find out my straitlaced sister turned into a secret criminal because my parents are poseurs. Kind of a letdown, you know? I mean, I'm supposed to be the rebel in the family."

Gaby's voice is light and playful, but I'm used to seeing through her "tough girl" act.

"Listen, I know today was a lot. And this case is now much more dangerous. Even if Caleb insists there's nothing to worry about, I've seen too much in my mom's case files alone to trust that. If you want to stop, I won't blame you. There are better PIs in the city."

She studies me for a moment before letting a small, sincere smile slip through. "Danika, you're good at this. You're going to find my sister. I don't believe in much, but I do believe in you."

Before I can embarrass myself by bursting into tears in front of her, Joemar knocks on my window, making me jump.

"What?" I ask after rolling it down.

"Sorry, was I interrupting something?" Joemar asks, his eyebrows raised. "Daniel's worried about you."

I immediately unclick my seat belt. "Gotta go, Gaby. I'll see you tomorrow?"

She hesitates as if there's so much more on her mind, but she only says, "Yeah, see you."

As I get out of the car, I make sure to keep my eyes away from her when I whisper, "Thanks for believing in me."

CHAPTER
TWENTY

AS SOON AS I SLIDE INTO THE PASSENGER SEAT THE
next day, Gaby asks, "Do you think Alex is involved?"

"Good morning to you too. Can I at least get some caffeine
before the interrogation?"

Without missing a beat, she hands me my usual iced Vietnamese coffee, absolutely brimming with condensed milk. Just
the way I like it.

Once we're on the road and I've had a few gulps of my morning nectar, I say, "Why do you think Alex is part of it? Because
he covered Caleb's shift that one time?"

"He's covered for Caleb more than once, according to your
cousins. And something about that guy bugs me."

"Yeah, you do act really weird around him, but I don't get it.
He's a nice guy. Probably the nicest one I've met since Junior."

"And that's what bugs me! No one's *that* nice. Not without
a reason."

"Anyone ever tell you you're an oddly suspicious person?"

"Anyone ever tell you you're not suspicious enough for a
detective?" she shoots back.

Ouch. I actually think I harbor a decent level of suspicion of people. Too much suspicion makes it harder for clients to open up to you. Why should they trust you if you won't trust them (at least a little)? It can also lead you down the wrong path in an investigation if you're so stuck on your initial impression that you're not open to other possibilities.

I've always been more of a Swords than a Cups girl, but I do have mad respect for the Wands. Lead with logic but trust your gut—that's how my parents operate, and it makes sense to me, both in tarot and in life. Though considering how Gaby's parents are, maybe she's got a legit reason to see everyone as sus.

"Agree to disagree," I say. "As for Alex, it's hard to picture him getting caught up in *The Bling Ring, Part Two,* but . . . I suppose the same could be said about your sister. His family situation does make him the right target for recruiters."

"See? You think we should ask him about it? We could meet him for lunch and try to feel him out."

"We definitely should *not* ask him outright. Let me text him and ask if he's free." I pull out my phone before glancing at her. "Felix will probably be there. You cool with that?"

She shrugs. "They're a package deal."

"He also works at the club and is supposedly broke despite wearing designer clothes, so it'd be good to watch him too," I say.

I try to word my text without being too obvious.

> **Danika:** hey you free for lunch? my dad packed way too much food for me and gaby

He responds so fast, I almost wonder if he was waiting phone in hand for me to message him.

> **Alex**: yeah! I got a lot too so we can share:)

> meet us at o entrance?

> **Danika**: See you there

I relay the info to Gaby as she pulls into a parking spot. She grabs my phone to read over our exchange, and her lip curls.

I take my phone back. "What's with that face?"

"Nothing. Just looking forward to lunch with your golden retriever friend."

What the hell does that mean?

"GOD, YOU SERIOUSLY EXUDE GOLDEN RETRIEVER energy," Gaby observes, watching Alex lay out all the food and fuss over everyone to make sure we have enough to eat.

"You keep saying that, and I still have no idea what that means," I say. "Alex, here are the napkins."

Felix shakes his head. "You're not wrong, but let's be real. Your friend is pretty similar."

"Don't you dare," Gaby warns.

"What's wrong with golden retrievers?" I ask. "I love them. They're the sweetest dogs."

"I'm more of a cat person," Gaby says.

"I bet you are." Felix grins at Gaby in a way I don't understand, but she seems to from the murderous look in her eye.

I glance at Alex, and he shrugs. I help myself to the rolled omelet he prepared.

"Oooh! It's sweet." I was expecting it to be salty, but after a few more bites, the unexpected mix of sweet and savory in the eggs really grows on me. "I've never had eggs like this. What made you add sugar?"

"Felix said the rolled omelets in anime always look so good, so he wanted to try them." Alex takes a big bite of one and grins. "My mom and sister both have sweet tooths too. I'll have to make it again for them soon."

"What a great guy, am I right?" Felix asks, helping himself to more rolled omelet and my dad's chicken teriyaki. "Trying out new recipes to make his loved ones happy."

"You two make an interesting duo," Gaby observes. "What's your deal? The brains and the brawn?"

"Pretty much," Felix says at the same time Alex asks, "What's 'brawn'?"

Gaby and I laugh, and Felix smirks. "It means I'm the brains and you're the muscle. I'm Beauty and you're the Beast. What about you two? You kinda have the same vibes, except, Danika, you're actually pretty smart too, aren't you?"

I shrug. "Smart enough."

Gaby raises her eyebrows. "What do you mean, 'smart enough'? You're in all AP classes!"

"Only 'cause I need a scholarship if I wanna go to college. I've just worked my ass off, that's all."

Felix gives me a look devoid of his usual humor and charm,

but it's one I like because I can tell it's sincere. A look that tells me he knows where I'm coming from. He gets it. Hell, he's probably in the same position.

"What's your story, Felix?" Gaby asks.

He narrows his eyes at her. "Why you wanna know?"

"You've already made all kinds of assumptions about who I am. Fair is fair."

Felix has the grace to look embarrassed. "I'm sorry for coming at you like that at the party. I know a little about your situation because of Eli, so, yeah. My bad."

"What did she say?"

Felix and Alex glance at each other. Felix shrugs, and Alex, who appears extremely uncomfortable, says, "Eli got really drunk at a party once and kind of . . . yelled at everyone about it?"

"Oh my God," Gaby says, covering her face with her hands. "So everyone at work knows?"

"Not everyone. Just most?" Alex says unhelpfully. "I don't think that many people know you're sisters. I mean, you don't really look alike. I doubt anyone would automatically assume you're related just because of your last name. The only reason I know is because Mrs. Whittle told me."

"And Alex told me at the party when he screamed at me for being rude to you. So unless you or Mrs. Whittle told anyone else, I don't think it's public knowledge," Felix adds.

"Caleb knows too, obviously," I say. "We know he and Eli were together."

"He's been pretty broken up about her leaving," Alex says.

"Are you two close?" I ask.

"I'm friendly with all the kitchen and dining staff. Plus, he knows about lots of cool music I've never heard of. Sometimes he gets me into shows for free if I carry and set up his equipment for him."

Felix rolls his eyes. "He's using you because you're strong and cool with being the designated driver."

"You don't drink?" I ask. "I saw you with a cup at the welcome party, though."

"What else did you notice about my boy?" Felix asks, smirking.

Alex shoves him, then responds to me. "I don't really like the taste of alcohol, but I'll have one drink to be polite, and then I'll stick with pop or juice for the rest of the night."

"Do you enjoy taking care of drunk people or something?"

Alex shrugs. "People usually give me money to drive them home since I'm cheaper than Uber and Lyft, so don't think I'm, like, that good of a guy. I like driving, I hate drinking, and I need money. It works out."

Felix musses up his hair. "Stop selling yourself short. You're not helping yourself."

"I'm not trying to?" Alex swats Felix's hand away. "If anything, you're the one who hypes me up way too much. That's why people get disappointed when they find out how boring I am."

"You're not boring," I blurt out. "I think you're really cool."

"I'm really not."

"Yes, you are."

"I—"

"Alex, when someone gives you a compliment, say thanks and accept it," Felix says.

Alex scratches the back of his head in, like, a super endearing way. "Sorry. Thanks, Danika. I think you're really cool too."

Gaby snorts. "See, there's that golden retriever energy again. You're a hot guy who, one, has no idea how hot he is, and, two, has no problem acknowledging his weak points. And not, like, as a tactic. Just because you're ridiculously honest. You're practically an endangered species, you know? I find you very annoying, but I also kind of want to protect you."

Felix points at her. "That. That's the perfect way to describe him. I'm glad someone gets what I have to put up with every day."

"Yeah, your dynamic makes more sense to me." Gaby glances at her watch. "We've got to get going, but I enjoyed this. Want to meet for lunch tomorrow too?"

"Yes!" Alex exclaims. "It's so much more fun with you two around. No offense," he adds to Felix.

Felix glances at me. "Please eat with us from now on and save me from his enthusiasm. I'd also love to try more of your dad's cooking."

"I'll let him know. He loves feeding people." I stand up and brush myself off. "See you guys at work later?"

"I'm in the kitchen most of the time, so probably not. But maybe I'll catch you on break." Felix holds out his hand for Alex to pull him up. "If not, see you tomorrow."

"I'll be there," Alex says as he assists his friend. "Maybe we can hang out during our break."

"Sounds good."

I help Gaby up, and we both make our way to our classes. "What do you think? Do you still think Alex is hiding something?"

Gaby shakes her head. "No, now I KNOW he's hiding something. And we're going to find out what it is."

"HEY, DANIKA, I HEARD YOU READ TAROT CARDS?"

I peer up from my sandwich to address Nadine, one of the servers who's also in the break room with me. She's one of the older servers, probably late twenties. "Yeah, it's a side hustle. Who told you?"

"Alex. I was joking about how my love life is so bad that I should consult a psychic about it, and he mentioned you." She glances at my half-eaten meal. "Sorry to interrupt you on break, but could you read for me when you have time? I'll pay."

"Yeah. Let me wash my hands and grab my deck." I cram the last of the sandwich into my mouth before doing those two tasks. When I return, Alex and Felix are at the table too.

"Can we join you? I've never seen a tarot reading," Alex says. "I hope you don't mind that I told Nadine about you."

"I appreciate you throwing more business my way. Up to Nadine if you can stick around."

Nadine laughs. "Sure, why not? It's all in good fun."

I have a feeling that she's underestimating me, which I HATE, but I don't say anything. Best to show her what I'm capable of. I spread my scarf on the table and set my deck on top. "Do you want a general love reading, or do you have a question?"

"When will I meet the love of my life?"

I groan inwardly. I hate when clients ask me questions as if I can predict the future, and time-based questions are always the worst. Any time a question starts with "When will . . ." I know it's going to be a tough reading. I have my own way of handling these questions, but not every client is happy when I tell them I can't and won't give them a specific date.

"I can't tell you exactly when you'll meet the love of your life, but I can give you advice on how to get there." I shuffle the cards several times and have Nadine cut the deck before laying three cards facedown and continuing my explanation. "The three things I can tell you are: what will help you find love, what's holding you back from finding love, and what you need to do if you want to be successful at it."

I flip over the cards. All reversed again. I'm noticing a pattern in my recent readings. But the fact that they're all Major Arcana is fascinating. This woman needs some big changes in her life, and as annoyed as I am by her slight, I'm glad she's come to me.

"The first card is the reversed High Priestess. The High Priestess is the card of intuition, knowledge, and the subconscious. Because it's reversed, my advice is that you spend more time looking inward. Is part of the reason why you have trouble finding love because you don't trust yourself? Do you ignore your gut feelings because you think you're being illogical or because you're too busy listening to other people's opinions? Learn to listen to and trust in yourself, and that will help you find love."

I continue to the next card. "The reversed Moon. Another card dealing with intuition and the subconscious, so it seems like this is a huge problem for you. What can help you is also what's been holding you back. You've been letting your fears and anxieties consume you to the point that you can barely hear your inner voice. You might not even realize you're doing this, but ugly emotions tend to lurk in the subconscious. You have to acknowledge them before you can fully free yourself."

Finally, I point at the Death card, and she flinches. Typical reaction, but I'm quick to reassure her as I did with Eli weeks ago. Hopefully, she'll take the news better. "The Death card doesn't mean a physical death. It's a symbol of endings and new beginnings, so you can almost think of it as, like, the death of your former self. Because it's reversed, it's a sign that you're on the cusp of major change, but you're fighting it. And I get that. Change is scary, and even when you know it's for the best, you can't help but resist. But to find love—if that's truly your goal— you need to embrace the possibilities that change can bring to your life. Let go of all that stuff in the past that's holding you back. Only then will you be ready to find love."

I'm so in my tarot zone that I don't realize that Nadine is full-on sobbing until she lets out a gurgly noise that snaps my attention back to the here and now. "Oh damn, I'm so sorry, Nadine. Was that too much? Tarot can get real personal some- times."

She shakes her head quickly, but tears are still streaming down her face, and Alex hands her a tissue box. She grabs a few to clean up her face and blow her nose, and after a few deep breaths, she's able to speak again.

"No, I'm the one who's sorry. I wasn't expecting you to be so . . . insightful. It's kind of embarrassing, you know? Like you can see all the parts no one is supposed to see."

She pulls out two twenties, which is twice my usual price. I try to hand her back the other twenty, but she refuses it. "No, you earned the money. I know you read for high school kids, but if you get the chance, you should raise your prices. Your gift is absolutely worth a little extra."

She gets up to leave and pats Alex on the shoulder. "She's a keeper, bud."

I glance at the clock and start gathering up my tarot stuff. I'm about to leave the break room when Alex suddenly stumbles toward me.

"Um, you okay?"

"Yeah, I'm fine." He turns to glare at Felix before focusing back on me. "I was wondering if you'd read my cards too. If you have time."

"I need to get back to the front desk, but I can read for you during lunch tomorrow?"

"That would be great!" He beams at me, and I can't help but smile back.

I glance over at Felix, who's grinning at us. "What about you, Felix? Interested in a reading?"

"After seeing how you took apart Nadine like that? I'mma pass. I don't need you getting in my head."

"Aww, don't be like that. Alex is willing to put himself out there."

"With Alex, what you see is what you get. My boy has depth or whatever, but you know what I mean."

"And what about you? You don't want me peering into your soul because it's bottomless?"

"Correct."

His answer is simple and straightforward and uttered in a way that lets me know not to push it. So I let it go.

But now he's piqued my interest.

"YOU STILL DOWN TO GIVE ALEX THAT TAROT READ-ing?"

Alex, Felix, Gaby, and I are passing around a bag of salted egg chips that Alex brought when Felix pops that question.

Alex freezes with his hand in the bag and stares at his friend.

"Don't worry; I'll pay for it. I know how much you've been wanting this," Felix says. "You've got your cards, right, Danika?"

"Um, yeah. But if Alex doesn't want me to read for him . . ."

"No! I mean, yeah, I want you to read for me. It's fine. I don't want to be a bother, though."

I pull my deck out of my backpack. "You're never a bother. Besides, I love reading for people almost as much as I love the money I make from it. So do you want to go somewhere private to do this, or . . . ?"

Alex sighs. "It's fine; they can stay."

"You sure?"

"Either I let him stay, or I hear about it later, so might as well."

It seems less like Alex wants a reading and more like Felix is demanding one, but whatever. If Alex is cool, then I'm cool.

"So do you want a general reading, or do you have a question to ask?"

"Do I have to ask this question out loud?"

"No, but it does make my job easier. There are so many ways to interpret the cards that knowing what kind of advice you're searching for can help me narrow things down."

Alex thinks it over for a moment. "Okay, so I'm in a situation where I can leave things as they are, and it's perfectly fine. Or, at least, it's fine for now. But I can also do something that will either make my life way better or ruin everything. And I don't know what to do."

"So you need help making a decision: keep the status quo or roll the dice. Am I right?"

"Exactly. I don't want to mess up a good thing, but if there's a chance . . ." He trails off, eyes on my hands as they shuffle the deck. "Anyway, I hope that's enough to go on."

"Yeah, plenty," I assure him. As I shuffle, a single card falls out, and I set it aside facedown. Whenever that happens, it means it's not meant to be part of the regular spread, but it wants to be known.

As usual, I lay three cards facedown in front of myself. "The first card represents what happens if you keep things the same. The second card is what happens if you try to change things. And the third card is advice on how to make that decision. I'll use the card I set to the side as a clarifying card if necessary."

I flip over the first one, and Alex flinches at the image of a multitude of swords impaling a dead phoenix. "The Ten of Swords. Based on your reaction, you have an idea of what this card means. This is a card that symbolizes defeat, failure, or a painful ending. If you keep the status quo, it means accepting defeat and moving on, since there's nothing left for you."

Felix claps Alex on the back. "That card couldn't be any clearer, could it?"

Alex elbows him away. "She's not done yet. Keep going, Danika."

The next card is the reversed Four of Chalices. "There are opportunities in front of you, but you don't seem to notice them. You're too afraid to open yourself up, to really express your thoughts and feelings, so you're stuck in your head. It's important to think over big decisions carefully, but take too long, and you'll miss out."

I turn over the last card. "Reversed Justice. You're not being honest with yourself and those around you. There's also a chance that you're trying to avoid accountability or responsibility. Maybe you find yourself blaming others for your mistakes or not wanting to accept that something was your fault. When it comes to making your decision, you need to examine your biases and be honest with yourself. Are you protecting your own comfort? Is your gain someone else's loss? What can you do to balance that and make the right decision?"

I lift my gaze from the cards and catch Alex's bewildered expression. "You have no idea how that's related to your question, do you?"

"Uh, yes and no? But it doesn't really help me with this decision."

"Then fingers crossed the clarifying card will help." I reach out for the card that slipped out when I was shuffling the deck and laugh when I see what it reveals. "The reversed Two of Wands. Basically, you're being too precious about this. Don't miss out on what can be a great opportunity 'cause you're afraid of making the wrong choice. That clear enough for you?"

Alex gazes at me and nods. "Yes, actually. That's exactly what I needed."

"Cool, glad I could help. So that'll be—"

"Will you go to prom with me?"

"—twenty bucks. Wait, what?"

"Sorry! Should I have waited until we were alone? It seemed like the perfect time, and I wanted to do it before I psyched myself out." Alex glances at Felix and Gaby. Felix takes the hint and drags a protesting Gaby away before Alex turns his attention back to me. "I really like you, Danika. But if you don't feel the same, all good. We can go as friends? Or not. That would be weird, right? I don't want to make things weird between us."

He's babbling now, and I'd be lying if I said it isn't super cute. I mean, I've always thought Alex is cute. But do I like him like that? I don't know.

Come on, Danika! He deserves an honest answer here.

"Alex, I think you're great, and I like spending time with you. But whether or not that means something more, I have no clue. Sorry," I add quickly. "That's not quite what you're asking, is it? You wanted to know about prom? Um . . ."

"No, that's fine! I'll take a maybe for now. If you're not sure, that means I've still got a chance, right?" He smiles gently at me. "I won't push. There's no time limit, so let me know when you're ready. Or, well, there's a time limit on prom, but that's not the important part. I want us to still hang out the way we've been doing, so don't think anything has to change. I like being around you however I can."

Hngh. His sincerity and puppy-dog look are like a shot right to my heart, and I can't take it anymore.

"I'll think about it for real. I promise," I say, touching his arm. "I don't mean to leave you hanging, but that's all I can do right now."

"It's more than enough, Danika. You're worth waiting for."

He walks me back to where Felix and Gaby are standing. They're eyeing us.

"So . . . ?" Felix's face drops as soon as we approach. "Ugh, seriously? Do I have to spell out why this guy is perfect for you? First off—"

"We gotta get to class! See you later!" Alex slings his arm around Felix's shoulders and drags his best friend away from us.

"So he finally asked you out," Gaby says.

I don't know why, but I feel oddly nervous telling Gaby about what happened.

"I mean, you heard him ask me to prom."

"And what did you tell him?"

"That I wasn't sure how I felt about him. He said that was okay and to take my time figuring it out." I chew on my lower lip. "You know, no one's ever confessed their feelings for me before."

"I find that hard to believe."

"Seriously. You've met my cousins. You've seen how overprotective they are. Everyone in my area knows not to approach me, or they'll have to answer to them. And no one I've liked ever seemed interested in me back." I shrug. "This is all new to me. I should text Nicole and Junior about this. They'll know what to do."

I pull out my phone, but Gaby covers it with her hand. "You honestly can't figure out how you feel without running it by your friends? You can't think for yourself? For once?"

"For once? What the hell does that mean?"

"All the decisions you make are based on how your parents operate or centered around your family or friends in some way. Everything you do revolves around what's best for them or what they think. But what do *you* want, Danika? You like to act like you have all the answers, but can you even tell me that?"

Gaby is leaning in close, practically screaming in my face as she jabs her finger into my chest.

I swat her hand away. "What do you even know about me and my family? Just because everyone in your life is selfish doesn't mean you get to judge the people in mine."

She staggers back as if I've shoved her, and I regret those words as soon as they pass my lips. Some things you just don't say out loud.

"Look—" I start, but my buzzing phone interrupts us, and Andrew's name flashes across the screen. My cousins never call, especially during a school day. "Hey, Andrew, what's up?"

"We found the address for that girl Emily, who worked the front desk before Eli, and went to check it out. Joemar swears he saw a girl matching Eli's description leaving the apartment and is tailing her now. What do you want us to do?"

I turn wide eyes to Gaby.

This is it. This is the break we've been waiting for.

"Stay there and keep an eye out for Eli. We're on the way."

GABY PARKS IN FRONT OF MY COUSINS' CAR, AND we get out to join Andrew.

"Anything new?" I ask.

Andrew's got Joemar on the car speakerphone, and he replies, "I followed the girl to a local grocery store roughly ten minutes away. She hasn't come out yet."

"Should we wait for her to come back to the apartment or head over there and see if it's actually her?" Gaby asks me.

"I think we go there now. If it's her, it's probably best for us to approach her in a public place. She won't want to cause a scene. She's in hiding, after all. If we wait until she's at the apartment, she can avoid us."

Joemar says, "Got it. Danika, I'm texting you the location. I'll alert you if anything changes."

Gaby and I drive to the grocery store and park in the lot. I give Joemar a small nod in acknowledgment before we head inside.

My eyes sweep the floor space of the small, locally owned chain. Since it's a weekday, the store isn't crowded, and the wide aisles should make the search fairly easy.

"Let's stick together," I tell Gaby. "It'll be easier to act if we see her."

Gaby nods, and we head toward the large produce section before systematically winding up and down the aisles in search of her sister. We find Eli in the cookie aisle—she's wearing a bucket hat and large sunglasses that cover most of her face, but I clock the rose gold ring on her right hand as she reaches out for a bag of Milano Mint Chocolate cookies. I gesture at Gaby to make her move.

"I still don't understand why you like mint chocolate. It tastes like toothpaste."

Eli's head whips around at the sound of her younger sister's voice. "Gaby! What the—why are you here?!"

"Do you have any idea how worried I've been?"

Gaby's harsh tone is softened by the bear hug she gives her older sister.

Eli's eyes quickly dart toward me. "Who's this?"

"My name's Danika. I've been helping Gaby look for you. Glad to see you're alive. Do you—"

"So you have been snooping around," Eli interrupts. "The friend I'm staying with heard you and some girl claiming to be a detective have been asking questions, and I need you to stop."

"But—"

A young woman pushing a shopping cart with a toddler in it interrupts us to get by.

"This isn't the place," I say. "Can we move somewhere else? Gaby really needs to talk to you."

Conflicting emotions war across Eli's face. Resignation wins.

"Fine," she says. "Let me just pay for these groceries. There's a café around the corner where we can talk."

Eventually she moves us to a Mexican café a few blocks away.

Eli puts in three orders of café de olla and waits until the spiced coffees arrive before tearing into her sister.

"Gaby, I'm fine. I got involved in something that was a total mistake. I need to lie low while I fix my mess, though, okay? Don't worry about me."

Her "don't worry about me" sounds a whole lot like "mind your business" to me. Gaby must feel the same, because she explodes.

"Don't worry about you? I find out that my sister ran away after having a secret boyfriend and becoming a freaking Hamburglar because our parents lost all our money, and that's all you have to say to me? DON'T WORRY ABOUT YOU?"

At this time of the day, there aren't a ton of people in the café, but we're sure as hell not alone. Eli calls out to all the people staring at us. "Sorry!"

I'm not sure if they know her or simply don't want drama at their place of business, but one of them, an older woman with brown skin and gray hair, likely the owner, approaches our table.

"You all right, mija?" she asks Eli, who nods. She studies her for a moment as if to call her out on her obvious lie, but then she shifts her focus to me. "You're Angelica Dizon's daughter, aren't you?"

"How—"

The woman gestures at me to follow her. "Excuse us for a moment."

I glance at Gaby, who remains mad AF, and then Eli, who clearly doesn't want me here, and decide my best bet is to follow the mystery woman.

"I'm not going to ask what you're doing here during school

hours, but I'll have to ask you not to cause trouble in my café," the woman says. "I'm Marcela, by the way."

"Sorry about that, Marcela. But how do you know who I am?"

"Your mom helped me a long time ago. We're friends."

Of course they're friends. If the school doesn't call my mom to tell her that I cut class, this woman probably will. I make a note to text my mom and explain the situation before anyone contacts her. Get ahead of everyone else, shape the narrative or whatever.

"Oh, um, it's nice to meet you. You've got a great shop."

It's warm and inviting and full of delicious smells like cinnamon and baking conchas. It feels good knowing my mom helped the woman who owns a place that can make others feel like they're at home.

Marcela smiles. "Thanks. I'll let you get back. I only wanted to introduce myself and gently remind you and your friends that this is a public place."

I thank her and apologize again. When she moves back behind the counter, I text my mom.

Danika: Before anyone else contacts you I want you to know I'm at your friend marcela's café

we found where eli's staying and gaby's talking to her now

We're all safe

I'll make a full report later

I send all those texts in a quick burst, and when she doesn't immediately answer, I message again.

> **Danika:** Please don't be mad I cut school its for the case

Nothing. Resigning myself to the lecture of a lifetime tonight, I rejoin Gaby and Eli.

Gaby says, "She won't tell me why she ran."

"I told you, it's for your own good! The more you know, the more danger I put you in. That was the whole point of me running, pendeja." Eli turns to me. "It took me a minute, but you're the girl who did the tarot reading for me, aren't you? Is that why Gaby got you mixed up in this?"

"Yes and no. Your reading wasn't exactly positive," I say. "But my mom runs a detective agency, so I gave Gaby a referral. TLDR version is, your parents suck and I took over the case."

The corners of Eli's lips quirk up in a bitter smile. "They're the worst. I wouldn't even be in this position if it weren't for them."

"I mean, they didn't make you turn to a life of crime," Gaby says. "Ugh, I can't believe I'm actually sticking up for them."

"God, I'm supposed to be the one who always makes the right decisions, and I've been doing nothing but screwing up my life nonstop." Eli squeezes her eyes shut and takes a deep breath before opening them and gazing at her sister. "I didn't mean to shut you out. Not at first. But after a while, I realized I was doing it because I was ashamed. And then I was doing it to keep you safe from the boss. It was never supposed to go this far. I was—"

And here she cuts off because the bells above the café's front door ring, drawing our attention to the new customer.

My mom.

Shit.

"Uh, hi, Mommy."

"Congrats on solving your first case."

Holy shit, yes. Technically, I found Eli. Or at least got her to resurface. I solved my first case.

So why does everything feel so wrong? There's something about my mom's expression, her overall vibe, that's off-putting.

"I wish you had told me you were coming."

My mom gives me a hard look. "This case involves a missing minor. I have to follow the law. I also—"

Eli bolts up out of her seat. "She called the cops!"

But they must've already been waiting outside, since two uniformed police officers enter the café before she can run.

"Eli Delgado? We have some questions for you."

"Wait!" Gaby tries to stop them. "Our parents never filed a report, so there's no need to take her in. She can come home with me."

"We're not here about a missing persons report. We're here about her connection to a string of burglaries happening around Chicago."

Both Gaby and Eli turn to stare at me.

"It wasn't me! I swear I never said anything!"

My mom steps in. "Your cousins told me. They were worried about you getting involved in something above your pay grade. Don't be mad at Danika. She's been trying to protect you both this whole time, even when it had her going against what I've taught her."

Those last words are said with a heavy emphasis toward me, and I have nothing to say in my defense. This isn't how it was supposed to go.

Gaby is still trying to keep the cops from taking her sister away, but my mom gently pulls her to the side.

"She's a minor, so your parents have been contacted. I tried calling them first, but they wouldn't answer. I was hoping they'd meet us here. Anyway, your sister won't be interrogated until your parents—and presumably your lawyer—are present. She'll be fine."

"Can I go with her?"

"Gaby . . ." Eli's eyes have been wide with terror since the police arrived, but they soften at her sister's inquiry.

"I'm afraid not. You can meet your parents at the precinct, though," one of the officers says. "Let's go."

The female officer holds out a pair of handcuffs, and Eli balks.

"Do you have to handcuff me?"

"Again, we are not bringing you in as a runaway. We're bringing you in for an investigation involving a criminal offense. Will you cooperate?"

Eli nods, and the officer handcuffs her while reading her rights, and then both officers lead her to their squad car. We follow them outside, and Eli pauses for a moment to stare me dead in the eyes, and I know—she blames me for all of this.

Then the female officer helps her get into the back of the

squad car, and they drive away, and me and my mom and Gaby are left standing in front of the café.

I can't look at Gaby. I simply can't. If I do, I'll probably see the same look that was in Eli's eyes.

But the world doesn't care about what I can deal with, because Gaby immediately gets in my face.

"WHAT. THE. HELL. We finally find Eli, and you do this to me?"

"It's not Danika's fault; she—"

Gaby ignores my mom. "Why did you call her?"

"The café owner is a friend of my mom's! I was worried that she'd tell my mom I cut class, so I figured I'd explain it was for the case. And anyway, I had to report we found her because of the agency—"

"I didn't hire the agency. I hired you! I should've known you—" She cuts herself off. "Forget it. Like I said, I shouldn't be surprised. Everything is so black and white for you, isn't it?"

"Gaby, you're being super unfair. Your sister is the one who—"

"Stay the hell away from me and my family. You've done enough damage. Oh, and your payment may take a while since I'm broke. I shouldn't bother paying you since you flat-out betrayed me, but you did help me find out that my sister is a criminal and my parents are liars, so go you. I'll leave it in your work locker on payday."

"Gaby, don't—"

But she turns away, walks over to her car, and leaves. Leaves me with my mom, a sick feeling in my stomach, and a ton of regret.

Bestie Group Chat

Junior: Why werent u at kali class?

Danika: Something came up

Nicole: u ok?

Danika: I'm fine

Nicole: I got work on Fri but u better tell us whats up next class

And no lying

Danika: Read

I MAY HAVE GOTTEN A LITTLE TOO USED TO GABY chauffeuring me around everywhere. But whatever, my student Ventra card still gets me around the city like a true Chicagoan. So what if the country club is inconvenient to get to from my house? The bus is sorta reliable and cheap. I'm being independent and environmentally conscious. And so what if it's embarrassing AF to have my dad pick me up from work like I'm a child? It's only until I can afford to fix up Veronica, which, thanks to my country club job, is only two paychecks away.

These self-righteous lies last literally two (2) workdays. On Sunday, Alex comes up to me during break at the club and asks if everything's okay with me and Gaby.

"You haven't had lunch with us. And I usually see the two of you arriving and leaving together for work, but yesterday I saw Gaby when she was about to leave, and I asked where you were."

"What did she say?"

"She glared at me as if she could set me on fire with her mind and left without saying anything."

I laugh. I can't help it. I can picture exactly the face Gaby made at him, and, yeah, that tracks.

"I messed up, and she's super pissed at me. Definitely my fault, so don't hold it against her."

"I'm sorry. Is there anything I can do? I mean, she doesn't seem to like me much, but I can try."

"She likes you fine. You're just very different people."

He's quiet for a moment. "Um, well, I know she always drove you to school and work and stuff. How are you getting around now?"

I shrug. "The same way I did before I met her."

"Do you want me to start giving you a ride?" When I stare at him, he adds, "Because I already pick up Felix, and you're on the way. Plus, it's not safe to be walking around alone at night. Not that you can't take care of yourself! Your cousins told me about your Kali lessons. But, you know, better safe than sorry."

He is babbling again, and it's so damn cute and sweet, and his kindness is a balm that I wasn't aware I needed.

"I'd like that. Thanks, Alex. I know you're super busy with work and family, so if you ever can't make it, no worries."

He laughs. "Who you talking to? You got even more than me going on! I have no idea how you handle everything."

"Poorly."

He laughs, but I'm being honest. Like, yeah, you can have it all, but something's gonna slip, and you're gonna mess up somehow, and you're gonna have zero boundaries, but whatever. Hashtag girlboss.

God, I sound like Nicole now. I haven't told her or Junior what happened, but if I see them tomorrow, I'm gonna have to. They always see straight through me.

"Hey, Danika. I—"

"I'll meet you at the entrance once I clock out, okay? Thanks again, Alex. Really."

I leave the break area and head back to the front desk before he can answer me. I feel bad for cutting him off, but he's gonna either ask me about prom again or pry more into what happened with Gaby, and I can't deal with either of those topics.

I text my dad that he doesn't need to pick me up anymore, and when he asks how I'm getting home, I tell him my friend is dropping me off.

> **Daddy:** Tell this "friend" to join us for dinner tonight.

> **Danika:** Daddy NO
>
> I swear he's only a friend

A friend who's expressed feelings for me and who I've left hanging for no good reason other than that I'm an emotionally stunted person who doesn't understand her own feelings, but, yeah, nothing else going on there.

> **Daddy:** Either he joins us for dinner, or I'll be waiting outside your job to pick you up later. Your choice.

> **Danika:** FINE

I groan and bury my head in my hands.

HAVING ALEX OVER FOR DINNER WITH MY FAMILY IS weird. Not "weird" as in "bad" or "awkward," but "weird" as in he kinda fits right in?

Daniel has always been way too friendly (he knows about stranger danger, but I guess he figures if I'm the one who brought them over, they must be okay), but since Alex is the reason he has Buchi, that makes him extra cool in his eyes. Not to mention his sports prowess. Like I said before, Daniel has a host of health problems, and possibly because of that he's a bit on the small side, despite the rest of our family being tall (or at least solid, like the twins). He's pushed himself to become as active as his health will allow, but that's not saying much. Maybe it's natural for him to idolize guys who are big and strong and the picture of health, like Alex.

It makes me a little uncomfortable, because the more Daniel points out Alex's physical attributes, the more I notice them as well. Like, yes, obviously I noticed he was tall. But I didn't think anything of just how tall he was until Daniel was like, "Woooow! You're so much taller than Ate! Ate, stand next to him! You only come up to his chin!"

And so now I notice how my head can tuck perfectly into his neck.

Thanks to Daniel, I also notice how big Alex's biceps are, how wide his shoulders are, and, above all, how kind and patient and sweet he is by how he interacts with my little brother. Add in the adorableness of him teaching Buchi how to sit and give her paw? Straight-up ten out of ten.

Worst of all, my parents love him. The way my mom talks to

him is like a complete one-eighty from the way she treated Gaby. With Gaby, it was like sometimes she understood that Gaby needed the familial warmth she was clearly missing from her parents, and other times it was like she thought Gaby wasn't to be trusted and needed to stay the hell away. Maybe because Gaby was supposed to be my client, not my friend? And my mom was trying to draw that line for me? All I know now is that she's staring adoringly at Alex like he's the child she's always wanted, and that's making me nervous.

My dad, who was shockingly the only member not to warm up to him immediately, thawed as soon as he found out Alex was a huge old-school hip-hop fan. He dragged him over to his record collection, and I thought he was going to cry knowing he had found a kindred soul.

And when my dad learned that Alex does most of the cooking at home since his single mom works multiple jobs and his older sister has school on top of her full-time job? He broke out the hallowed Dizon family notebook that houses all his recipes. He doesn't use recipes for his everyday cooking. These are ones he wrote down himself to prepare me and Daniel for having to feed ourselves when we eventually leave home.

A neighbor once asked for my dad's lumpia recipe, and he listed a bunch of ingredients with no proportions or instructions. He also didn't mention at least two of the ingredients, something he probably didn't realize I knew after watching him cook for years. But here he is, giving away his recipes all willy-nilly to the first guy I bring home. Well, the first guy since Junior, but he doesn't count.

Things remain frosty between me and my mom. Like, I get why she did what she did. She's an adult; she's beholden to certain expectations. And I think it's a good thing that she has a strong moral code, both as a person and as a professional. But I don't see why this one time she had to play by the book. She's bent the rules for her clients several times over the years in pursuit of a justice she knows the law would never bring. But for my very first case, she couldn't let me handle it my way?

Seeing her fawn over Alex when she only showed Gaby how unwelcome she was pisses me off even more. Well, I guess she got what she wanted, since Gaby's never speaking to me again.

At the end of the night, after my dad piles containers of food in Alex's arms and my whole family lets him know they'd love to see him again, I walk him to the door to say good night.

"Sorry about all that. I know my family can be a lot, but they really liked you. Not sure if they made that obvious enough."

He laughs, his smile so bright, I actually have to glance away from him like he's the damn sun or something. "Your family is so cool. I mean, I love my mom and sister, but your parents are so interesting! A mom who's a private detective and a dad who writes books? Like, how many people can say that? And Daniel's a really good kid. I always wanted a little brother."

"Yeah, Daniel's the sweetest. Sometimes I worry he's a little behind socially since he's sick all the time and was homeschooled for a few years. He hasn't had a chance to hang out with other kids much. It was really nice of you to pay attention to him."

He seems surprised. "Why wouldn't I? Speaking of, he asked me to help with his homework, but I told him that wasn't really my strong point. I promised him that, instead, I'd teach him to play basketball sometime. If that's cool with your parents."

"I'm sure they'd love that."

"Cool. So then I'll see you tomorrow?"

"Yeah."

"You're still cool with me picking you up in the morning?"

I nod.

He hesitates outside the door and starts to lean toward me before stopping himself. "Good night, Danika."

"Good night, Alex."

He jogs over to his car and waves goodbye. I watch him drive away before closing the door and leaning against it with my eyes closed.

What was that?

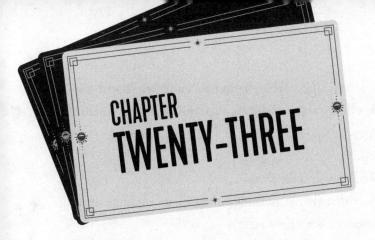

CHAPTER
TWENTY-THREE

"ALEX IS A VERY NICE BOY, DANIKA."

"I know, Mommy. You made it very obvious how you felt about him."

"What's wrong with that?"

It's the morning after Alex came over for dinner, and I'm trying to get ready for school without blowing up at my mom, but she's making that real difficult.

"Nothing. You also made it pretty obvious how you felt about Gaby. And I couldn't help noticing the difference."

My mom purses her lips and studies me for a moment. "Do you think the way I treated Gaby was because she's a girl? And that I have a problem with you dating girls?"

"What? No! Gaby and I aren't like that. I want to know why you treated her so differently; that's all. Especially since you knew her family situation."

"It was because I knew her family situation. I know what parents like that are capable of. I know the kinds of secrets a girl like that can hide. I know that someone like that can't help but be drawn to your kindness. And I know the many ways someone like that can drag you down. I don't want that for you."

The longer she speaks, the more I can't help but think she isn't only talking about Gaby. But before I ask her to explain, she says, "Anyway, things are going to get even uglier for that family, I'm afraid."

"What do you mean?"

"I hear that they're pushing to try Eli as an adult since she won't cooperate with the case."

"But she's only seventeen!"

"They're going to have a tough time making a case since Illinois has strong juvenile protection laws, but it's not impossible if the charges are solid enough."

I scoff. "What charges? So she helped scam rich people out of a couple thousand dollars. She wasn't even directly involved in the robberies. It's not like she's a hardened criminal."

"If she's involved in the suspicious deaths surrounding the country club robberies, then, yes, she is."

"I'm sorry, what?"

"I don't think—"

The sound of a phone ringing cuts off my mom and makes us both jump. I check my phone and see that Alex is calling.

"Hello?"

"Hey, sorry, but you weren't answering your texts. I've been outside for the last five minutes. You did say you wanted a ride, right?"

I glance at my phone and see several missed texts, as well as the time. "So sorry. Be right out!"

I hang up and sling my backpack over my shoulders. "I have more questions for you later."

My mom points at me. "Watch your tone. But sure. This is your case. It's only right you get the follow-up details."

I run outside and slide into the passenger seat of Alex's car. "Where's Felix?"

"He said he had something to take care of, so he was going to drive himself from now on." The tips of Alex's ears turn red, and he keeps his eyes on the road. "He's had a car for a while now but never bothered driving since I always do. I think he wanted to give us some space. He's not very subtle. If it makes you uncomfortable, let me know."

I smile reassuringly at him. "Nah, it's cool. Thanks for the ride."

We chat aimlessly the whole way to school, our topics mindless enough for me to obsess over what my mom told me. I'm gonna have to risk public humiliation to try and get Gaby to talk to me about this, because my head is spinning. Suspicious deaths? I mean, yeah, there was that one senior at our school, Alberto. He died while working at the club, but that was an accident. The way my mom phrased it makes it seem like Eli is mixed up in murder. And there's no way she'd go that far, right? Though she did run for a reason . . .

"Danika?"

"Huh? Oh, ham, I guess."

"We stopped talking about sandwiches, like, ten minutes ago. Are you okay?"

"Not really. But I know what I need to do, so it's a start."

He turns off the car after pulling into his spot in the parking lot. Oh, that's right. I forgot that seniors were allowed to park in the lot. Nice perk of riding with him.

"I won't push you, but you know you can talk to me about anything, right?"

He's so earnest, I can't help but reach out and ruffle his hair. God, it's so soft and fluffy. He really is a golden retriever. "Thanks, Alex. I appreciate it. See you at lunch?"

He nods, and I head to my first period class while planning out what to say to Gaby once I finally track her down. It's not going to be easy, but there has to be some way to approach her that won't have her screaming at me in the halls in front of everyone, right?

WRONG. For someone who had to spread a fake story to cover up her sister's absence and save face for her family, she sure doesn't care about putting their business on blast for everyone to hear.

"I don't have your money yet, Danika. My family's too busy trying to afford a lawyer for my sister. The one you got arrested, remember?" Gaby slams her locker closed and glares at me. "So if you're looking to mess up my life even more, I don't really have time for that."

Sheesh, straight heat out of the gate? And why is she talking like I'm the one acting out of pocket when her sister was legit involved in multiple robberies? Committing whole-ass felonies, and I'm the bad guy here?

Yes, I feel guilty about how the case ended. Yes, I hate that Eli is in jail and in danger of being tried as an adult. And yes, I wish everything had gone differently. But I'm not the one who put Eli in this situation. I'm not even the one who pursued this case in the first place. She came to ME.

Maybe it's time that I remind her.

"You need to stop talking to me like I'm the one who got us here. Your parents made those decisions. So did your sister. And guess what? You did too." I step closer and closer to her as I make my point, until she's trapped against her locker and I'm up in her face. "Don't be mad at me because you all fucked around and found out."

Gaby and I are locked in a staring contest, and I'm standing so close, I can feel her trembling. With anger? Fear? Both? Neither?

I don't know how long this standoff would've gone on for if the bell hadn't rung and startled us out of whatever was going on.

Gaby's the first to turn away. "Well, you don't have to worry about me or my dysfunctional family anymore. You're free to enjoy your happy family and perfect boyfriend."

Before I can respond, she shoulders me out of the way and hurries down the hall. So that's it, huh? I watch her back as she disappears into the crowd, and all I can think is *Ingat.*

Take care, Gaby.

"THAT'S IT? THAT'S HOW YOUR FIRST BIG CASE ends?"

It's family mealtime after Kali class, and I'm finally coming clean to Junior and Nicole about all that happened last week. I didn't bother going last Wednesday since that's when shit hit the fan with Eli, and on Friday, Nicole wasn't there and it was easy to keep myself busy helping my aunt so that I didn't have to face Junior and risk spilling everything. But with both of my best friends present (and Gaby noticeably absent), I can't keep avoiding the topic, and I spill every little detail of the case. Gaby already hates me, so might as well add "breaking client confidentiality" to the list of things she can be pissed about.

"I don't know if I should be upset or super impressed that you managed to keep this much a secret for so long," Nicole says. "And, yeah, whatever, you were trying to be professional, but still. How do you find yourself in the middle of cracking a burglary ring with potential murder AND a love triangle and you don't say nothing? I thought we were friends."

"How did you get a love triangle out of everything I said?" I ask.

Junior and Nicole exchange glances, and Nicole gestures for Junior to answer that.

"Gaby's kind of in love with you."

I snort and end up choking on a mouthful of fried rice. After I chug some water to clear my throat, I say, "I told you she hates me five seconds ago. She made that very clear to me and everyone else in the hallway."

Junior sighs. "She's messed up after this thing with her sister, but she's taking it out on you because she's jealous of whatever you've got going on with Alex. Well, that's probably not the only reason, but I bet that's part of it."

"Based on what? You've talked to her, like, twice."

"We've seen how she looks at you, and I did go shopping with her. Half the time we talked fashion, and the other half was her asking questions about you." Nicole rolls her eyes. "She wasn't subtle, and she wasn't trying to be, asking me what's your type and your dating history and all that."

Nicole wouldn't lie to me, so I think back over every time Gaby acted weird and her hostility toward Alex.

"Is that why she's so suspicious of Alex?"

"She legit thinks he's too nice and doesn't trust him, but, yeah, pretty much."

I sit with that. Gaby is—or at least was—interested in me. Is it even worth worrying about considering (a) she won't talk to me, and (b) I don't know how I feel about Alex yet, and he at least confessed to me directly? Oh, and (c) she's my client. Or I guess ex-client now. Do the rules still apply there?

I say as much to my friends. "Why was it easier for me to track down a teenage runaway than figure out my own feelings?"

Junior and Nicole reply in unison, "Because you're you."

Yeah, I am me. Which means I need to tackle this problem Danika Dizon–style.

"I gotta consult the cards."

I'VE BEEN SO BUSY READING CARDS AND GIVING advice to other people that I haven't taken the time to pull for myself in over a month. My Lola Rita (my dad's artsy, woo-woo mom) was the one who gave me my first deck of tarot cards. She taught me how to use the pictures in the cards to interpret them, to understand how they tell a story. From her I learned how to use daily one-card pulls as journal prompts, both to sharpen my skills and also because my Lola Rita worried about the fact that I could analyze other people so well but didn't seem to understand myself in the slightest. Her words, not mine. She's what Filipino people would describe as "maarte," a word that translated literally means "artistic" but basically means "dramatic and extra AF."

She and my Lolo Carlos are currently touring Europe with some of their artist friends. Otherwise I would've gone to her for advice ages ago.

I pull out my OG deck, a classic Rider-Waite-Smith since my lola wanted me to start with the basics before expanding into the more modern interpretations. It's been a while since I've used it, because my clients favor the newer, prettier Star Spinner deck that Junior and Nicole got me for my birthday. The cards in my

OG deck are well worn and fit in my hands as if they belong there. I go through my usual ritual of shuffling while keeping my focus questions in my mind.

What do I do next?

How do I deal with everything that's happened lately?

What decisions do I need to make?

I do a three-card pull as usual, but it's not a spread. A spread is where each card's position means something and can be read as an answer to a particular question. What I'm doing is examining things as a whole, reading the story of the cards like my lola taught me.

Reversed Justice. The High Priestess. Five of Cups.

I have to laugh. For all my talk of not believing in the woo-woo aspect of the cards, sometimes I'll get a pull like this and wonder how the cards can perfectly illustrate my mind.

Wrongs that need to be made right.

Trusting in myself and my intuition.

Emotional conflict and regret.

The cards love putting me on blast. They might as well be yelling, *You know deep down that the case is being mishandled! Trust your gut! You're letting your guilt over the situation hold you back. Pick yourself up and move on.*

I study the Five of Cups. In the image, three of the cups are knocked over, their contents spilled to the ground, wasted. But two cups remain upright. I can spend my time grieving over what was spilled and lost. Or I can focus on those other two cups and the opportunities that I have to make things right.

I gather up the cards, hoping that my gratitude and energy

seep from my fingers to the cards so the deck understands how I'm feeling. Thanks to them, I now have a plan and a way forward.

I've spent so long trying to do things the way I thought my mom would that I never stopped to think about how *I* want to lead my own investigations. If I truly want my mom to respect me as a detective, I need to show her I have my own way of getting things done.

But first, I kinda need her help.

MY MOM GETS ME A MEETING WITH ELI ON WEDNES-day at the Cook County Juvenile Temporary Detention Center. I'm led to a room that's empty except for a table, a couple chairs, and Eli. I dive right in.

"Let me start by saying, I'm so sorry, Eli. You don't have to forgive me, but this is not what I wanted to happen. I would never want to hurt Gaby like that."

She leans back in her chair and studies me. She's not wearing handcuffs or restraints, but my mom told me they'd make her wear them if she started acting aggressive.

"And yet, she's hurt. So your intentions don't really mean a lot to me." I flinch, and she smiles. It's not a nice smile. "She won't talk to you, huh? I refuse to speak to her when she comes here, but I know my sister. Let me guess, she's doing the ice queen routine?"

She continues talking before I say anything. "No, she really likes you, which means she can't ignore you. She wants you to hurt the way she is. She probably blew up at you when you tried to talk to her at school. Made sure it was loud and public, like she was trying to burn everything down."

I nod.

"That's my little sister. Loyal, even to a screwup like me. She feels too much, too often."

Eli falls silent, tracing a pattern over and over on the tabletop with her fingertip.

"Why did you agree to see me?" I ask her.

"Because you didn't only ruin my life by prompting your mom to call the cops. You also put Gaby in danger. There's a reason I won't talk to her. There's a reason I was in hiding. But no one cares about that. They only want me to spill so that all the rich people who lost pocket change will feel safer."

Okay, the Gaby tidbit is very, VERY alarming, but I need to make sure I get all the facts first so I know what my next steps should be.

"You wanna talk about the suspicious deaths?"

"I didn't kill anybody, if that's what you're asking."

"Do you know anything?"

She studies her cuticles, not bothering to answer me.

"Eli, you wanted me here for a reason. You mentioned that Gaby is in danger. I can't help if I don't know what's going on. In danger from what? From who?"

She curls her fingers into a fist but doesn't lift her head.

"Please, Eli. This is about more than the case for me. You're clearly scared about something. What is it?"

"I . . . may have seen something. Overheard something about one of the burglaries that went wrong. About the rich old guy they found beaten to death. It's been on the news a lot lately."

I flash back to my mom watching the news story about her old lawyer acquaintance who was murdered. "You *saw* that old guy get killed?"

She shakes her head. "I wasn't there when he was murdered. But I might know who did it. They didn't admit to anything. But they got into an argument over it, and I watched . . . I watched Alberto get pushed down the stairs."

"Was he part of the burglaries?"

"Yeah, but he was trying to get out. I don't think he killed the old guy, but I think he was there when it happened. I heard him say that he didn't sign on for murder, that he was out, and then . . . and then they pushed him. It wasn't an accident like the cops are saying."

Holy. Crap.

"Who did it?"

She shakes her head. Yeah, that'd be too easy, wouldn't it?

"Did they see you?"

Her faces crumples. "That's why I ran away. I didn't want to be next. Emily, the girl I'm staying with . . . is in the same position as me. That's why she took me in. She's got someone at Chicago Glen who lets us know what's going on. But then Gaby started poking her nose into my business, and now she works at the country club. If I talk, they'll hurt her. I know how they operate. I've seen how brutal they can be. The only way I can protect her is by not talking."

I can see her picturing the horrifying fate that awaits her sister if she does.

I grab her hand and squeeze. "We can protect her. If you don't trust the cops, Gaby can stay with my family. Between a private detective, a world-famous martial artist, a mystery author, plus me and my cousins, we've got enough brains and muscle to handle it."

I can see in her eyes that she doesn't trust me. But I can also see that she's near her breaking point. Despite my actions being the reason she's in juvie, I think she can feel my sincerity in wanting to keep Gaby safe. Maybe that's enough.

"If you can get Gaby and my parents to agree to let her stay with you, have all of them come to me, and say that they'll do it, then, yeah. I'll cooperate. But I won't talk until then."

I need to convince Gaby, who hates me, and their parents, who also hate me, to entrust the safety of their other daughter to me after putting their eldest daughter in jail. Cool cool cool.

"I'll do my best. Thanks, Eli. And, again, I'm sorry."

"You better take care of my sister. I got myself into this mess, so I don't care what happens to me anymore. But she didn't do anything wrong. Keep her out of trouble."

"I will."

"I mean it, Danika."

"So do I. Your sister means a lot to me. I won't let anything happen to her."

"You better not. I haven't approved of your relationship, by the way. You better prove you deserve her."

"What're you—"

The juvenile detention officer who's been keeping an eye on the room opens the door. "Time's up!"

Before I leave, I ask one last question. "Does Caleb know why you left?"

Her eyes soften, and she shakes her head. "I didn't want to endanger him either. I'm mad that I let myself get talked into this, but that's my fault, not his. He's well meaning, not scheming."

"Good to know. Thanks again, Eli."

My mom's waiting for me in the lobby, and as we make our way back to the car, I report everything Eli told me.

"I don't think Eli has any particular loyalty to whoever's at the top, so I figured she had to be scared about retaliation. I've already talked to the detectives on the case, and they suspected the same thing, but she refuses to speak to them, so their hands are tied. If doing this will get Eli to open up, I'm sure we can get them to provide additional support." My mom glances over at me. "Do you want me to approach Mr. and Mrs. Delgado?"

I nod. "I'll text Gaby, but I doubt it'll do any good. Probably best for you to talk to their parents and have them persuade Gaby to cooperate. I know you don't like her, but this is our best option if we want to help Eli."

"I don't dislike Gaby. I understand her a little too well, and that makes me nervous for you. But I would never turn her away, not with so much chaos around her. I'll do my best to make them see reason."

"Thanks, Mommy."

I kind of always thought of my mom as perfect, even when she was making choices about my life that I didn't agree with.

But after this whole thing, I finally see that my mom is a regular person. She tries her best, does what she thinks is right, and her actions are not always going to have the best consequences. Same as anyone else. That's both reassuring and scary, and I sorta hate it. There's only one thing that'll help when I'm feeling mixed-up like this.

I turn to my mom. "Can we pick up Daddy and Daniel and go out for boba tea?"

CHAPTER
TWENTY-FIVE

"YOU WANTED TO SEE ME, MRS. WHITTLE?"

She glances up from a sheaf of documents that she stuffs into a file folder when she sees me. "Ah yes, Danika. Please sit down."

Mrs. Whittle smiles. "I would like to extend an opportunity to you. Some of the other staff members have had wonderful things to say about your tarot reading talents, and I thought it would be fun if we could set aside some time during your usual hours on the weekend to read cards for our interested members. Because you'll be on the clock, you'll get your usual wages, but you can earn tips from the members you read for. Would that be something you're interested in?"

I only earn fifteen dollars an hour at the club while my readings cost twenty dollars each and take maybe ten minutes, tops. Reading cards is way more fun than working the front desk, but it consumes a lot of my energy. But it'll be worth it when I get Veronica up and running, right?

Mrs. Whittle must understand the reason behind my hesitation because she adds, "Our members can be very generous tippers. How about we book you for a couple hours this Saturday as a trial? If you like it, we can continue doing it every weekend. If not, you can work your regular shift as always. Does that work for you?"

"Yes, that's perfect. Thanks, Mrs. Whittle."

She stands up, and I follow suit. "I look forward to this experiment, Danika. I'll make sure to stop by for a reading myself. I can't wait to see what revelations you have for me."

She holds out her hand, and we shake on it.

"HEY, YOU'RE RIDING WITH ME."

Gaby steps in front of me and Alex as we're about to exit to the school parking lot Friday afternoon.

"Excuse me? You've ignored my texts, screamed at me in front of a bunch of people, dodged me at work, and now I'm just supposed to be like, 'Oh yeah, sure, thanks for the ride'?" I gesture toward Alex. "I have a ride, and we've got places to be, so . . ."

I try to step around her, but she plants herself solidly in my way and wraps both of her hands around my wrists. Her hold is loose, almost tentative. Her touch is like a question, a plea. Her voice comes out just as soft.

"I'm sorry. Please. I really need to talk to you." She pauses, glancing over at Alex, who's watching us carefully. He would step in if he thought it was necessary, but he's waiting for me to signal if I want him to or not.

I shake my head at him. "It's fine, Alex. She's right; we do need to talk. I'll text you later, okay?"

He smiles, but his heart isn't in it. "Tell your family I said hi. Pick you up at the usual time tomorrow?"

Before I can respond, Gaby says, "You don't have to worry about that anymore. She'll be riding with me."

Irritation flashes over his face. "You don't get to decide that for her. And you also don't get to start and stop your friendship whenever it's convenient for you. Do you have any idea how bad you hurt her? You—"

Alex starts getting more and more heated as he talks, stepping so close to Gaby that she's forced to let go of my wrists and hold her hands up to stop him from getting in her face. It's easy for me to forget how big Alex is because he wears his height a little awkwardly and he gives off "gentle giant" vibes. I've never witnessed him being anything but super chill and thoughtful. But seeing his face flushed and twisted in anger, seeing how he towers over Gaby, who no one would ever call petite, I have to admit . . . he's intimidating AF. Even Gaby, with all her bravado, has nothing to say.

Alex glances down at Gaby's hands on his chest, trying to keep him at a distance, and I think we both notice that her hands are trembling. He places his hands gently over hers before closing his eyes and taking a few deep breaths. When he opens his eyes, it's like he's come back to himself.

"I'm so sorry. I didn't mean to scare you." His voice is soft and a little raspy.

Gaby snatches her hands away. "You didn't scare me. You—"

"No, I'm sorry. I shouldn't have done that. I know better. *I know better*," he repeats. He wipes his hands furiously at his eyes, as if trying to stop himself from crying. "I need to go. Danika, you should start riding with Gaby again."

"Why? I thought—"

"I'll see you around. Bye!" Alex throws the door open and sprints to the parking lot without looking back.

"That was weird." I turn back to Gaby. "What did you want to talk about?"

"Not here. Let's wait till we're in the car."

We walk to her parking spot in silence, and as I slide into the passenger seat, I can't help but notice the stuffed duffel bag and suitcase in the back seat.

"You going somewhere?"

"I'm staying at your place for a while. Your mom talked to my parents and convinced them it was for the best. For me and also for Eli."

"I'm surprised they actually listened to her."

"My dad was the one who was against it, actually. He had some macho idea that it was his job to protect his family, but your mom shut that down quick. He eventually agreed that I could stay with your family if the police also promised to keep an eye on me. The cops said they couldn't assign someone to follow me everywhere, but they'd increase patrols around school, work, and your place. Your mom said your family would handle the rest."

I sit there digesting. "So Eli's finally going to talk, huh?"

"Once her lawyer confirms that protections are in place like she asked." Gaby laughs. "Weird way for me to find out how much my sister cares about me, huh?"

She says it jokingly, but I can hear the edges of sadness in that statement. "I guess we never really know how we feel about someone until it gets tested like this. There's a chance for your family to fix your relationships."

"You say you've seen some dark stuff as part of your mom's cases, but you're still disgustingly optimistic." Gaby shakes her head slightly, a hint of a smile on her lips. "I don't know how you do it."

"It's like the Star card in tarot. You have to keep moving toward that light at the end of the tunnel. You have to believe things will get better. You have to believe that what you do makes a difference." I glance out the window at the familiar worn-down buildings as we draw close to my aunt's martial arts studio. "My dad says that's why he and my mom are drawn to the work that they do. That their jobs involve them digging deep down and seeing the absolute worst sides of people. But also sometimes the best. And that bit of hope keeps them going day after day."

Gaby parallel parks in front of the studio and leans back in her seat, keeping her eyes straight ahead. "That sounds like something your dad would say. You're lucky to have him."

"I know."

AFTER CLASS, I'M SITTING WITH GABY, JUNIOR, AND Nicole around the low table when my cousins come join us.

"I hear we're on bodyguard duty," Joemar says, plopping

down next to Gaby. "You've got nothing to fear now that I'm here."

He strikes an All Might pose, which I'm sure goes over her head since she doesn't seem like an anime fan. Though I can probably change that.

Gaby laughs and acts like she's swooning. "My hero!"

Andrew takes a seat across from her. "Seriously, though, how are you doing? Anything we need to know?"

Gaby shakes her head. "I haven't noticed anything weird, so I think Eli's overreacting. I appreciate everyone's help, though. Your family has been way too nice to mine."

"You never know," I warn her. "The way she was talking, it seemed like whoever's in charge is either someone with easy access to us or someone with mad connections. Maybe to a particular gang or something."

"You think someone at your job bangs?" Joemar asks.

"It's hard to say. Because of the dress code, everyone wears a uniform and none of us can have visible tattoos. I don't see most of them outside of work, so I can't check for logos or colors or anything like that."

Andrew says, "We'll keep an eye out to see if we recognize anyone. Maybe your mom can check out their employee files to see if she can find a link."

"I know she only managed a surface-level search since she was on the case for such a short time. Maybe she can convince Mrs. Whittle to cooperate if she offers to help with the burglary ring problem. It can't look good for the club for their members to be among the targets."

"Sounds good. You talk to your mom, and we'll handle the rest."

My aunt calls for my cousins, and they go to help her finish setting up.

"I'm guessing you two know what's going on? Considering they were talking about the case in front of you?" Gaby asks Junior and Nicole. When they nod, she turns to me with a scowl. "What happened to client confidentiality?"

"We only found out recently. You know, after the case was over and you stopped talking to her? So maybe watch the attitude, yeah?" Nicole swells up protectively, and I can tell she's ready to throw hands for me.

Junior jumps in too. "Danika was super messed up by how the case ended, and she came to us for advice on how to fix things with you. But I'm starting to think there ain't nothing to fix. You're only around when it's convenient for you. Then things get a little tough, and you bounce. She don't need someone like that in her life."

I stare at Junior and Nicole, my two best friends in the world seated on either side of me, and wonder what I did to deserve them. Before, my instinct would be to step in and smooth things over, to make things less awkward. Not anymore. As much as I want to make up with Gaby, they're right. She's hurt me enough when I'm only trying to help. So I'm gonna let their words cook for a bit.

I reach down to squeeze my friends' hands in appreciation and smile at them both before getting up. "I've got to help Tita Baby. Talk to you all later."

Gaby's eyes widen, and she looks like I've thrown her to the wolves. Good.

After family meal is over and we've all cleaned up, I rejoin Gaby and my friends.

"See you two on Monday?" I ask.

"You know it." Nicole smiles sweetly at Gaby. "Don't forget what we talked about."

It may be my imagination, but Gaby appears pale AF as she returns Nicole's smile.

I pull Junior aside. "Do I want to know what happened?"

"She knows what's up now, and that's all that matters." He tugs at the end of my braid. "Be careful, okay?"

I give him a hug, and he squeezes me tight in return. I pull Nicole in for a hug too.

"Thanks," I whisper to them both.

Nicole gives me a lip-smacking kiss on the cheek. "We got you, girl. Now go handle your business."

Gaby and I make our way to her car, with my cousins trailing close behind to follow us home in their car. We don't talk much on the drive to my house, and we arrive at the same time as my dad and Daniel and my cousins. Joemar and Andrew help Gaby bring her things inside and check in with my mom real quick.

"You're leaving at eight tomorrow morning, right?" Joemar asks. When we confirm the time, he says, "Sounds good. I'll be here in the morning to escort you to work, and my brother will be waiting for you once you finish. Don't leave the building until you know he's outside."

"You guys won't be able to get close to the building, though," I say. "We park in the employee lot behind the club, so it should be fine. We'll meet up with you once we're on the street."

"I don't like that. Someone could easily attack you while you're walking to your car," Andrew says. "Maybe we can get Alex to walk you? We don't want him to know why, though, so we'll need to think of a good excuse."

"No way. I don't trust him," Gaby says.

"Alex?!" my cousins say in unison.

"Alex is the best guy I know, and I'm including me and my brother in that statement," Joemar says.

Daniel, who wasn't really following the conversation since he was busy feeding Buchi, runs over when he hears Alex's name. "I love Alex! He taught me how to train Buchi, and she can do lots of tricks now. Want to see?"

Gaby's expression is growing strained, and my mom—of all people—steps in to help. "Anak, it's getting late. Let's go over your homework and get ready for your shower and bed, okay? You can talk to Gaby more tomorrow. I'm sure she'll be happy to watch Buchi's tricks when she's not so tired."

Gaby smiles in relief. "I'd love to see those tricks when we get home from work tomorrow. Is that okay?"

"Of course! Buchi would love that. Right, Buchi?" The puppy at Daniel's feet wags her tail rapidly as if agreeing with him. "She says yes."

At my mom's urging, Daniel says good night to everyone, and Buchi follows her human to his room. We all wait until he's out of earshot before my cousins continue our previous discussion.

"Why don't you trust Alex? Has he done or said anything weird? Do you think he's involved?" Andrew asks.

Gaby refuses to meet my eye. "We shouldn't let our guard down around him. We don't know who Eli's boss is, and Alex seems to know everyone at work. He might be completely innocent, but he could let something slip to the wrong person. The fewer people who know, the better."

Andrew nods. "All right, how about you call me and keep me on speakerphone until we meet at my car on the street? At least I'll be able to hear if anything goes wrong."

We agree on that course of action, and my cousins head home. My dad is the only one left in the living room with us.

"Welcome back, Gaby. We'll try to make things as comfortable as possible. Can I get you anything to drink?"

"No thanks, Ben. Can you point me to where I'm sleeping, please? I'd like to get my things set up."

"You can either sleep on the pullout sofa downstairs in my office or on a mat on the floor of Danika's room," my dad says. "The sofa bed is more comfortable, but we thought we'd give you a choice."

"You said the sofa is in your office? I don't want to disturb your work. I'm okay with the floor as long as I can get some pillows and blankets."

"Of course. Let me just grab a banig, and I'll meet you in her room."

My dad goes to find the old woven mats we sometimes sleep on in the summertime while I lead Gaby to my room.

It's small, and most of the space is taken up by my twin bed and the cheap table I use as a desk. A used dresser and secondhand bookshelf take up almost an entire wall, and the latter is full of my dad's books and other mystery novels he's given me, puzzle games, old journals and notebooks, plus some comics and manga, most of which were passed down from my cousins.

Gaby selects a volume of *My Dress-Up Darling* and reads the back before opening it up to a random page. "This sounds cute. What do you—WHOA!"

She has it open to a particular two-page spread, and I jump forward to yank it from her hands. "It's not what you think! The story is actually really wholesome and sweet; only certain parts can be a little spicy and—"

I am SWEATING as I try to explain my way out of some anime BS, and my dad chooses that moment to knock on the partially closed door. "Can I come in?"

"Yes!" I yank the door fully open, and my dad comes in with one of our smaller banigs.

Gaby stands by my desk while he unrolls the mat and lays it down between my bed and bookshelf. It barely fits. While he's doing that, I go grab her a couple blankets, pillows, and my dad's old sleeping bag in case that's not enough.

"I figured you're not used to sleeping on the floor, so hopefully these will help," I say, setting everything on top of the banig.

"I'm not that much of a princess," Gaby says, holding up the sleeping bag. "My dad used to take us camping when we were kids. My mom made him eventually upgrade to a cabin on the lake, but for a while we did the whole tent thing. It was fun."

"Do you girls need anything else?" my dad asks.

I glance over at Gaby, who shakes her head. "I think we're good. Thanks, Daddy. Good night."

"Thanks, Ben. Good night."

My dad closes the door, and it's the two of us again. We seem to do fine whenever we're around people, but when we're alone, it's like we don't know where to look or what to say or what we should do with our hands.

I clear my throat. "We only have one bathroom, so you might want to get in there before Daniel takes his bath. Do you need anything?"

"I brought all my stuff, so no worries. And it's still pretty early. I can wait until after he's done to take my shower."

I sit on my bed and pick at my threadbare bedsheets while watching Gaby arrange her sleeping area and unpack her paja-mas. "I don't have a closet, but I cleared out the bottom drawer of my dresser if you want to unpack some of your clothes."

"Thanks, but I don't want to put you out. Besides, it's prob-ably better for me to stay packed since I don't want to stay too long." Gaby sits cross-legged on top of the sleeping bag. "Dan-ika . . . I'm so sorry. I know that everything that happened with Eli was not your fault. You were only trying to help and I've been the absolute worst lately. I want you to know that I'm grateful for everything. And that your friendship means a lot to me."

I raise an eyebrow. "Could've fooled me."

She winces. "I deserve that. Ugh . . . There are so many things going on right now that piss me off, and I took it out on you because you're safe."

"I'm safe?" My voice weirdly breaks, and I clear my throat

and try again. "I mean, I'm glad you feel safe with me. And there's a lot we both got wrong, so I appreciate your apology. Friends?"

I stick out my hand to shake on it, and she kinda stares at it for a moment. I can't read the expression on her face, and I worry I messed up again, but she sighs and shakes my hand.

"Sure. Friends."

We sit in companionable silence for a bit, Gaby reading the first volume of My Dress-Up Darling and me going over an English essay I've pushed to the last minute that's due on Monday. I close my Chromebook and am about to sit beside Gaby on the floor when there's a knock on my door. I open it, and my mom enters, leaning on the doorway.

"Daniel finished his bath. He's got enough time for a hot drink before bed, and he wanted to know if you can join us."

Gaby scrambles up off the floor. "Of course. I'll have whatever you're having."

My mom raises an eyebrow. "I'm having red wine. And before you ask, no, I am not one of those 'cool' moms."

"Then I'll have whatever Daniel's having."

"Hot chocolate it is."

We follow my mom to the kitchen, where my dad is heating a small pot of water and soy milk for him and Daniel since Daniel's lactose intolerant.

"Can you add extra for us, Daddy? We'll both have some."

"Way ahead of you." My dad drops in a few discs of tablea and whisks the mixture over low heat until the chocolate is melted and the drink is nice and foamy. He pours the tsokolate into four small mugs and brings them to the table, then plates a few suman and a cut-up mango before sitting down. "Help yourselves."

We settle around the table, and everyone but my mom helps themselves to the snacks. She seems content sipping her glass of wine. Buchi is curled up under Daniel's chair, and Gaby asks him questions about the dog, which he happily chatters about for the next half hour or so. He eventually runs out of steam, though, and once his head and eyelids start drooping, my mom sets down her glass.

"Bedtime, Daniel. Say good night."

He obediently gets up and sets his dirty cup in the sink before gesturing for Buchi to follow him. "Good"—yawn—"night."

My parents go to put Daniel to bed and soon return. We begin the talk we've all been waiting for.

Gaby starts by saying, "Thank you again for taking me in. I know my sister is being unreasonable, but I appreciate you supporting us." She fiddles with the banana leaf on her plate for a moment before adding, "I know this isn't your case anymore, but I was wondering if you could dig up more information on that burglary ring?"

"Why would we do that?" My mom can be HARSH.

But that doesn't stop Gaby. "Eli says she has no proof that the person she saw push Alberto is also the big boss, since she doesn't know who that is. She can't even prove what she saw because it's not like she has pictures or video. It's her word against theirs. And she's not sure that the police will care enough about Alberto's death to cut her a deal if they can't also tie it to the burglary ring and the rich old guy who was killed."

"You want my family to find evidence connecting what Eli

witnessed to the larger criminal enterprise? In the hopes that it will reduce her sentence?" Mom responds.

"You put it way better than I did, but, yes."

"And why should I continue to put my family's lives in danger to do that? Isn't it enough that we're letting you stay here and offering protection?"

"Is it money? I'm sure if you talk to Mrs. Whittle, she'll be able to get the funds since you'll be helping the reputation of the country club."

"The money would certainly help my livelihood, which would be at stake if I ruin the club's reputation, but I repeat: Why should I let my daughter continue risking her life for this case? Or my nephews? Don't you think we've already done our part?"

Gaby glances at me, but I stay quiet. My mom has a point. Our family has spent weeks investigating and protecting and extending a hand. She must realize that because she meets my mother's gaze. Not in defiance or anything like the last time Gaby was here. But out of respect.

"You're right. You've all gone above and beyond, and I promise I'll find a way to make sure you get paid. Because I need your help. Desperately. I'm also sure plenty of news outlets will want to interview the person who took down a gang of thieves. Danika told me you love good publicity."

Well, good FREE publicity, that is. It's not like my mom wants her face on a bus stop bench or anything. That's cringe. Give her an opportunity to rub her success in her family's face for zero dollars, however? She will absolutely jump on that.

My mom finally smiles. "Danika is right. Okay, Gaby. You make sure that my family stays safe and I get paid, and I'm on the case."

Gaby holds out her hand, and my mother shakes it. "You've got yourself a deal."

CHAPTER
TWENTY-SIX

WEALTHY COUNTRY CLUB MEMBERS LOVE TAROT readings. I spent most of my shift on Saturday doing consultations. By Sunday, because of its popularity, Mrs. Whittle pulls me from my front desk duties and has me cater exclusively to our members. She even makes sure to stop by for a reading at the end.

"What kind of reading would you like, Mrs. Whittle? You can ask about something you need advice for, or I can do a general reading focusing on life, work, love, et cetera."

"A general life reading should be fine. I've never had a tarot consultation before, but I'd love to see why our members and employees are so fond of them."

"I'll do a basic past, present, and future reading, then." After shuffling and cutting the cards, I lay the three cards facedown in front of me. "It's exactly what it sounds like, with the cards representing what your life was like in the past, what your present situation is like, and what your future could be."

She nods in understanding, and I proceed to flip over the cards. "The World. You used to be on top of the world and managed to accomplish big things. You've probably enjoyed quite a bit of travel, and your life was infused with a feeling of satisfaction. You felt whole. Complete."

Mrs. Whittle perks up. "Not to brag, but you're absolutely right. I've worked hard to get to where I am."

I tap on the reversed Four of Swords. "Unfortunately, no one stays on top forever. This card in the present position implies a feeling of stagnation. You might be frustrated at your current lack of progress or how the life or relationship you worked hard for is now stuck in a rut. This card, combined with the reversed Page of Coins, which is in the future position, hints at you having big dreams and goals but not taking the action you need to make them happen. If you want to be back on top again, you need to remember your original motivation and make the appropriate moves."

Mrs. Whittle stares down at the cards. "Anything else?"

"Um, the cards also indicate burnout and/or restlessness. It's okay to step away from a relationship or situation until you have the energy to make a proper decision. Also, failure can be a learning experience."

Mrs. Whittle grabs my hands and squeezes them. "Danika, I'm truly impressed. I've been wrestling with something for a long time, something that could affect everyone here with my selfishness, but I didn't know what to do. You've given me the courage to do the right thing." She reaches into her clutch and pulls out a crisp one-hundred-dollar bill. "Please don't tell anyone about this reading. And thanks again."

She slides the money toward me and hurries away before I can respond. It's not like I'd fight her over the amount, but I can't help but feel like it's meant to cover up something. She mentioned a decision that affects everyone here at the club . . . Could she be the boss that Caleb and Eli were talking about? Did she intentionally hire Gaby as leverage?

Sounds a little far-fetched, but is it? I mean, she's the one in charge of hiring. No one knows as much about each employee's background and personality as she does. That means she knows who's desperate or ballsy enough to want in. The more I think about it, the more I'm convinced I'm right, and my reading was a sign for her to stop. Ordinarily, giving up a life of crime would be a good thing, but if she wants out, she'll likely destroy any evidence connecting her to the burglaries in the city, and I can't have that.

Luckily, it's the end of my shift, and I can share my suspicions with Gaby and my family soon. I clear my space and grab my things out of my locker and meet up with Gaby. I hustle Gaby out of the building and call Andrew on speakerphone as promised, since it's a long walk to where we're parked.

"Hey, I might have a lead. I can't talk about it yet, but we're walking to the car now. Can you—" I cut myself off and whip around to see if anyone's following us. No one's there, but I can't shake off the feeling that we're being watched.

"Danika? Are you okay? Do you need me to—"

"No, it's fine. I'm being paranoid." Gaby and I get into her Audi, and I continue the conversation. "We're in the car now, and we'll head to the meeting spot."

"Keep me on speakerphone till we all reach the house."

"Got it." I set the phone in the cupholder space between me and Gaby. "Gaby, how was your shift?"

We chitchat for a few minutes as Gaby makes her way out of the parking lot and we meet Andrew at his car. After a brief greeting, we continue driving toward my house with Andrew following behind us.

We're about halfway there when Andrew's voice suddenly comes from the phone. "Danika, five o'clock, two cars back. Gray SUV."

"I clock it. It's been following us since we met up with you, hasn't it?"

Despite the situation we're in, Andrew sounds pleased that I detected it. "Your training is really coming along. I didn't think you'd notice."

"Yeah, good for Danika for leveling up her detective skills, but what the hell should I do?" Gaby is gripping the steering wheel and glancing over her shoulder every five seconds.

"First, focus on the road. Don't get distracted. We can't lead them to the house, so we should go somewhere else. Preferably public and busy and well lit." Andrew's quiet for a moment. "Head to Chinatown."

"Chi Cafe or Three Happiness?" I ask. Both are open late and would make a great place to kill time.

"Chi Cafe is open later, so head there. Can you call Joemar and let him know what's up? We might need backup. But don't hang up. Put me on hold and merge the call."

"Got it." I follow his instructions, and his brother picks up. "Hey, Joemar. Gaby and I are being followed. Andrew wants us to meet up at Chi Cafe. Are you free?"

There's some rustling in the background before Joemar

responds. "Just grabbed my keys. I'll meet you there. You probably don't want to, but you better tell your mom what's happening."

When I don't answer, Andrew chimes in. "You're going to have to eventually. Who knows how long we've gotta wait out this person? Your mom is gonna wonder why you're not back from work yet. Plus, Joemar and I report to her. I don't wanna snitch, and you don't want your mom asking why you weren't being up-front."

Joemar says, "Handle it, cuzzo. I gotta stop by your house anyway to borrow your mom's car. See y'all soon."

And he hangs up on us.

"He's got a point," Gaby says. "Your mom is already upset that I'm putting you all in danger. She's going to hate me if something happens and she wasn't kept in the loop."

I groan. "Fine, calling my mom. Putting you on hold again, Andrew."

I select her contact, and she answers immediately. "Danika, are you okay?"

"We're fine, Mommy. But, um, we think there's someone following us. Andrew is having us meet at Chi Cafe in Chinatown. Joemar's heading there too, but he's stopping at the house first." I pause, wondering if there's anything else I should add. "It's probably nothing, but I thought I should give you a heads-up just in case."

My mom's silence is so loud, I can almost hear her processing everything I said and trying to come up with a plan. "I need to talk to your father. I'll call you back."

She hangs up, and I switch back to Andrew to relay

everything. "I contacted her. She's supposed to get back to me after she talks to my dad."

A call from my mom comes in.

"Dang, that was fast. Hold on. That's her." I change over to my mom. "Hey, Mommy. What's the plan?"

"Tita Baby's going to meet you there. Since you'll be with your cousins, it will hopefully look like you and Gaby are meeting up with the family for a late dinner in Chinatown. And if they try to approach you, Tita Baby is better equipped to handle the situation than I am. She's got both combat and de-escalation training, though I hope it won't come to that."

"Thanks, Mommy. Let me tell Andrew and Joemar."

"Keep me updated, and don't do anything foolish, Danika. Ingat."

I check the rearview mirror and spot the gray SUV still trailing us. It could be nothing, since gray is the most common car color and there's a possibility it's not the same car that we first spotted. It's too far away for me to see the license plate. That said, I'm not taking any chances.

I three-way call my cousins to go over the plan. "Andrew, can you tell if that car is the same one that's been following us? I can't see the license plate."

"It definitely is. The windows are tinted, so I can't see inside, but I got a picture of the license plate. I sent it to your mom already."

"Cool. Well, not cool. But what's everyone's ETA? We're about fifteen minutes away."

Even on a Sunday night, Chinatown is packed. Great for

trying to shake off a tail, not so great for trying to find parking. Luckily, a few spots open up in the lot across from the plaza, and my cousins meet us at Gaby's car. My instinct is to rush to the restaurant and get out of the open space, but I don't want to tip off the person following us by acting strange. The four of us deliberately take our time walking through the square, even stopping by to pet the zodiac statues as we head for our destination.

We're about to enter Chi Cafe when Joemar pulls out his phone. "Hello? Yeah, we just got here. You're where? Hold on. I'll go find you."

He "hangs up"—from my vantage point, I can see that he faked that call—and says, "That was my mom. She needs help finding the place, so you all go on ahead and get a table for us."

"Got it." Andrew nods, and the two hold a silent conversation with their eyes before Joemar hurries off.

The restaurant is bustling, but there are still plenty of seats, so we're shown to our table immediately. Andrew fires off a text real quick before leaning toward me and Gaby.

"Joemar's scoping out the area. I let my mom know to call him when she gets here so they can meet up. If there's more than one person watching, we don't want to draw their attention."

"Makes sense," I say, opening up the huge menu. "Gaby, is this your first time here?"

"I've been to Chinatown before but not this place. What do you recommend?"

"Depends on your mood. The menu can be overwhelming, so for you, I'd recommend the 'Congee' and 'On Rice' sections. We can also order family style and share whatever looks good to you."

By the time Joemar and Tita Baby join us, we've decided on a big bowl of salty chicken congee, salt-and-pepper smelt, walnut shrimp, and two stir-fried dishes to share. Joemar adds on some beef ribs, and Tita Baby asks for crab and corn soup. The table is absolutely brimming with the fifty million dishes we've ordered, and we waste no time digging in.

"Thanks for inviting us, Gaby. I know you want to show your appreciation for the Kali lessons, but you don't have to treat me. I'm just happy to have a night out," Tita Baby says a little too loudly.

So that's the cover story we're going with.

"Way to make us look bad, Gaby," Joemar jokes. "Now Andrew and I are gonna have to hear about what a nice girl you are and why don't we ever do things like this, et cetera, et cetera."

Andrew adds, "At least we remembered the name of your favorite restaurant."

I take a sip of tea. "Were you able to find parking nearby, Tita? We had to circle a couple times before we found a spot."

"I ended up parking on Wentworth. It's a bit of a walk, but I prefer stretching my legs after a big meal. So it all works out."

That walk also means she can survey the area and see if that gray SUV is still around or if anyone else is watching us.

The rest of the night passes in idle chitchat like that—nothing about the case or that hints that we're still investigating. Just a normal night out.

After a couple hours of feasting and endless pots of tea, my aunt decides enough time has passed for her to do some surveillance outside. She returns a couple minutes later to report that she didn't spot anything. She orders Hong Kong French toast for us to split as our dessert, and after about fifteen minutes or so, my cousins get up to do their recon. By the time they make it back, the French toast is all gone, and we're sipping our final cups of tea. Tita Baby pays the bill while we're in the bathroom even though Gaby said she'd take care of it, which is totally a sneaky Asian auntie thing to do.

My cousins and aunt follow me and Gaby as we make the twentysomething-minute drive to my place. None of us spot the gray SUV at any point, so whoever was driving must've gotten tired of waiting and left. When we get home, we go straight to my mom.

"It's a Sunday night, so I haven't been able to run that license plate yet, but I'll take care of that tomorrow. I'm glad nothing happened. Thanks for helping out with so little notice," my mom says to Tita Baby and my cousins.

"Anytime," Tita Baby says. "It's been a long day, and I'm sure the girls need their rest. You've all got school tomorrow."

MONDAY AT SCHOOL IS AS UNEVENTFUL AS OUR anticlimactic Sunday night.

I start to think that creepy SUV was a coincidence and maybe we weren't being followed, that maybe we're being paranoid.

Until Gaby and I get to her car and see that all the windows have been smashed in.

CHAPTER TWENTY-SEVEN

"I THOUGHT YOU WERE GOING TO PROTECT HER."

Mrs. Delgado and my mom rushed to meet us after Gaby and I called them. My mom helped Gaby file a police report, and once the proper paperwork is done and the cops are gone, Mrs. Delgado confronts my mother.

Gaby tries to get between them. "Mom, stop! This isn't her fault."

Mrs. Delgado ignores her. "You promised that your family and the police would all be watching out for my daughter. So how did this happen?"

"Mrs. Delgado, I'm sorry. I can't imagine how scary it was to receive that call, but luckily, your daughter is fine. I'm sure she's a little shaken up, so maybe you could—"

"Fine? She is not fine! Do you see this?" Mrs. Delgado sweeps her arm toward the wrecked car. "Do you have any idea how much it'll cost to fix this?"

Gaby gapes. "Is that all you care about? The money? I could've—"

Mrs. Delgado continues screaming at my mom. "What if she was inside when they attacked? What if they decide this isn't enough and they come after her?" Mrs. Delgado starts sobbing. "Eli is already going to jail because I'm a terrible mother. I can't lose Gaby too!"

Mrs. Delgado's whole body is heaving with the strength of her cries, and Gaby wraps her arms around her mother in a tight hug.

"I'm here, Mom. I'm here. It'll be okay." Gaby repeats this over and over as she and her mother rock slowly in place until her mother's sobs die down.

"I must look like such a mess." Mrs. Delgado digs around in her purse for something that she can't seem to find. My mom reaches into her own bag and pulls out a packet of tissues, which Gaby's mom accepts. She wipes her face and blows her nose, taking a moment to compose herself. "Thank you. I'm sorry for snapping at you like that. But you must understand—"

"Of course I do. Did you forget that my own daughter is putting herself on the line to support yours?"

Mrs. Delgado's eyebrows shoot up. "Truly, I didn't even think of the toll this could be taking on you, Danika. Thank you so much for watching over my Gaby."

I nod at her in acknowledgment but don't say anything. I nudge Gaby forward, signaling that she shouldn't let this moment pass by.

Gaby hesitates before taking her mom's hands in hers. "We have a lot to talk about. You and me and Dad and hopefully Eli. When this is all over, we really need to sit down as a family. But right now, I need to be with the Dizons. Please don't make this any more difficult than it has to be."

Mrs. Delgado straightens up and squeezes her daughter's hands before releasing them. "I'll explain everything to your father. Call him later, okay? He'll never say it, but he misses you."

"Will do. And I . . . I miss him too."

"Well, then." Mrs. Delgado hikes her purse higher before turning her attention to my mom. "She's in your care."

"Thank you for trusting us," my mom says.

I echo her statement, and Mrs. Delgado nods at us before heading to her car and driving away.

"You two ready to head back home? I already told Tita Baby that you wouldn't be at Kali tonight. Your father and Daniel are busy preparing a special dinner for us."

"I'm starving. Let's go home, Danika."

I smile at Gaby referring to my house as "home," but on the drive there, I can't help but wonder: *Followed on Sunday, smashed car windows on Monday. What is Tuesday going to bring?*

AS SOON AS I WALK INTO WORK THE NEXT DAY, I know something is off. There's a weird energy in the air, like everyone's on edge, both guests and staff alike. People who usually greet me with a smile and maybe a bit of gossip barely acknowledge my greetings. They stop talking when I enter the staff lounge. Even the kitchen staff and servers, who would usually come out to tease me during my break and share their snacks, maybe ask for a tarot reading, are icing me out. Alex is the only one treating me the way he usually does, but even he's holding something back. He's incapable of lying, though, so when the uncomfortable vibes finally get to me, I seek him out.

"What's going on?" I approach him on the pretense of double-checking the dinner reservations for tonight before surprising him with that question.

"What do you mean? There aren't any special events, if that's what you're worried about."

"Alex."

He blinks rapidly at me, either trying to appear innocent, like he's fluttering his eyelashes, or because he's nervous. "Yes, Danika?"

"You know what I'm talking about. Why are you hiding things from me?"

"I'm not. There are just some things I can't talk about yet. Because someone else needs to talk to you first. But it's not my business. And I don't have a problem with you, obviously. But maybe some people do?"

His rambling somehow makes things clearer without actually enlightening me as to what the problem is. I don't find out what everyone's beef is until the end of my shift, when Mrs. Whittle calls me into her office.

"Danika, would you happen to know why the police were disturbing our guests earlier?"

Of course they'd come here with Eli being in custody. From what my mom has said, the cops have been conducting their investigation on the low for a while. But now that they arrested someone and my mom reported what happened to me and Gaby, as well as my suspicions about Mrs. Whittle, the cops must be ready to make a move.

"I might have an idea," I say. There's no playing this off. Clearly she knows I'm involved in the investigation somehow, or she wouldn't have called me in here.

"I've heard some disturbing rumors that you've been using your position at the Chicago Glen Country Club to nose into the business of our members and employees. Is that true?"

"Not exactly."

"Unfortunately for you, I have a trustworthy source that says otherwise." Mrs. Whittle sighs. "You realize this means I have to terminate your employment, yes? Effective immediately."

You can't do that! I want to scream. How can I keep an eye on Gaby after someone busted up her car in broad daylight? How can I figure out who's behind this burglary ring and the murders? How can I help Eli if I'm not on the premises, searching for more clues?

But all I say is "Of course, Mrs. Whittle."

"You were a good worker, Danika. I'm sorry to lose you. But the privacy of our members matters above all. Let's hope I don't find out you were doing anything untoward to obtain the information you were seeking. I would hate to press charges."

She stares at me as if I'm about to break down and confess, but I say, "I understand."

She summons a security guard, who escorts me to the exit, where Alex and Gaby are waiting for me.

"I'll take it from here, man. Thanks," Alex says, giving the security guard a head nod. They must know each other well enough for the security guard to trust him, because the security guard returns the gesture and leaves us alone. "You, uh, need a ride home?"

I glance at Gaby, who scrutinizes Alex for a minute before pulling me aside. "Ride with him and find out what he knows. I'll call Andrew and tell him what's going on. We'll try to follow you, so make sure he takes you straight home."

She hurries off, and I go back to Alex, who's still waiting near the exit.

"I'll gladly ride with you, but you don't ask any questions, and you have to answer all of mine."

"Deal," he says, motioning for me to follow him to the parking lot. "Or, at least, I'll answer anything that I actually know."

"Did you know I was going to get fired?"

He winces. "No, but I had a strong feeling that might happen. I got here after the police left, but some of the older staff told me that Mrs. Whittle was PISSED at you. Said it looked bad for the club to have the cops crawling around, and our reputation will be ruined if word gets out."

"Gets out about what?"

"About Eli. You know she was arrested, right?"

"Everyone knows about Eli? And what she was doing?"

"I heard she got arrested, and it has something to do with the club. But I have no idea why. Either the people I talked to don't know, or they think I don't need to know. I didn't want to pry, anyway. It's not my business, and it's gotta be hard enough for Gaby without everyone at work talking about her sister."

Do I believe him?

Has he ever given me a reason not to?

"Do you know why I got fired?"

He nods. "I wondered why you started working here when

you already had a job at your mom's detective agency, but, like, of course. It would be weird for your mom to get a job here for her case, but it makes sense to send you."

"Are you upset that I was investigating you and everyone at the club?"

"You were investigating me?" He takes his eyes off the road for a split second to glance at me. He appears utterly bewildered, and I can't help but laugh.

"I was investigating *everyone*. You didn't think it was weird that my cousins introduced us out of nowhere?"

"I thought that was because . . ."

"Because what?"

It's dark in the car, so I might be wrong, but I could swear that a deep red flush has spread across his face. "Your cousins told me to go to the lesson because they wanted to introduce us. They know I haven't had a girlfriend in a while, and they thought—"

"My cousins said they wanted to hook us up?"

"Basically." Awkward beat. "Are you mad?"

"I'm not mad. I . . . Why did you go along with it?"

"I like your cousins, and I needed help finding homes for those puppies. And your cousins really talked you up, so I thought, 'What's the harm in meeting you? It doesn't have to mean anything.'"

As embarrassing as it is to hear that we only met because my meddling cousins think I need assistance getting a date, I can't help but wonder what they told him about me. And what he thought when we first met. Was he disappointed? Did they overhype me, only for him to see me in my workout gear and no makeup and think, *Really? Her?*

I have so many questions, but I absolutely don't want the answers at the same time. Especially after what happened not even an hour ago. So I change the subject.

"How did everyone find out that I was investigating? I doubt the police said anything."

His fingers flex around the steering wheel as if he's nervous or upset. Because I changed the subject away from us? Or because I changed it to a topic he's not comfortable with?

"I guess the police left right before we got to work. My direct supervisor pulled me aside and asked me if I knew about you snooping around. His words, not mine," he adds quickly. "Obviously, I had no idea what he was talking about, so he filled me in. Mrs. Whittle held a staff meeting for the management types to share what was going on, and then word got around."

Which begs the question: Who told Mrs. Whittle?

I ask him as much, and he shrugs. "Like I said, I found out from my supervisor, and then everyone else was gossiping about it. I'm surprised no one came out and asked you."

Something suddenly occurs to me.

"Do you know if she fired Gaby too?"

"Why would she fire Gaby? Was she working with you on your investigation?"

Yes. "No, I . . . I assumed people would be suspicious of her since we are always together and with Eli getting arrested and all. But it would be messed up if she got fired because she associated with us. She didn't do anything wrong."

Alex doesn't have any other useful information for me, so we spend the last fifteen minutes of the ride chatting about school and music and food to ease the awkwardness. When he drops me off in front of my house, he puts the car in park. "Do you think I could check in on Buchi, maybe say hi to your family?"

"I'd love that, Alex. But maybe some other time?"

"Right. Sorry. You probably have to talk to your parents about . . . Yeah. I'll see you at school tomorrow?"

"Sure. Thanks for the ride."

He stops me before I get out of the car. "I meant at lunch. You haven't sat with us for lunch lately. Did I do something?"

I bite my lip. "I swear it's not you. There's just a lot going on. Can I text you later?"

He tries to smile, and somehow that makes me even sadder. "Of course. Good night, Danika."

"Good night, Alex. Thanks again."

I watch him drive away and signal to Andrew, who parked across the street moments after Alex pulled in front of my house, that I'm okay. Gaby's car is already here, so she must've sped home ahead of us. I assume she's already inside. Sure enough, my parents and Gaby are waiting for me around the dining room table.

"Where's Daniel?"

"We told him we had important adult stuff to talk about, so he's playing with Buchi in his room," my dad says. "Gaby told us what happened. You look like you could use some sugar."

He slides a mug of hot chocolate my way, as well as a big slice of sapin-sapin. "I stopped by the store to get some. I must've sensed it'd be needed."

I help myself to a big forkful of my favorite dessert. "Mrs.

Whittle fired me because she found out I was investigating. The cops were poking around earlier, and she didn't appreciate the negative exposure."

My mother sighs. "I was worried that would happen. Well, that wasn't your real job, anyway. But at least you're close to affording those car repairs by now, right?"

A jolt runs through me, and I almost drop my fork. I completely forgot about Veronica. Considering that's a huge step in getting my mom to take me seriously as a PI, I can't believe I didn't remember.

"I'll need to double-check, but I think I only need one more paycheck, and then I'm done. Anyway, that's not important right now. I feel like I'm missing something," I say. "Well, I know I'm missing something. Someone had to tell Mrs. Whittle about my investigation. But who? And why?"

"It's got to be Caleb, right? No one else knows about your mom, and he's probably suspicious about why we were asking him about Eli. He's simple, but he's also sharp, you know?" Gaby says.

"True. We need to talk to him again. Too bad he moved. Now that I don't work at the country club anymore, I can't really corner him. Plus, he's probably put two and two together to figure out that Eli's been arrested because of me, so I doubt he'd wanna meet up with me if I text him. Could you talk to him? Make sure you're not alone when you approach him, though."

"Yeah, about that . . . I quit."

"You what?"

My voice rises, and even I can't tell if it's in shock or anger.

My dad gives my mom a look, and they both leave us alone at the table.

"I quit. When I heard they fired you, I may have had words with Mrs. Whittle, and, well, I'm now unemployed."

"Gaby, you didn't have to do that! I at least have a job at my mom's place. Not that she pays me, but still. What about you?"

She waves her hand at me. "Don't worry about me. I hated that place, and Eli begged me to quit, anyway. She also said to stick with you at all times, and Mrs. Whittle probably won't let you past the parking lot."

I snort. "Now I'm a bodyguard? Another thing to add to my resume. Too bad none of these jobs make me any money."

Gaby fiddles with her rings. "I'm sorry I can't—"

Now it's my turn to wave her off. "It's cool. If money were that important to me, I would choose a different career."

But she insists. "Friday is payday, right? I'm supposed to go to the country club to pick up my last paycheck. You need yours too, right? Let's go together, and I'll give you a cut of mine."

I start to argue with her, but she points out that it's not like our last minimum wage paycheck is gonna go far. And that if I want to stay on her good side now that we've made up, I should do what she says.

I laugh. "Whatever you say, princess. I got your back."

She grabs my hand and squeezes. "And I've got yours. No matter what."

I squeeze back. "No matter what."

IT'S ONLY BEEN A FEW DAYS, AND YET IT ALREADY feels weird being back at the country club. Not that I ever felt like I belonged here, exactly, but at least the staff was always nice to me. Now, though, people are either shooting me dirty looks or outright ignoring me as I walk in. (They must be involved in the scam and pissed I nearly got this place shut down, *or* they simply don't like anything that gets them involved with the police, which, fair.) It's the latter response—the silence—that bothers me more. I can deal with confrontation. It's the passive-aggressive stuff that gets to me.

Mrs. Whittle's assistant, Annette, sees us enter and hurries over to us. "I'm sorry, ladies, but I'm going to have to ask you to leave. You know you're no longer allowed on the premises."

"Relax, Annette. We're here to pick up our last paycheck. Mrs. Whittle said it was okay."

"She did? She didn't mention it to me."

Probably because Gaby didn't give a date, time, or mention me when the vague plans to pick up her check were made the day she quit, but whatever.

Annette glances at her watch. "I'll escort you to her office, then. Come along."

Once we get to Mrs. Whittle's office, Annette knocks on the closed door. When there's no answer, Annette knocks again, then looks up Mrs. Whittle's schedule in her planner. "I was right. You're not on her schedule. She's in a meeting right now. Sorry to make you come all this way for nothing, but next time call ahead and—"

"It's fine. We'll wait," Gaby says.

"Excuse me?"

"We actually got here a little early. Didn't want to leave Mrs. Whittle waiting. She's a busy woman. I figured we'd wait in her office until she arrives."

My previous investigation into Mrs. Whittle didn't go so well, but she must have information about who the boss is. Even though some of the burglaries were unrelated to club members, I'm positive the leader is in the building. Why else would Eli insist that Gaby quit? Working here, especially without me around, would put her in direct contact with the ringleader, and Eli thought they might do something to her.

Even if the big boss isn't a member of the managerial staff, I still think they're at least being helped by someone higher up the food chain. The actual act of breaking and entering is pretty bold, but all the planning involved, like gathering member data, creating copies of their keys, and boosting the merchandise, speaks to someone fairly intelligent and highly organized. And considering that our members were being targeted, someone senior must've noticed what was going on and covered things up. If I can't shake out the boss, maybe I can find their number two.

Annette glances over at me. "I'm sorry, dear, but I really can't leave anyone in Mrs. Whittle's office unattended. I'd stay with you until she arrives, but I have my own work to do."

"Can we wait out here?" I ask, gesturing to the seats we used back when we first interviewed for our positions.

Annette narrows her eyes at me. What does she think I'm gonna do? Steal some fancy stationery? Pocket a paperweight? Hack into Mrs. Whittle's computer? Okay, I actually am planning on doing that last one, but that's beside the point.

When Annette doesn't budge, I make a big show of rolling my eyes. "The door's locked, Annette. Once I get my paycheck, I'm out of here. Not like I want to be here, anyway."

She bristles at that, as if everyone should feel honored to step into the hallowed halls of the Chicago Glen Country Club. But then she glances at her watch and lets out an aggravated huff. "Fine. Don't cause any trouble. I'll let Mrs. Whittle know you're here."

Then she hurries off.

"She's so suspicious," I say as I pull out my lockpicking kit. Again, being the daughter of a PI and a mystery writer has its perks. Most kids had, like, LEGOs or something to play with when they were young. I got logic puzzles and lockpicking lessons. "Keep an eye out."

I'm about to get to work on the lock when Gaby suddenly calls out, "Hey, Alex! What brings you here?"

I quickly shove my tools into my pocket and straighten up.

"I heard Annette tell Mrs. Whittle that you two were here. She wanted to send a security guard to watch you, but I convinced her to let me go instead."

"Why do they trust you so much?" Gaby asks, eyes narrowed at him. I've never been suspicious of him the way she is, but it's a good question.

He stares down at the floor. "My mom is Mrs. Whittle's housekeeper. She's the one who got me this job. The staff knows I need it, so they trust me to handle random things around the club."

Gaby's eyes meet mine. A trusted member of staff. Someone who needs money. Access to the higher-ups. Could it be . . . ? Gaby seems convinced. But I can't picture it. Alex, the head of a criminal organization? Sweet, honest, simple Alex, a murderer? There's no way.

But then Eli hardly seemed like the type to get involved in this kind of mess, and yet . . .

So I take a gamble.

"Alex, do you ever get the feeling that something . . . shady is going on here?"

"Danika!" Gaby hisses.

"No, seriously, Alex. You've worked here way longer than us, and you know everyone and everything that goes down around the club. Are you that surprised that the police are investigating this place?"

Alex rubs the back of his head. "Honestly, I try not to think about it. It's not my business, and I need this job. Pretty sure most of the staff feel the same way."

"Okay, but what if it IS your business? Or everyone's business, really. I mean, people are dying. How can you not—"

"Wait, what are you talking about?"

Gaby nudges me and points to the time on her phone.

"Alex, I don't have the time to explain everything right now. All I can say is that Alberto's death was not an accident, and the police know it, but they need more evidence." I'm getting desperate now. "Trust me. I need to get into Mrs. Whittle's office, and I need you to look the other way. Please."

He stares at me for a moment, and I wonder if he's thinking about the fact that I, after all this time, haven't even properly given him an answer about prom. Is he going to be petty at a time like this? Or I guess I'm not exactly making it easy for him. It's not like I'm explaining why I need to break into his boss's office. The boss who holds not only his job but also his mom's main job in her hands . . . He's not gonna help me out, is he?

But he's nothing if not full of surprises. He reaches into his pocket and pulls out a bunch of keys. "Mrs. Whittle is constantly locking herself out, and Annette's not always around. I have one of the spares."

He hesitates, hand on the doorknob. "How sure are you that Alberto's death wasn't an accident?"

"One hundred percent. I wouldn't play about something like that."

"And you promise this will help find justice for Alberto?"

"I can't promise anything. But, if nothing else, his family deserves the truth."

"Good enough." He lets us into the office, glancing over his shoulder nervously. "Make it quick, okay? I trust you, but I seriously can't afford any trouble."

"Then you really shouldn't be friends with me," I say, half

joking. "Gaby, check the shelves. I'm going to go through her desk and maybe her computer if I can get in."

My computer skills are pretty basic (my dad has a hacker friend who my mom reaches out to when she needs that kind of help), so I'm hoping that Mrs. Whittle makes the amateur mistake of leaving her password written down somewhere if I need it.

"What should I do?" Alex asks.

"Close the door and keep an eye out. If anyone comes by, especially if it's Mrs. Whittle or Annette, stall them. Get them to leave if you can, so Gaby and I can get out without them seeing us. Can you do that?"

He hesitates but nods and closes the door. I make my way to Mrs. Whittle's massive desk. Her planner is open on her desk, and I skim the pages, trying to see if there are any patterns or if she meets with a particular person regularly. Nothing. I don't see a password out in the open, so I leave her computer for last as I go through the folders on her desk and check each of her drawers. Again, nothing. I'm about to head to Annette's much smaller desk to see if maybe she has the password written down somewhere when I hear Alex's overly loud voice outside the door.

"Felix! Hey, man, what're you doing here?"

"Where are Danika and Gaby?"

"What?"

"Alex, I ain't playing. Where are they?"

"What makes you think they're here?"

"I heard Annette talking to Caleb, and I think something's up. I think they might be in trouble."

Gaby waves her hand to get my attention, points to the door, and gives me a "what do we do?" face. I sigh and make my way to the door. Alex is going to give in any second now, so I might as well get it over with.

"What kind of trouble?" I ask, flinging open the door.

Both guys jump, and I hear Felix swear under his breath.

"Why are you here, Felix?"

"Trying to make sure my best friend doesn't lose his job doing something stupid."

"I'm fine, man, don't worry about me."

"Then why were they in an office that's usually locked? Where everyone knows you got a key, so it'll be pretty damn obvious who let them in if they get caught?"

He's right, and I say that, but Alex stands by us nonetheless. "You said doing this will bring peace to Alberto's family. I want to help."

Felix freezes. "Alberto? What's he got to do with this?"

"They said the police have evidence that Alberto's death wasn't an accident."

"Alex," I say sharply. Boy does not know how to keep his mouth shut, does he?

"I get it. That's why you're really here, huh?" Felix says to Gaby. "The police think Eli did it."

Alex already opened his big mouth, so might as well run with this if that's what Felix thinks.

"We know she didn't, but the police don't wanna listen. We want to find proof to clear her name. That's all," I say. "You understand, right?"

"What, you think I'm a snitch like you? I know how to keep my mouth shut," Felix says. Then he stops and thinks for a moment. "Alberto, huh? He was a good guy. His death never sat right with me, but if you're saying it wasn't an accident, that means he was murdered, right?"

I shrug. "That's what the police think, anyway."

"So then, what, someone at the club covered it up? Who would have the power to do that?" He glances over at Alex, and I can almost see the calculations going on in his head. "I didn't want to do this, but you leave me no choice. If I leave you all here, you're gonna end up getting caught. And I wanna know the truth about Alberto too. So follow me."

"Follow you where?" I ask. There's something in his eyes I don't like—following him could get me answers, but something tells me it's the wrong move.

"If there's something to hide, it won't be in Mrs. Whittle's office, where anyone can find it. I know where they'd hide it. Come on." Felix gestures for us to follow him and walks off.

"How do you know so much?"

Over his shoulder, Felix says, "You're not the only one who pays attention, Danika."

Alex goes with him and so does Gaby after I nod at her to follow them. I quickly start emergency sharing on my phone to send my location to my mom and hurry after the others. Felix leads us down an empty hall and out one of the side exits. Nobody's around as he guides us past the golf course toward what I think are the storage sheds for the recreational area.

"Tell us more about this secret hiding place," I say.

"I caught Mrs. Whittle sneaking around with the head chef a while back. I was using one of the abandoned sheds to nap, dealing a little on the side—don't judge me, bro—and I caught them doing the deed. The chef's wife is on the board of directors and got him this job, and Mrs. Whittle's husband is also someone in management. Things would get real ugly for them if I said anything, so they made me a deal: keep my mouth shut and stay the hell away from this area, and I get to be assistant to the head of kitchen staff. Major pay increase, looks good on my resume, all that good stuff."

"Wait, so you think they're hiding evidence in their sex shed? How does that make sense?" I ask. But, also, I understand Mrs. Whittle's reading a little better now. I did say that the relationship she worked hard for is now stuck in a rut. And the head chef is obviously getting her to shake that restlessness.

"Eww, please don't refer to it as a sex shed. That sounds so gross," Gaby says.

"The club calls it a shed, but it's pretty big," Felix says. "You'll see."

I know what's going on, and I'm pretty sure he knows that I know. But I don't think the other two have quite pieced it together. Or at least I don't think Gaby does until Felix leads us farther and farther away from where the guests and employees are.

"Hey, where is this place exactly?" she asks. "I don't see anyone around."

"Almost there. Sorry, I know it's far, but it makes sense if you're doing stuff on the low, right?" Felix says. "What better place to hide your stash?"

Gaby grabs my wrist to signal that she wants to turn around and leave, but I gesture for her to follow my lead. We've gotten this far. We might as well see it through. Besides, I told her I'd protect her, and I will. She has nothing to worry about.

At least, I think that until Felix finally stops in front of a small cabin and motions for us to go inside. "After you."

Of course.

I pull Gaby with me into the cabin and stand in front of her as Alex and Felix follow us in.

"Bro, I'm getting some weird vibes," Alex says.

Felix sighs. "I'm sorry, man. I didn't want to get you involved."

Before Alex can respond, Felix reaches into his pocket and pulls out a switchblade, flicking his wrist.

"I wouldn't have figured you the type to get your hands dirty, Felix," I say, keeping my eyes on the blade.

I should be freaking out, but I'm not. Either I'm in shock, or all my training is finally coming in handy. Whatever it is that's keeping me calm, I'm grateful for it. Kali is a martial art based on stick-and-knife fighting, so I've literally been training for this moment almost since birth. I mean, yeah, the most important lesson Tita Baby drilled into our heads is that if we ever come across an opponent with a weapon, we should run, but that's not really an option now. And, okay, we've only ever used blunt practice knives while training. But I got this. Right? Right.

As I'm giving myself this mental pep talk, Felix draws closer, and I move so that I stay between him and Gaby while also keeping the two of us as far away from him as possible. A quick scan of the room shows a gross bed, a bookshelf, a small table with a couple chairs around it, and several very full garbage bags tied shut. There's not much in the small space, so there's only so much distance I can keep.

"I'm not, but you know what they say. Snitches get stitches. And I can't have you running your mouth again."

"Felix, what the hell is going on?" Oh, Alex. You sweet summer child. He's standing by the door, looking like his best friend's heel turn is the biggest shock of his life. It probably is.

Felix's eyes flicker toward Alex, and I take that moment to close the distance between me and Felix and disarm him.

He scrambles for the dropped knife, but I grab him and kick it away. "Gaby, run! Get help!"

You gotta give it to her—that girl does not hesitate. She sprints past Alex and out the door without turning back.

I go to follow her, but Felix tackles me, and we both hit the ground. My arms instinctively move up to protect my head, so I'm a little slow to react when Felix suddenly starts choking me.

When he sees this, Alex grabs the knife and holds it out at both of us. "Felix, man, stop it!"

Felix lets go and holds his hands up. "Alex, it's cool. I'll admit, I went a little overboard with the strangling, but you don't wanna do anything you'll regret."

"Explain everything. Now."

So he does. He tells Alex everything. How one of his uncles works at a locksmith, and he got the idea to use his uncle's resources to con the country club members. How he started small, swiping the occasional key to make copies and having one of his fellow kitchen staffers do some petty thieving, but soon he recruited people to steal bigger and more expensive things, even expanding to identity fraud and all other kinds of things based on what info the burglary ring members could find.

"That was you in that gray SUV that followed us after work one day, wasn't it?" I ask. My mom had run the plates and it belonged to a stolen car, so we figured it was a dead end.

"I needed to keep an eye on you. You were asking too many questions."

"And what were you planning to do to us?"

He ignores my question and turns back to Alex. "I didn't tell you any of this because I know how important it is for you to stay clean, go on to college and all that for your family. But you've benefitted from all this too."

Alex pales. "What do you mean?"

Felix shakes his head. "Like I said, I wanted to make sure you stayed clean. But those bonuses you've been getting? All those generous tips from satisfied members? Yeah, those were from me. Passing on some of the money I made because I knew you wouldn't accept it otherwise."

"But Annette's the one who's been giving those to me."

"Because I've been paying her off."

Alex stares at him, but Felix smiles at him again. "Come on, don't look at me like that. It's me. Your best friend since second grade. You got my back, and I got yours."

Alex finally lowers the knife he's been holding out. "You've just been stealing from our members? That's all you've done?"

"Of course. I'm only in it for the money; you know how it is."

Alex takes several deep breaths. "I don't approve of anything you're doing. But I know that you're looking out for me in your own way. Like you always have."

"Alex, no!" I say.

He places the knife on the table and turns to me. "Danika, I'm sorry that he tried to hurt you, but you've gotta stay quiet on this. Please."

"How can you just—"

"He's my best friend! All he's done is steal money from some rich people; it's not that bad. Can you please call off your investigation and—"

"No, Alex. He's done way more than steal money."

"What do you—"

"God, would you shut up?" Felix moves to attack me, but I easily dodge him.

"He killed that lawyer, Walter Abbot, in his own home during a burglary gone wrong, and then he killed Alberto when Alberto told him he wanted out."

"Alberto's death was an accident," Alex says reflexively. Then he pauses. "Wait, that's not right. You said the police found evidence . . . ?"

They didn't—not that I'm aware of, anyway—but this moment might be the push I need.

I glance at Felix. "You gonna tell him, or should I?"

Alex shakes his head frantically. "No. Alberto was our friend. Felix would never do something like that."

For a moment, I swear I see tears in Felix's eyes, but then they harden again as he shifts toward Alex. "He was going to ruin everything. He threatened to snitch after he saw what happened to that old man if I didn't pay him off and let him out. I knew him. I knew his type. Even if I agreed, he was gonna talk the second someone put pressure on him."

"Felix . . ."

"I handled him like I handle everything nobody else wants to do. And now I've gotta handle her. I'm not going to ask for your help, since I know you caught feelings. But you better not get in my way either."

Before Alex or I can react, Felix springs forward and grabs the knife. This time, he's not standing between me and the door, so I make a run for it.

Then a loud scream makes me whirl around.

Alex is bleeding from a cut on his arm and has Felix restrained on the floor, the knife on the ground next to them.

"Oh my God, Alex, are you—"

"I'm fine; he grazed me. Grab the knife!"

I grasp it and point the blade at the boy on the floor, who stops struggling. "It's over, Felix."

CHAPTER
TWENTY-NINE

"LET ME GET THIS STRAIGHT: YOU FOUND THE MISS-ing girl and solved your first case, which we already knew. Cool. But that led to you also catching a murderer and shutting down a criminal operation."

"Yes."

"And to catch the killer, you had to follow him into a sex shed, where you got into a knife fight?"

"Yes."

"And in the process, you had not one but two absolute hotties fall for you?"

"Um . . ."

"And while this was going down, you've been ignoring our texts and avoiding us because . . . ?"

". . . I'm telling you now. Does that count?" When Junior makes a disgusted noise, I say, "I'm sorry, but I couldn't talk about it! You know how important client privacy is. And the cops made a big deal about keeping quiet since it's an ongoing investigation. I did tell you most of it after Gaby and I got into that big fight. I just haven't had a chance to tell you about all the dangerous stuff at the end . . ."

It's been almost two weeks since everything went down, and I was finally catching up with Junior and Nicole at our favorite café. I hadn't talked to them at all about what happened—they found out because their parents saw the news stories and told them.

"On God, you are so annoying. I am your oldest friend! You're basically my sister! And you couldn't think of some way to let me know about all this life-changing and dangerous stuff going down? I don't care about your client's secrets, DD. I want to know that you're okay!"

Nicole and I stare at Junior after his outburst. He's not the type to let his emotions show like this. He's more likely to play it off as a joke or avoid an argument by acting like a clown. Usually it's me and Nicole who get heated, which means he's deadass. And that's when I realize how much I've taken both him and Nicole for granted, again, by expecting them to understand what I've been going through without ever having to explain myself.

Like how I expect them not to get mad at me for not hanging out since they should understand my family issues. How I expect them to accept how secretive I can be around my work. And, most of all, how I expect them to keep putting in the work in our relationship without me giving them a single thing in return.

I burst into tears and hug Junior.

"Whoa, wait, no, that's not how this was supposed to go. You can't cry; you never cry . . ." Junior is freaking out and rubbing my back, trying to comfort me even though I'm the one who screwed up.

"I'm sorry. I'm so sorry to both of you. I know I haven't been a good friend lately. Or, well, for a long time now. But I love you guys. I'm trying to be better about . . . emotions and things."

"You realize calling them 'emotions and things' doesn't exactly fill me with confidence, yes?" Nicole says. "But, whatever, you say you're gonna do it, so you'll do it. That's who you are."

"Thanks, Nicole."

She shrugs. "You're important to me. I will always give you another chance. Always. But you gotta show me that you actually want one."

I swallow the lump in my throat. "You two are my family. I would never let another person, client, love interest, whatever, get between us."

"Speaking of, what's up with you and Gaby? And Alex? I know your cousins were trying to hook you up with him, but Gaby's really cool. I think she's good for you. Expand your horizons and all that."

"Alex is solid, though," Junior argues. "Honest, hardworking, uncomplicated. Danika needs someone she can count on, someone who can keep her grounded, remind her of what's important." To me, he says, "And it seems like he values family the way you do, DD."

"You're both shockingly on point. I can't choose between the two of them, so I'm not going to."

"So, what, you're not going to date either of them? That seems like a waste of hotness. I mean, you have feelings for them, don't you?" Junior asks.

When I don't respond right away, Nicole puts one hand on

Junior's forearm and the other on her chest. "Danika de la Paz Dizon. Are you telling us that you want to date both of them? Junior, our little girl has become a player!"

"It's not like that! Or, actually, maybe it is?"

"Spill. Immediately."

ONE WEEK AGO

AFTER FELIX WAS ARRESTED, IT TOOK A WHILE FOR things to calm down. Eli is still in juvie for her crimes, but the prosecutor dropped any talk of trying her as an adult. Her cooperation in the burglary ring case meant she'd get a reduced sentence but still have to serve time in juvie. Luckily, she had a great lawyer (my mom pulled some strings), and even with all the ugly aftermath, she told me and Gaby that she's feeling more positive about her future than she has in a long time.

Once things with Eli were settled, Gaby asked me out. As much as I hate to admit it, Junior and Nicole were right about her having feelings for me.

I still hadn't given Alex a straight answer about prom or whether I wanted him to keep waiting for me. So I proposed that the three of us meet somewhere. I thought about meeting at a café or something, but I'd die if anyone overheard us, so I invited them to my house on a day I knew my family would be out.

Once all three of us were seated around my dining room table, I said, "I'm just gonna come out and say it: I like both of you."

"Yeah, I figured," Gaby and Alex said at the same time.

"I'm sorry. I don't mean to be indecisive, but you're both so different, and I like each of you for different reasons." I turned to Gaby. "You're so much fun, and you made my world so much bigger."

"I also almost got you killed, but, yeah. I have fun with you too," she said.

"And, Alex, you're so sweet and kind, and you gave my brother a dog, and you freakin' got stabbed for me—"

"I didn't exactly get stabbed FOR you—"

"That's actually pretty metal, I gotta say," Gaby added.

The three of us all laughed, and the tension left the room.

"So where does that leave things?" Gaby asked.

"I've never dated anyone before," I said. "So I'm not sure if I'm ready for anything serious or exclusive or anything like that. I don't think I can choose."

Gaby and Alex both nodded, as if they expected that as well.

"So don't," Alex said. "I like you a lot, Danika. A lot, a lot. But we've only known each other for, what, a month or two? I understand if you still need time to get to know us."

Gaby chimed in, "Yeah. It's not like I was proposing to you or anything. We're still in high school; it's not that deep. I mean, I don't want to lose out to the golden retriever or anything, but I'm not asking to be exclusive. Not yet, anyway."

"So I can date you both?"

"Yeah, until you figure things out. But not, like, in a throuple kind of way. No offense," Gaby said to Alex. "You don't really do it for me."

"I doubt I could handle both of you, so that's fine by me," Alex said. "Oh, and don't worry about prom. I'm not exactly in the mood to go anymore."

I was glad the pressure was off but wished there was a better reason for him to take it off the table. Finding out your best friend is a murderer is a pretty good reason to skip, but I knew he was struggling. He tried to visit Felix a few times in prison, but Felix refused to see him. Even though he's a criminal who tried to kill us, I think this is Felix's way of doing right by Alex and making sure he doesn't get further involved in his mess.

I wished I could say something to ease his pain, but my only response was "I get it." When I grabbed his hand, he squeezed. And when Gaby tucked a loose piece of hair behind my ear, I shivered.

So . . . Are we dating? Is this what dating is?

Whatever was happening, I was glad to have gotten this far, and from the smiles on their faces, I could tell Alex and Gaby felt the same.

"SO, YEAH, THAT'S WHAT HAPPENED."

Junior and Nicole stare at me with their mouths hanging open, and I'm honestly kind of annoyed that they're more shocked by my story about dating than they are about me catching a killer and almost dying. Like, hello. Priorities, people.

But I'm also happy that I get to talk about something fun and seminormal with my two best friends.

I glance at my phone and note the time. "You both are coming over for dinner, right? We better get going soon, or my dad's gonna go overboard with the cooking. Apparently Alberto's family brought over a dessert to complement his main dish."

"Of course. You're driving, right? I know you wanna show off V," Nicole says.

That's right. I managed to fix up Veronica. Not only were my country club paychecks enough to finish the last of the repairs but I also received a sizeable reward from Walter Abbot's estate. Since we helped catch the killer, the Dizon Detective Agency got front-page billing in the news and also the promised reward. My mom put nearly all of it into a college fund for me.

"You did a great job, Danika," my mom said after we left the Abbot family's law office. "But I want you to continue your education. So let's make a deal: You will continue to work part-time at the agency, actual paid work, but you have to get a degree. Once you're done with school, we'll revisit the idea of you becoming a licensed private investigator. How does that sound?"

I stuck out my hand, and she shook it. "You've got yourself a deal."

Mentally, I'm still riding a high as Junior, Nicole, and I get up to head out. But before the three of us can leave, a girl I recognize as the tarot client with terrible taste in guys approaches our table.

"Um, sorry to interrupt, but—"

"Sorry, I don't have time for a tarot reading right now. Talk to me at school, and we can—"

"No, I'm not here for a tarot reading. Someone told me you were a detective? I've got a case for you."

I glance at my best friends, who sigh and motion for me to continue the conversation. I unlock Veronica for them before turning back to the girl.

"Oh? Tell me more."

ACKNOWLEDGMENTS

This book literally would not exist without the tireless efforts of my awesome editor, Bria Ragin. Bria, thank you so much for seeing my potential all those years ago, and for your patience and guidance in getting me to where I am now. The same goes for my amazing agent, Jill Marsal. Thank you for your support and expertise that saw me through many, *many* iterations of the proposal that would eventually become *Death in the Cards*. You both are the absolute best.

Writing is often a solitary journey, but publishing is a team effort. Thank you to the team in charge of my YA debut: Ray Shappell, cover designer; Alex Cabal, cover artist; Megan Shortt, interior designer; Liz Sutton, production manager; Colleen Fellingham and Cindy Durand, copy editors; Wendy Loggia, VP and publisher, Delacorte Press; Barbara Marcus, president and publisher, RH Children's Books; Joey Ho, publicist; and Stephania Villar, marketer.

Huge thanks to Gloria Chao, Randy Ribay, Elle Cosimano, Jumata Emill, and everyone else who read an early version and kindly provided blurbs. I appreciate you all so much!

This book centers on two hobbies/beliefs of mine, which are tarot and Kali. I want to thank Imee of the Mayari Moon for her

Sacred Kali teachings; Tina Whittle for her guidance in some of my early tarot readings; Kellye Garrett, my rock star mentor who encourages and shares my tarot deck obsession; Biddy Tarot for their extremely helpful resources; and the creators of the two tarot decks that I used while writing this story: Trung Lê Capecchi-Nguyễn/Trungles (Star Spinner Tarot Deck) and Latisha Shelton and Roberta Rodrigues (The Black Femme Tarot Deck).

To my Chicagoland kidlit crew, particularly Samira Ahmed, Rena Barron, and Gloria Chao, who all screamed when I told them about my book deal. I finally get to be one of the cool kids!

Much love to the Asian and Asian American Voices In-Community Highlights Retreat group, who first heard about this book while I was still struggling to get the proposal together, and then a year later cheered me on as I read the opening for the very first time. Debbi Michiko Florence and Grace Lin, you two have created a very special space that I hope I can return to again and again.

As always, thanks to my family for their love and support and for being the best street team. And to my husband, James, who keeps me going when the stress and self-doubt and overwhelm start kicking in—thank you for always, *always* believing in me. I love you. Maybe not as much as I love Gumiho and Max, but you're definitely up there. <3

Finally, shout out to *The Mystery Files of Shelby Woo*. I loved that show as a kid, and it meant so much to see a young Asian American girl in such a fun leading role.

Representation matters.

ABOUT THE AUTHOR

MIA P. MANANSALA is the award-winning author of the Tita Rosie's Kitchen mysteries and a book coach from Chicago. She uses humor (and murder) to explore aspects of the Filipino diaspora, queerness, and her obsession with pop culture. A lover of all things geeky, Mia spends her days procrastibaking, playing RPGs and dating sims, reading cozy mysteries and diverse romance, and cuddling her dog, Gumiho. *Death in the Cards* is her first novel for young adults.

MIAPMANANSALA.COM

Ⓕ 𝕏 ⓘ